CASTING

DARKER

SHADOWS

Acknowledgements

Many thanks to Jim O Keefe for his detailed knowledge on the inner workings of the Gardai. To Brendan Murphy for his fine eye in the editing process and to Geraldine O Neill or her invaluable insights.

Thanks also to Elaine, Chris, Donna, John and Darragh for their love and support. In particular I want to thank my better half, Eileen. Without her care, encouragement and love I would be lost.

A special thanks to Paul Dunne and Irish Dew Photography, whom I put to a lot of trouble to get the picture I needed for the cover. www.irishdew.com

Casting

Darker

Shadows

The journey of life is like all trips taken, it's not the places we visit or the sites we see that make them memorable—but the company we keep along the way.

About the Author

Hugh Flanagan lives in Kilbeggan County Westmeath. He is a postman in Kinnegad. Married to Eileen since 1980. They have three children and a dog called Ella, who thinks she's a Kangaroo.
Casting Darker Shadows is Hugh's second novel. It is a follow-up to *Hiding Ugly Children.*

Email address. hughpflanagan@gmail.com

CASTING DARKER SHADOWS

CHAPTER 1

Nellie Roe of Rose cottage had passed away.

Father Tom Nolan was reassuring the congregation that Nellie was now safely in the arms of Jesus in heaven. Joggy doubted this. Nellie deserved to be in her utopia, of that he had no doubt. She was his Godmother and she deserved to go to somewhere beautiful. But Heaven! In Joggy's mind, Heaven was unattainable. It was for the holy, for the saints, and while Nellie was a good woman, she was no saint. He left his musings behind, when Alice tapped him on the arm to stand. Of late, he had found his mind wandered during mass and attributed this to Fr Nolan's nasal drone. It lulled his mind and sent it to engage something more interesting.

The sermon was all about forgiveness and reconciliation and once again Joggys mind wandered, but only to the previous evening. Because of heavy downpours, he and his son Danny had come home early from the bog. They knew the rain was coming. However, the weather forecast had not been precise and so they had hoped to get as much out of the day as possible. By midday it was a downpour. They arrived home with the full expectation of putting their feet up for the afternoon, but as soon as they came in the kitchen, Alice, told her husband that the two calves he kept in his one acre of ground behind the house, had escaped. He knew which one to blame; the Friesian. He had bought it only recently and as soon as he had released it into the field, he saw why he had got it at a bargain price. It was wild and uncontrollable and spent all of its time looking for gaps in the hedges.

The rain was still falling heavily when he and a reluctant Danny went looking for them. It did not take them long to find the escape route. Unfortunately, it was onto Harry Butler's land. Her real name was Harriet, but everyone called her Harry. She dressed like a man and had a temper so vile, few neighbours spoke to her.

Joggy hoped that the heavy rain would keep her indoors and thus prevent her from seeing them. But unfortunately it was not to be; she was waiting for them. She approached them, her steps purposeful, in Wellington boots that were a size too big. The open tops wobbled and slapped against her dung stained denim trouser legs. She wore a black floppy hat and a heavy black coat, tied around the waist with baler twine. The grin on her deeply wrinkled face took Joggy by surprise. It was almost as if she was happy to see him. "You wouldn't by any chance be looking for two calves now Joggy, would you?"

"I am, and you've obviously seen them."

"I have. I found them eating my grass. You see Joggy, I've a golden rule. No animal grazes my land but my own. So I put them off my land."

"And where are they now?"

"Grazing to their heart's content on grass nobody owns."

"And where might that be?"

"By the side of the railway tracks."

Joggy glanced at his watch. The one-thirty to Galway was due soon. He gave Harry a withering look and then the two men ran and did not stop until they reached the railway line. They looked quickly in both directions, but could see nothing.

"This way Dad," said Danny, picking up a trail of manure droppings. Three hundred yards further down the line they found the two calves grazing close to a hedge. With great difficulty they herded the calves off the line and through the gates of the unmanned level crossing on Barterstown lane. It ran parallel to the main road on which Joggy lived.

Just as they closed the gate, the one-thirty rumbled past at high speed. With Danny in front and Joggy behind they eventually got the calves home and into a shed. They removed their saturated clothes and dried off. For the rest of the afternoon Joggy sat in the armchair by the window, quietly brooding.

Outside, the water raced down the opposing hills and began collecting under the old stone railway bridge that spanned the road. With the drainage unable to cope with the deluge, the area usually flooded.

Later that evening, after the rain having passed over, Joggy and Danny climbed into the slate-grey Morris Traveller. Danny had a hurling match in Kilpatrick. He did a quick check in his kitbag; all were there, boots, socks and shorts. His father drove off and it quickly became apparent to Danny that something was not right. The engine was revving hard and they were going faster than normal down the hill. Danny looked up and saw the cyclist coming down the opposite slope towards the floodwater under the bridge. He turned to his father and shouted in alarm "Dad, slow down. You'll drown her."

Joggys face was dark and malevolent but with the hint of a smirk lingering on the corner of his lips. Coming down the other incline on a bicycle, was Harry Butler. She saw Joggy too late. They met in the middle and a wave of ice cold water washed over her. She shrieked. Joggy regarded the scene in the rear-view mirror and smiled. Harry was standing, straddling her bicycle, with both feet in the water, drenched from head to toe.

"Fucking bitch," he spat. "You won't put my calves on the railway line again."

The tinkling of the Eucharist bells brought Joggy back to the present. He now considered forgiveness. Then slowly shook his head: the lingering taste was still too sweet. *Maybe later,* he thought; *when it has soured some.*

The presence of Victoria Parker, Danny's girlfriend, raised many disapproving eyebrows: Church of Ireland in a Catholic Church. She was there for Danny. Over the previous two years he had become fond of Nellie, visiting her on his weekend's home from college. It was he who had found her slumped in her armchair by the fireside. There was no pulse and she was cool to the touch. The smouldering embers of the fire indicated she had not been dead long.

After the holy Sacrament was served, Fr Nolan read out Kilpatrick's upcoming events: the baptism of the fourteenth and latest Flynn sibling; the wedding notice of John Purdy and Sandra Moore, the dates and times of several local meetings and finally he announced with much glee, the imminent arrival of one Fr P J Hayes; the new curate.

The burial was a small, tidy affair. At the graveside, Joggy and Danny stood shoulder to shoulder. At six-foot-two, Danny stood a few inches taller than his father. To the neutral observer there was no mistaking them, with their black mops of tousled hair, for anything other than father and son.

Joggy stood close to the edge and peered down into the deep empty grave. He noticed that the base was covered in boot prints. It raised a curious thought. Some time ago he had read an article in a magazine about red Indians and their belief that photographs captured their souls. It now made him wonder, what they would make of the footprints of the living being buried with the dead; did the owners of those, lose something of themselves every time they dug a grave?

Joggy and Danny helped lower Nellie's coffin. Nellie had not left her rundown cottage for several years and people had sort of forgotten about her. But Joggy and Danny had not forgotten; each shed silent tears.

"Small funeral, Joggy," said Sergeant McNeill as he fell into step on the way back from the graveyard. He was in uniform.

"Aye, probably because she was out of circulation for so long." Joggy had a good idea of what McNeill wanted.

"I had a very irate lady on the phone to me yesterday evening, Joggy. Says, you tried to kill her."

"An unfortunate accident, Ed. That's all that was. Danny had a match and we were running late. I was trying to make time. Unfortunately, we came together at the flood. I was going to stop but as I said we were already late."

"I see. An accident you say. So where did she get the notion that you were trying to kill her?"

"Well, earlier my calves had broken out onto her land and she then moved them onto the railway line. She probably got the silly idea into her head that I was somehow taking my revenge on her."

"And were you?"

"The thought never crossed my mind, Ed." Joggy tried to look serious but a smile kept breaking out. "Look, I'll tell you what I'll do. When I get time, I'll call and apologize to her."

"Well," said McNeill, as he slid the peak of his cap to a higher position on his bald head, "I can't ask for fairer than that, it being an accident an all. I'll let her know you'll call."

They both knew as they parted that hell would freeze over before that happened.

Victoria now drove a violet-blue Ford Capri. It was the first thing she had bought with her inheritance and she adored it. After the funeral, Danny climbed in beside her and they drove off. He was having dinner today with her parents; Terry and Elizabeth Parker. Terry had sold his travel business and their home in Northern Ireland and now shared the farmhouse with their daughter. Unlike Danny, Victoria, had no interest in going to college. She had grown to love the farm.

Danny's weekend routine was now well defined. He spent his nights with Victoria, which her parents disapproved of. But as Victoria pointed out to them, on more than one occasion; it was her house. His mother however, still had the honour of washing his clothes and supplying him with fresh ones and some of his daily meals.

On arriving home, Joggy, changed out of his Sunday best and into casual clothes. As it was drizzling rain, he slipped on his Wellingtons and pulled down a navy blue anorak from the back of the kitchen door. He was setting out for Barterstown House. The day before as he stood at the un-manned railway gates, the now abandoned house had pricked his curiosity. He had walked passed it on several occasions but had never gone in. The last person to live there had died six years previous. There were only three houses on Barterstown lane; Kelly's occupied one side of the level crossing while Butlers and Barterstown House occupied the other. The lane was a cul-de-sac of sorts. It was only a dead-end for motorised transport. A narrow grass pathway led on past Barterstown house, past the back of Victoria's land and reconnected to Joggy's road further down.

He told Alice he would not be long and set out across Parker's fields. He intentionally avoided Harry Butlers land. Crossing her fields under normal circumstances was not a problem, but for the moment he thought it wise to avoid any further unpleasantness.

However....Terry Parker, Victoria's father, was also giving him grief. He had taken it upon himself to act as custodian of his daughter's property. On several occasions he had caught Joggy, accused him of trespassing and then ordered him off the land. At first Joggy had laughed, ignored him and continued on his way, but that soon wore thin. It then slowly escalated into a war of words and that is where it now stood.

As he crossed the field, he heard the shout. The hood of his anorak blocked his view so he turned completely around.

"Mister Jackson," said Parker, his words as sharp and as cold as the north-east wind that blew. "How many times do I have to tell you to stay off our land?"

"Why Terry, it's nice to see you too," Joggy replied with a wide grin. It was a vain attempt to hide his frustration. "Tell me, do you ever smile? You're here two years and for the life of me I don't believe I've ever seen you smile."

"I don't appreciate your sarcasm, Mister Jackson," said Parker, a breeched and loaded shotgun hung from his left arm.

"Trust me Terry when I say, I do have sympathy for your situation."

"My situation? What are you talking about?"

"You having to sell up and move down to live among us Catholics. It can't be easy. And to add insult to injury, you find your daughter has taken up with one of them."

"For your information, Mister Jackson, not that I feel I have to justify myself to you, I have nothing against Catholics. I moved down here to be close to my daughter. I also do not have a problem with Danny dating Victoria, although.... I'd prefer it if they were not sleeping with one another."

"But you do have a problem with me crossing these fields!"

"Yes, you are trespassing. If you wish to cross my land, please ask for permission."

"Don't you mean Victoria's land and Victoria's permission?"

"Victoria, mine, it's all the same, we're.... all the one family." He said, with an air closer to diffidence than confidence.

Joggy picked up on it and went on the attack. He figured if he played it right, Terry Parker just might leave him be in the future. He walked slowly and menacingly towards Parker, his eyes never leaving his. "Yes," he almost shouted, "but you're the only one that has a fucking problem. Victoria has no problem with it, nor might I add, had Fred Winter, and he was a right bastard. So I'm going to tell you this once and once only."

Parker began backing away as Joggy kept coming.

"I have been walking these fields around here for twenty years and nobody has ever told me to get off their land. Do you know why, Terry? I'll tell you why, because I don't damage fences or leave gates open and besides that my neighbours are my friends. So if you want to live around here, learn to be friendly not embittered. Now fuck off home and don't ever come near me again."

Without another word, a horrified Terry Parker turned and walked away.

Joggy opened the galvanised round iron gate that leads onto Barterstown Lane, closed it and then leaned on it, arms flat along the top rung. With furrowed brow he watched the retreating figure of Terry Parker until he had disappeared over the hill. He was already regretting his rash words.

Barterstown house stood on a small hill surrounded by yew trees and evergreens. The house was once visible through them but not any longer. It had been empty for many years and all Joggy knew about the place was that the previous owners were Fitzgerald's. He climbed the padlocked and rusted flat iron-gate at the base of the hill leading up to the house. The small front gate and the path leading to the front door were entombed by a privy hedge, making it impassable. He went around the back and tried to gain entry by the farmyard. The gate at the entrance to the back pathway opened easily. He stooped to pass under the outstretched branches of the evergreen trees on either side, his feet treading on a thick carpet of twigs and pine needles, emerging into an open and grassy backyard. Because of the trees and the ivy, the roof of this once magnificent two-storey house was now no longer visible. It was now home to a colony of rooks; their raucous cries, unrelenting. It was as if nature was reclaiming its space. The heavy white back door lay flat on the ground opposite where it once stood. Joggy walked over it and into the back hallway where a stair led up to a landing. He turned right and into what was once a dining room or sitting room. Rubble and clutter were everywhere.

He picked up a large black and white photograph. It was of a young married couple. She stood behind her husband who was seated. Her hair seemed short and was brushed back off her lightly smiling face. She wore a long-sleeved blouse with a bow at the neck that was secured by a broach. He sported a full moustache; the ends pointed up. A pair of bright eyes stared out at him. He presumed, not knowing the Fitzgerald's, it was of the parents. Peter Fitzgerald, the last occupant, had died six years previous and for a long number of years before that he just worked the farm, shunned all contact and was basically seldom seen.

Joggy then walked down the short hallway to where another open door led into the kitchen. Every cupboard was open. It was obvious the place had been ransacked several times. He then made his way back to the stairs and carefully climbed them. The fireplace surround in one of the three bedrooms was gone. He was surprised to find in the main bedroom, gentlemen's clothes. Suits and ties, all still hanging in the wardrobe and several pairs of tan and black leather shoes lay by the side of the unmade bed. A brier pipe and tobacco tin stood on the peeling teak dressing table. He felt a tinge of sadness as he stood in the eerie silence. A fine house that was once possibly a happy home, with its furniture and personal belongings, left to rot. As he walked away, the harsh riotous sounds of the rooks struck up again: it only seemed to highlight the loneliness of the place.

"Victoria," said her mother. She never abbreviated the name always loving the way it sounded in the full. She lifted the roast chicken from the oven. "Will you go and see what's keeping your father."

Danny went with her. They met him in the farmyard. He looked at Danny. "I met your father down the fields," he said, his anger barely concealed. "He swore at me ... used the f-word."

"I'm sorry about that," said Danny.

"What did you say to him this time, Dad?"

"We had words over his trespassing, that's all. I never once swore at him."

"Dad, why do you not listen to me? I asked you to leave it alone."

"But Victoria, you cannot have people walking around on your land. God only knows what harm they could be up to."

"Dad, it's Danny's father, not a black stranger, and anyway, people go for walks across other people's land all the time."

"What about the areas of flattened grass I found at the back of the sheds the other day?"

Victoria gave a long sigh. "I had a look. Yes, grass was pressed down in a few spots but that could have happened in any number of ways. A rabbit, a fox, birds even could have lain down." Her father was about to further argue the point, when Victoria put her hand up, fingers outstretched. "Dad, I've had enough of this. Leave Danny's father alone. I see nothing wrong with him walking across my fields; it's the country way"

"And what about his use of profanity. Are you going to let him away with that as well?"

"I'll talk to him about that," said Danny.

"Everyone's very quiet today," remarked Alice, observing her two daughters, sixteen-year-old Helen and nine-year-old Kate and Joggy in turn. No one said anything. They just gave a half smile and continued eating their dinner.

The table was cleared and the dishes washed, dried and put away. Kate and Helen, who had helped their mother, went to their bedroom to listen to Helen's newest David Bowie L.P.

Alice made tea and then joined her husband on the three-seat settee that nestled close to the Stanley range. Twenty two years of marriage had created a certain rhythm and ritual to their lives. They were now fully in sync with each other, knew their roles and how to play them. In the tone of their words and in the simple things they did for one another, there was a discreet and understood intimacy. Joggy was perusing the local paper and in particular a full page of photographs taken at the annual Garda dinner dance. He read the names underneath one particular photo. *Mrs Lucille Murray, Mrs Grace Matthews, Inspector Martin Murray and retired Ex-Inspector Peter Matthews.* He scoured the rest of the photo's but could find no trace of Sergeant Ed McNeill. He did however see a picture of Detective Sergeant Owen O Reilly, looking very smug and seemingly holding court, in the centre of a group of fellow officers.

"What has you so quiet?" she asked, handing him his tea.

He removed his reading glasses, put down his Sunday paper and then told her what had happened. Being a little embarrassed, he omitted the swearing.

"It's not been your weekend has it?"

"I'll be glad when it's over. Butting heads with the neighbours is not exactly my idea of fun." He sipped his tea. "Anyway, I don't understand Victoria's father. It's like he doesn't trust anyone. I hope after today, that that's the end of it." He picked up his spectacles and paper again. "Did you see Matthews?" he asked, pointing to the pictures.

"I did. They all look very chummy in their dickey bows."

"Yeah, retired or active, that crowd still stick together like shit to a boot."

Later that night in Victoria's double bed, Danny put his arm around her and pulled her close. She laid her head on his chest and playfully toyed with the few hairs he had.

"What are we going to do with our fathers?" Victoria asked eventually.

"Do you think I should ask dad to apologise?"

"Would he?"

"I don't know. He's always had a problem with authority. I could well imagine him baulking at an outsider, telling him to get off land he's been walking unhindered on for years."

"I can understand that, but it still doesn't give him the right to swear at my father," she said, feeling protective.

"I know it doesn't and as I told your father, I'll talk to him. You've got your driving test tomorrow, haven't you?" Danny asked, changing the subject. He gently pulled her closer.

"Yeah, at eleven."

"Do you want to practice your gear changing? It's all ready if you do."

Victoria lifted herself onto one elbow. Danny was grinning mischievously at her.

"What are you talking about?" she asked, lightly blushing.

"The morning after you got your first driving lesson, remember, you thought I was asleep, but I wasn't."

"No," she said, blushing a little more. "No, can't say I do. If I did I must have been still asleep."

"If you were asleep how come you were saying the words as you changed my gear stick; first, second, third, fourth, over and over."

"Nothing wrong with that, a lot of people talk in their sleep."

"Well my offer still stands, if you know what I mean," he said, the impish smile still playing on his lips.

"Actually, you're right Danny," said Victoria suddenly brightening up. "I could do with a little practise. Lately, I've been having trouble getting reverse."

The impish grin abruptly disappeared and a pained expression appeared in his eyes as Danny suddenly remembered. To get reverse in her car she had to push the gear stick down hard, to the right and then straight back. The pain in his right testicle had lasted for several days after she had attempted it the last time.

"God, you won't believe it, but," he gave an exaggerated yawn, "for some reason, I suddenly feel very tired."

"Can I have a quick go before you go asleep?" Victoria pleaded, the moonlight shadows hiding her delight at his discomfort.

"No, I'm sorry, maybe some other time. I've college tomorrow so I've to be up early."

He kissed her goodnight and then turned on to his side. He fell asleep with his right hand over the wounded memory, while Victoria fell asleep with a smirk that just would not leave her face.

Early on Monday morning, Joggy pulled up at the head of the avenue that leads to Victoria's farm. Through the tall black heavy wrought iron gates, he spied Danny, with his knapsack slung over one shoulder, and in no particular hurry, making his way towards him. Normally he headed back to college on a Sunday evening. But because he had no classes until after lunch, he took advantage of the extra night.

From an upstairs window, Victoria, with her arms folded across her chest holding together the loose ends of her red towelling bathrobe, watched him leave.

"Morning," said Danny as he climbed into the back seat.

"Good morning," replied Joggy and then drove off.

Danny emptied his knapsack of his weekend wear and then refilled it with the fresh clothes his mother had washed and ironed and left on the back seat for him. All loaded up, he climbed into the front passenger seat.

"Did you have a good weekend?" Joggy enquired.

"By all reports, better than yours. You do know you're not exactly flavour of the month in the Parker household at the moment."

"I guessed as much. It wasn't exactly my finest hour. Though, in my own defence, the man did drive me to it."

"That's pretty flimsy, dad."

"Yes, well.... I'm not going looking for him, mind you..... but, the next time I bump into him, I'll .... apologise."

"That must be a record, two promises of apologies in one weekend."

"Yes, but only one of them is based in truth."

Later that evening after supper, Joggy, ambled down the road and under the grey stone railway bridge. He gave Tom Bakers back door a rhythmic tap and walked in.

"Joggy," said Tom through a mouthful of food. "There's tea in the pot, help yourself."

Joggy took a cup down from the press, rinsed it under the cold tap and then passed up on drying it when he saw the blackened state of the tea towel. He poured the tea and then sat down. The conversation flowed as you would expect between two people who were good friends all their lives. He eventually got to telling Tom all about his run-ins with Harry Butler and Terry Parker and his visit to Barterstown House. "You've lived all of your life here Tom, you must remember the Fitzgeralds?"

"Gawnee, the Fitzgeralds," he said in mild surprise. He scratched the side of his skull. "It's been awhile since I heard anyone talk about that family. Apart from Peter, the rest of them have been gone a long time."

"What do you know of them?"

Tom gave him a quizzical look. "Why are you so interested?"

"Ah, you know me, I love a good mystery," said Joggy dismissively. And there was some truth in that, but really, he was bored and the signs were evident. Clearing his good friend, Luke Baker, Tom's brother's, name of murder, had whetted his appetite for more adventure. For two years now he had given Alice, his wife, nothing to concern herself with. After the last fright he gave her, when he nearly drowned in Winter's slurry pit; it had taken her a long time to forgive him, a lot longer than Joggy had anticipated for her to show she had forgiven him by cooking his favourite meal of lamb chops, new potatoes, mushrooms, onions and gravy. "Curious; a fine house like that... left to rot. Just wondered why it was never claimed. There was children in the family, wasn't there?"

"Three boys, but gawnee Joggy, they're gone a long time. Could even be dead some of them. If you remember, none of them turned up for their fathers funeral."

"Yeah, I wonder why."

"Oh I don't think there was much mystery in that, Joggy. Would you come back to the house where the leather belt and the open hand was meted out without mercy?"

"I suppose not."

"The first chance those boys got, they ran and it seems they've not looked back ."

"Yeah, but the land is leased, so that has to go to somebody?"

Tom smirked. "To get the answer to that, you'll have to ask Harry Butler who she pays."

CHAPTER 2

Victoria was busy the following Sunday morning doing what she loved best, driving her Ford Capri. It was a bright and sunny morning when she attended with her mother and father, the nine-thirty service in the Church of Ireland in Knockeen. Then she and Danny travelled to the Catholic church in Kilpatrick. They picked up his sisters Helen and Kate on the way. Like Victoria, they also loved her car and the sweet way it smelt. Their fathers smelt of 10-10-20 fertiliser. While they attended eleven o clock mass, she listened to the radio. After mass they dropped the girls off.

Danny was having dinner at home today, but since it would not be ready for another hour or so, he and Victoria went for a short drive.

Joggy took off when he came home. He told Alice he was going back to Barterstown House for another look around and was in a buoyant mood as he crossed Parkers field. He kept a wary eye out but saw no sign of Terry Parker. This time however he did notice the tufts of daffodils, sticking up everywhere like clumps of yellow hair. He also heard the joyful singing of the smaller birds; thrushs, blackbirds and starlings all busy with their nests. They, like the daffodils, had all been there the previous week, but for some reason he had not seen or heard them and as he approached the house. This time the raucous cries of the rooks did not seem so loud. What he had hoped to find on this second visit, he did not entirely know; perhaps a sense of what went on there. He walked over the fallen back door into the back hallway before turning right and entering what was once the living room. He found another black and white photograph, this time of a tall, elegant gentleman standing in the sunshine beside a car. Beneath a black fedora hat, he was dressed in a dark suit, waistcoat, white shirt and tie. Behind him were the neatly trimmed ivy-covered walls of Barterstown House. The shortened shadows told him the photo had been taken shortly after midday. He slipped the photo into his pocket and then climbed the stairs. In one of the bedrooms he found some farm account ledgers and recorded in them was the everyday running of the farm. He brought one into the light of a side window. As he scanned some of the entries, his peripheral vision picked up a flash of light. It came from outside. At first he could not see where it came from but then it flashed again and that's when he spotted Harry Butler. Something she was wearing, a badge or shiny button, kept catching the sunlight. She peered at him from behind a heavy whitethorn bush that sat in the field next door; land that once belonged to the Fitzgerald's but was now being leased by her. He left without finding anything more.

Victoria parked the Capri close to the back door.

"Victoria, will you go and see what's keeping your father?" her mother asked. "He went down the yard a while ago to feed the chickens. I shouted that dinner was nearly ready, but he mustn't have heard me."

"Dad," Victoria shouted out several times as she walked down the yard, but got no reply. She became worried when she found his double barrel shotgun and the galvanised bucket of chicken feed lying on their sides outside the hen run on the rough gravel yard. She searched each out-building in turn until she reached the hay shed, slid back the door and screamed. Her mother came running. She found Victoria outside, leaning against the shed wall, her hands over her face and her sobs in time with her short sharp breaths.

"Victoria, what's wrong? Where's your father?"

She moved towards the door but Victoria gripped her by the shoulders. "You don't want to go in there, Mum."

"What's happened? Let me pass," she said, trying to shrug out of her daughter's hold.

"No, mammy, you don't want to see this. Its daddy....he's...he's...he's dead." Elizabeth Parker's face drained of all colour and her mouth dropped open in shock.

"He can't be," she said, as panic took hold. She wrenched herself free of Victoria's grip. "He's probable only just asleep." Missus Parker stood in the doorway and saw her husband. He was hanging motionless from the end of a blue nylon rope Without uttering another word, she passed out.

CHAPTER 3

"It's probably Victoria," said Danny as he rose from the dinner table to answer the phone. They had plans for the afternoon and she had said she would ring when she was about to leave.

"Daddy's dead, daddy's dead," sobbed Victoria.

"Oh my God," Danny exclaimed loud enough for everyone at the table to stop eating their dessert of strawberry jelly and vanilla ice cream and to look at him with puzzled expressions. "I'll be there right away," he said and hung up. "Dad, can I have the car?"

"What's happened?" enquired Alice.

"Victoria's father has died."

Alice pushed her chair back and stood up. "Right, we'd better go down so." Alice had been in this situation a couple of times before, when near-neighbours had died. She knew how to take charge. She and Joggy took their coats from the back of the kitchen door. "Helen, you and Kate clean up and we'll try not to be too long."

They met Victoria in the back kitchen. She immediately fell sobbing into Danny's arms. "Where is.... your Father," he asked softly.

"He's still down in the hayshed," she said between sobs. "I rang Sergeant McNeill. He said he was on his way and not to touch anything."

As the shockwave passed around the room, Joggy slipped quietly out the back door and down the yard.

"And where's your poor Mother, pet?" Alice enquired.

"She's through there," she said, pointing to the sitting room.

She found Elizabeth Parker sitting on the settee, staring, unseeing, straight ahead.

"Your Mother's in shock," said Alice when she returned to the kitchen. "Have you rung your doctor?"

"Sergeant McNeill said he'd do it."

The lifeless body hanging from the end of the blue rope did not shock Joggy. He thought it would and had tried to prepare himself for it by remembering all the other dead people he had seen and how they looked. Terry Parker however, to all appearances, just seemed to be asleep on the end of a rope. Looking at him, Joggy began to feel very uncomfortable. He felt he was overheating and his skin was covered in pins and needles. He couldn't help wondering if it was something he had said that drove Terry Parker to take his own life. He then moved away from the hayshed and towards the shotgun and the spilled chicken feed and then glanced back up at the house just as a car came to an abrupt halt outside the entrance to the farmyard.

Sergeant Ed McNeill jumped out. "What are you doing here," he asked sharply. "Oh, right, I forgot," he said suddenly remembering, Danny and Victoria. "I hope you haven't interfered with anything?"

"Nope, didn't even go in."

"Good."

Joggy showed McNeill where the body was. McNeill then took a couple of measured footsteps towards the body and stopped. A few seconds later he carefully retraced his footsteps. "I need you, Joggy, to leave this area now and go back to the house."

"Why, it's a suicide isn't it ?"

"I'm sure it is. It's just precautionary."

As they passed the overturned bucket of chicken-feed and the breeched shotgun lying on the yard, Joggy remarked, "Who drops what they're doing and just goes and hangs themselves?"

McNeill made no reply.

They parted at the car and McNeill got on the radio.

McNeill had all the pertinent areas taped off, including the entrance to the yard, when two Garda cars pulled up. Two plain-clothes policemen climbed out of the first one and five uniform Gardai from the second. Detective Sergeant Owen Reilly was one of the two detectives. McNeill recognised the other, fresh-faced man as Sergeant Alan Cole.

"I hope you're not wasting my time, McNeill," said Reilly. "It takes a real Detective to call a suspicious death, not a fucking glorified village guard."

"Gee, I'm so sorry. Did I wake you from an afternoon nap or maybe you were just tallying up all the innocent people you sent to jail recently?"

The humiliation of been found to have sent an innocent man to jail had hurt him badly and was now burnt deep into Reilly's mind. After the Luke Baker affair, Inspector Murray had spent the best part of an hour tearing strips off him. Reilly had tried to make plausible excuses but Murray would have none of it. As far as he was concerned, Reilly was the investigating officer and the fault lay with him.

Reilly stepped towards McNeill, his right hand curled into a tight knot.

Cole stepped in. "Gentlemen," he said, "can we put this aside and be professional; were being watched."

Reilly turned around and spotted Joggy standing in the back doorway of the house dragging on a cigarette with an amused look on his face. "What's Jackson doing here?" he said.

"He lives up the road. His son is going out with the deceased man's daughter," explained McNeill.

"Great, that's all I need," said Reilly as he, Cole and four Gardai moved off. The fifth, a new recruit, straight out of Templemore, was left to guard the entrance. He had a hard cover, navy blue ledger tucked under his arm, into which he would write the names of everyone who came and left the cordoned off scene. McNeill stayed with him. A few minutes later Reilly was back.

"You're not needed here any longer," he said to McNeill, "Now fuck off back to your poxy little village."

McNeill climbed into his car and drove back out the avenue, pleased that he had made the right call.

While Reilly scrutinized the hay covered concrete floor for clues, Cole wandered around the farmyard. He stood close to the shotgun and then looked back towards the house. He had a scenario playing in his head and he wanted to see if he could make it fit in with reality. A few minutes later he stood in the shed doorway. "You'd better come and see this," he said to Reilly. Cole brought him around to the side of the hayshed and showed him a trampled patch of nettles. Reilly hunkered down. He took a silver ballpoint pen from an inside pocket of his brown tweed jacket and poked at the three cigarette butts and the empty Sweet Afton cigarette packet.

"It looks like someone was lying in wait," said Cole.

"And for a while," agreed Reilly. "Three fags, if he was anxious, represents at least a half-hour of hanging around." He stood up and looked out over the barbwire fence into the large hilly field beyond. "I want an ordinance survey map of this area and I want all the neighbours houses marked on it." He then turned his attention back to the trampled patch. "Make damn sure that this evidence is processed properly. I don't want any mistakes made."

Beginning to envisage the full picture for the first time, he and Cole strolled back to the yard and then stopped. "He must have heard Parker feeding the chickens," said Reilly, looking down to the hen run. "And because Parker was probably going chuck, chuck, chuck or some such nonsense, and had his back turned, he mustn't have heard the killer sneak up on him, who then knocks him out or kills him. The absence of drag marks means he most likely carried him back into the shed and then sets it up to make it look like a suicide."

"One other thing I noticed," added Cole, "if you look back to the house from where the gun lies, you can't be seen from the lower windows."

"Right," said Reilly, "Who ever did this has been here before and knew the lie of the land. So I reckon we're looking for someone fairly strong and with local knowledge."

Reilly then gathered all his men around him. "Gentlemen," he said, "it seems we may have a murder on our hands." He then issued orders for his men to search the farmyard and the fields, with specific instructions for what to look for.

"Sergeant, you and I have some questions to ask. Let's start with him," he said nodding in the direction of Joggy, who after receiving Victoria's permission, was framed in an upstairs window looking down on them.

"What about the firearm?" enquired Cole, as they made their way towards the house. "Why do you reckon he had that with him?"

"No idea. Let's hope we get an answer inside."

"Right," he said to Cole. "You talk to Danny Jackson and Parkers daughter in the sitting room and I'll have his father and mother in the kitchen."

Joggy sat at the end of the kitchen table while Alice sat around the angle to his right. Reilly sat at the other end.

"Will you have a cup of tea?" she asked.

Joggy grasped Alice by the wrist and held her in position. "Owen won't be staying long enough to enjoy it," he said, his eyes fully on Reilly and his words full of distain. The grip Joggy had on her wrist was strong enough for Alice to realise he was serious.

"Thank you for the offer," said Reilly, his voice saccharin sweet. "But I'm fine. Let's get down to business. Mister Jackson, can you give me your whereabouts since nine this morning?"

"Owen, why do you need to know that?" enquired Alice. "I thought the poor man had taken his own life?"

"It's Detective Sergeant, Missus Jackson and.... "

"I bet he insists on his mammy calling him that too," Joggy mocked. Reilly quietly bristled, but kept calm and ignored the jibe. "For the moment we are treating it as a suspicious death."

"Now Mister Jackson, can you get back to my question, where were you this morning?"

Joggy reluctantly explained his morning. He thought of the photo in his pocket, but then thought better of it. All it would prove, he reckoned, was that he was in Barterstown house. It would not prove he was there that morning.

"And is there anyone who can attest to you been in Barterstown House?"

"As a matter-of-fact yes, Harry Butler saw me. She was spying on me from behind a whitethorn bush."

"She?" said Reilly.

"Yes," said Alice. "Her real name is Harriet, but everyone calls her Harry and when you see her you'll understand why."

In the sitting room, Danny and Victoria sat on the settee. Sergeant Cole leaned forward from the front edge of the armchair. "Could you Miss Parker, tell me why your father had a loaded firearm with him?"

"He never went anywhere on the farm without it."

"Did he use it for hunting?"

"No, he never shot anything."

"So why did he carry the gun?"

"I don't know. Why does that matter now, he's dead," she said, and broke down.

"I'm sorry to have to ask you these questions now, but in a case of a suspicious death, we have to look at all angles."

"A suspicious death!" said Danny. "Why is it suspicious?"

"Until after the autopsy results become known, we treat all suicides as suspicious; it's just routine procedure."

"Look," said Danny, "Mister Parker was a very secretive man. He bought the gun about six months ago and wouldn't say why.

All we know is that from the time he brought it home he never went anywhere without it. He even slept with it, fully loaded, under his bed."

"And what did Missus Parker think of that?"

"She was less than pleased. I believe they had several rows over it."

"I see. Now, Danny, can you give me your whereabouts from early this morning?"

"I was with Victoria until she dropped me at my parent's house."

"And what time was that?"

"Half-one. I was there until she rang to tell me what happened"

"And what time was that?"

"Just before two."

The young Garda entered the kitchen. He looked a little nervous. "Excuse me, Sir," he said to Reilly, "Doctor Kelly is here."

Reilly and Cole finished up and went out. Joggy stood up and watched them through the back window go back down the yard.

"What was that all about?" snapped Alice, "you hurt my wrist, so you did."

Joggy turned around. "I'm sorry about that Alice, but I wouldn't give that bastard the steam of my..."

"There's no need to be vulgar, remember where you are."

"Sorry. Do you not remember him?"

"Should I?"

"Yes you should. It was Reilly who sent Luke Baker to prison, it was Reilly who nearly lost me two of my best customers, Cedric Mercer and Doc Kelly a couple of years ago and I'm pretty sure it was Reilly who attacked me in Kilpatrick then. "

"Joggy," she said, keeping her voice to a loud whisper, "you can't go around saying things like that without proof.... you'll get yourself into trouble."

"Give me some credit, Alice. I'm only saying it to you, but I know in my heart and soul it was him. McNeill told me there was no evidence to charge anyone, but that was to be expected, since they were investigating their own."

The rope had two nooses. One noose was tossed over the steel rafter and then fed through the other. It had then slid up and tightened around the steel. One of the Gardai climbed the stepped bales and cut the rope while the other three held Terry Parkers lifeless body.

"He's not been dead long," said Dr Kelly, on first examination.

"Murder or suicide, Doc?" Reilly asked.

Dr Kelly opened the mouth and pushed back the eye lids before standing to face Reilly. "There is an absence of petechiae haemorrhaging. You won't know for sure until after the autopsy. I believe we may be looking at foul play here. But you already suspected that, Detective?"

"Yes, I thought he looked a bit too peaceful for a suicide. My guess is he was dead before he was strung up."

Dr Kelly then left to attend to Mrs Parker.

Later, with the ambulance gone and the young Garda left to secure the yard, Cole and Reilly climbed back into their car. Reilly banged the passenger door closed.

"What's eating you?" Cole asked as they drove up the avenue.

"Jackson, that's who," he said, his jaw clenched. "That cunt gets up my nose. What I wouldn't give to be able to pin this on him."

Cole glanced quickly at Reilly.

That night as Joggy lay in the bed beside his softly snoring wife, the events of the day fizzed through his brain. Terry Parker's "suicide" just did not make sense and questions with no obvious answers, just kept coming. *If he was intent on suicide, why did he abandon everything in the yard? Why did he not bring the bucket of chicken feed and the gun into the shed and leave them there neatly? It was almost as if he had a sudden thought and then hurried to do it. Why did he go to all the rounds of setting up a rope when he held a better, faster and less painful way in his hands?* He concluded that this was a disorganised suicide, completely the opposite of what he knew Terry Parker to be. He then began to analyse the other possibility. *What if it wasn't a suicide?* From his vantage point that afternoon, he had seen Cole and Reilly going around to the side of the hayshed. *What did they find and why was Reilly so animated when he came back out?. What did they see that made them call it suspicious?* Then he remembered how urgent McNeill became after seeing Parker. *What had McNeill seen that I hadn't?* All he could recall was how peaceful Parker looked. And then a memory popped up, like a duck in a shooting gallery, and he had to check it out.

He eased out of bed, being careful not to wake Alice. In the kitchen he opened a door on the dresser and pulled out a couple of True Detective magazines. They were bought several months ago on a whim one Saturday morning while waiting for Alice to finish the weekly shopping. He thought he remembered there being a photo of a hanging in one of them. He leafed through the pages and there it was. Slipping on his reading glasses, he carefully examined the black and white picture of a grotesquely disfigured face; bulging eyes and the tongue jutting out at an angle from the mouth.

"What are you doing?" Alice asked from the doorway, squinting at him through sleepy eyes.

"Terry Parker didn't hang himself, Alice." The picture having validated his suspicions. "He was murdered," he concluded with the faintest hint of joy. Relieved now, that the harsh words he had used had not contributed to the mans untimely death.

Across the fields in a darkened room, slouched in a tattered armchair, in front of the dying embers of an open log and turf fire, was Harry Butler. Dangling from the nicotine stained fingers of her left hand was a cigarette, its long ash about to fall to the floor and in her right hand was a teacup. Her right arm hung limp over the side of the armchair, precariously close to the floor, with the dregs of a whiskey about to spill. The fire crackled and a spray of sparks flew out like fire works, momentarily awaking her from her stupor. She lifted her head and in the faint flickering light, her sad brown eyes, heavy with sleep, fell on a small faded and yellowed framed photo in the centre of the mantelpiece. As her eyelids closed again, a teardrop slipped out and ran slowly down her ruddy weather-beaten cheek.

Constant heavy rain forced Joggy home earlier than he had wanted on Wednesday afternoon from Heatherville house. He reached Oldbridge just after four and so decided to swing round by Henry Street to where the secondary school bus stop was. If the bus was not gone he could pick up his daughter, Helen. It would save her from walking home in the rain from where the bus would drop her off.

A large group of teenagers, boys and girls, their school uniforms matching the sky above, were huddled together under the bus shelter. Joggy stopped just short and scrutinized the group, but could see no sign of Helen. He then spotted, under the blue and white striped awning of Flynn's shop, two couples, completely oblivious to their surroundings, kissing, and one of them looked remarkably like Helen; shoulder length strawberry blonde hair and rosy cheeks. To be certain, he waited for them to break for air. When they finally did; he was certain. This was a first for him and he wasn't at all sure how he should handle it. He wished Alice was here. He blew the horn. Helen looked aghast when she saw her father and he did not need to be able to lip-read to understand what she said, "shit, it's daddy."

The young fella she was with, wore the crimson red jumper of the Christian Brother School. He turned around and gave Joggy a little wave; his face unconcerned.

Helen flustered with her school bag and then, without a backward glance, bolted for the car.

"See you tomorrow," the young man shouted after her.

There was silence as they drove home. Helen was edgy. She wanted to get it over with. She wanted her father to say what he had to say. She did not want to wait until they got home and have both her parents gang up on her. "Aren't you go to say something," she said eventually, "give out or whatever?"

A short silence ensued before Joggy spoke. "I'm a little disappointed really, could you not have picked someone a little taller and with a bit less acne?"

"We're teenagers dad; we've all got acne."

"What's his name?"

"Robert."

"Does Robert have a last name?"

"Nice try, dad, but you'll have to boil me in oil to get that."

"Well, is he a good kisser at least?"

"DAD!" Helen exclaimed. She then smirked. "He's not bad."

"You're experienced then are you?"

"He's not my first, if that's what you mean." Her rosy cheeks heated up.

"More than two, less than ten?"

"Again, nice try dad, but that's for me to know and you to find out."

"Look Helen," Joggy said solemnly. He was uncomfortable with what he felt he had to say. "You're at a stage in your life when boys are a major part of it. I have no problem with that, your mother will have no problem with it, it's part of growing up. So for our sakes keep it simple, please; preferably kissing only."

"I'm not going to do anything stupid, dad."

"Good. Has your mother had the *talk* with you?"

"The birds and bee's talk you mean? Yes she has."

"Good, good," said Joggy, relieved that he didn't have to fill in the blanks.

"So tell me, when you're not swapping spit with the acne king, what do ye do, groom each other like monkeys and burst each others pimples?"

"DAD! that's gross," she shrieked with disgust. But after a short while she started to laugh.

They drove up the short rutted avenue and around by the gable-end of the long low thatched farm house and came to a halt outside the front porch door. Hens scattered across the rough stone yard. The pebbledash house had not received a lick of paint in years and old yellowed newspapers and other bric-a-brac were piled high in the two dirty windows, one each side of the porch. The discoloured and battered porch door scraped open and Harry Butler stepped out. The two men saw instantly why she was called Harry. Beneath a head of short dirty grey hair, that looked as if it had been styled by a hedge shears, was the frayed collar of a navy check shirt. Over that was a grey v-neck jumper with holes in the sleeves where her elbows stuck out and below that a dark grey man's trousers, several sizes to big, which was held up by a slim brown leather belt.

"What do ye want?" she asked sharply as the men began to step out of the car. "Stay where ye are." She took a step back into the porch. "Ye can talk to me from inside the car."

The men sat back in. Cole rolled down the driver's side window. "We're policemen, Missus Butler," he said. "This is Detective Sergeant Reilly and I'm Sergeant Cole. We're investigating the death of Terry Parker. Did you know him?"

"Of course I did. What sort of a silly question is that? I know all my neighbours, old and new."

"Yesterday... Sunday... were you in the vicinity of Barterstown House?"

"Why?" She looked at the men suspiciously.

"Someone has said that they saw you there, is that true?"

"What time would that have been then?"

"Between twelve and one."

"Oh dear no, I would have been having a bite to eat at that time. Who ever it was must be mistaken."

"Have you seen anyone up at Barterstown House recently?"

"Well now that you mention it, I did clap eyes on two men up there a week ago, one of them was Joggy Jackson. He was there on the Sunday. But the other man was there the day before. Didn't know him, too well covered up. Was it Jackson that saw me? If it is, he must be mixing up the Sundays."

"There goes Jackson's alibi," said Reilly, as they turned in the yard.

Cole waved at her as he passed the door and drove out of the yard. "She seems a bit cuckoo to me. Do you think she's reliable?"

Reilly stayed silent.

Reilly remained in the passenger seat as Cole got out in the driving rain and opened Parker's heavy wrought iron gates. Earlier that Tuesday morning, Reilly had rung the house and Victoria had told him that her mother was well enough to answer questions.

Victoria met them in the kitchen. "Let me take your overcoat," she said to Cole. "I'll put it on the rack over the range. It'll be dry by the time you leave."

"Thank you, that's very kind of you," said Cole.

Reilly rolled his eyes at all the fuss and made his way into the sitting room. "I'm so sorry for your loss," he said to Elizabeth Parker, who was sitting in an armchair beside a blazing open fire.

"Thank you," she said in a voice barely above a whisper.

"I'm Detective Sergeant Reilly and this is my colleague, Sergeant Cole. Do you mind if we sit?"

She shook her head and gestured for them to sit on the settee. Reilly started by asking a few preliminary questions to establish her whereabouts on the day of her husband's death, then moved on to what he really wanted to know. "Could you tell us, Missus Parker, why your husband carried his shotgun with him everywhere?"

"He always said it was for security. Because of the troubles, you know. He thought, being down here, we were at risk. I don't like guns. But he had applied for his license and bought the gun without any of us knowing."

"Did he fear someone or was there a threat made against him or the family?" Cole asked.

"Apart from the few words he had with Danny's father, there was no animosity from anybody. In fact we were made feel very welcome here."

"Words! What words?" Reilly asked abruptly.

Mrs Parker raised a quizzical eyebrow. "Oh, it was nothing." She raised a hand into the air and attempted to swat away the inference Reilly was obviously drawing.

"Two stubborn men each set in their own ways..... schoolyard stuff"

"Nevertheless, Missus Parker, could you tell us what the argument was about?"

Mrs Parker explained.

"Did your husband fear Joggy Jackson?" Reilly asked.

"I don't believe so."

"You've been here two years," said Cole, "Why do you think your husband waited until six months ago to buy a gun?"

"I can't answer that Detective. My husband kept a lot of things close to his chest. When we lived up North, he was involved with the Orange Order, in fact, at the time he resigned to move down here, he was grand master of his local lodge. That part of his life interested me little, so we didn't talk about it much."

"When did the arguments with Joggy Jackson begin, do you recall?" enquired Reilly.

"Oh... I should think about the same time as he bought the gun."

Reilly's eyes brightened. "Really."

"The heavy gates at the head of the avenue Missus Parker," said Cole, "They're new are they not?"

"Yes, my husband had them erected about five months ago."

"Did he have anything else done?"

"Well, yes," she said, perplexed by what the two Detectives wanted to know. "He had deadbolts put on the doors and security locks on the windows. Why are you asking these kind of questions? Is there some doubt over Terry's death?"

"It's normal practice to rule out all suspicions in these cases," said Reilly, trying to deflect her fears. "We have to be thorough. There's nothing to worry about."

As Cole collected his coat from Victoria, a thought crossed his mind. "Was it your fathers habit to feed the chickens at that time every Sunday morning?"

"Oh no, I usually feed them, but he took it upon himself to feed them that morning."

A few hours later, Inspector Murray with the autopsy report in his hand, stood on the second of the two steps to the main entrance of the Garda Station and declared to the waiting press that he had a murder investigation on his hands.

"Inspector," enquired the Tribune reporter, "has your investigation so far unearthed any clues as to who might have done this?"

"Let's just say that we are following a definite line of enquiry. That is all gentlemen."

With the reporters still firing questions at him, Murray turned and walked back into the station

To everybody's surprise, Terry Parker was buried in the Church of Ireland cemetery in Knockeen. Danny told Joggy that a letter was found which stated that in the case of death, he wanted to be buried locally. It was not a large funeral, mostly near neighbours, local Church of Ireland members and family members who travelled from Northern Ireland. Afterwards, everyone who wanted to come were invited back to the house. Alice, along with a few other neighbours, made tea and sandwiches.

The family were barely in the back door when the phone rang in the hallway. Victoria answered it and then listened aghast at what she was hearing. "I have nothing to say," she said, and hung up. Seconds later the phone rang again. She listened and then shouted, "leave us alone," hung up and burst into tears. Danny rushed to her.

"Dad was murdered," she said, almost in a daze. "That was a reporter asking questions."

The phone rang again. "It's them again," she sobbed.

This time Danny answered it and listened. He said nothing, then depressed the cradle and left the receiver by the side of the phone. He wrapped his arms around her.

"Dad was murdered, Dad was murdered," she repeated against his chest, the words came slow like a mantra. It was almost as if saying them again and again, gave her some form of comfort, now that the stigma and shame of suicide had been lifted.

She leaned back from Danny. "Who would kill my dad?" Her eyes pleaded for an answer, but he had none to offer.

CHAPTER 4

Two weeks after Fr Nolan had announced it from the pulpit, the new curate made his first appearance on the altar. He was a tall slim man who looked to be in his fifties; bald and as brown as boot polish. "My name is Father Patrick Joseph Hayes," he said, in a clear crisp voice. I have spent the years since my ordination working as a missionary in Kenya, Chad and Uganda."

He then continued on explaining how the faith had taken hold and was now spreading throughout those countries. Somewhere in the middle he raised a laugh when he said that his only regret for having come home was that the lovely brown colour he had acquired, would soon vanish and that before long his skin would be as pale as his congregation. He then smiled cheekily at them and said, "Have the kettle on the boil ladies, I intend over the next month to call and get to know all my new parishioners."

After Mass, Joggy, Alice and the two girls retired to O Mara's pub. The ladies found seats while Joggy waited to be served at the bar. The buzz of conversation in the room was centred around only one subject; the Terry Parker murder. Joggy's turn came and he ordered a pint, a Babycham and two bottles of orange. The orange with two straws sticking out of them arrived on the counter. He brought them down to the girls. A few minutes later the Babycham and the pint arrived. He paid, and as he turned away with them in his hands, the bar door opened. All conversation ceased and the bar went deathly quiet. All eyes turned to look at Detective Sergeant O Reilly and an older uniformed Garda standing behind him in the doorway. Reilly walked towards Joggy; his eyes square on his target. He was, as usual, well turned-out, smart navy suit, crisp white shirt, navy tie, neatly trimmed black moustache and with his Brylcreamed hair parted to the right. "Mister Jackson," he said aloud, removing the drinks from Joggy's hands and placing them back on the counter, "I'm arresting you on suspicion of murder." He produced a pair of cast-iron, lock and screw handcuffs. He did not need them. They were primarily used for the violent and the dangerous. He wanted to cause Joggy the greatest discomfort. Reilly was still smarting over Joggy's role in the Luke Baker debacle he wanted to cause maximum embarrassment by arresting him in front of his family and friends.

"Murder?"

"Yes, of Terry Parker."

Shocked, but still thinking straight, Joggy, realised what he was up too and was not about to let him get away with it. He was not going to give Reilly the satisfaction of leaving quietly.

"You're a fucking joke' Reilly," said Joggy equally loud. "A week's investigation and this is the best you can come up with?"

"Are you sure you've got it right this time' Reilly," Spit Sweeney shouted. "The last innocent man you sent to prison died there."

"This is what you did to Luke Baker and now you want to do it to another one of our own," shouted a woman.

Reilly no longer looked smug. The crowd became more vocal and more animated. The Garda, fearing for their safety, grabbed Joggy's arm and marched him to the door.

Alice blocked the doorway. "You can't take my husband," she said. "You've made a mistake, he'd never do anything like that."

"Then you don't know your husband very well, Missus Jackson," said Reilly. "Now, get out of the way or I'll have you forcibly removed."

Joggy turned towards the room. "Is there anyone here that would allow such a thing to happen?" he asked.

To a man the patrons stood up and bellowed their support.

Reilly became alarmed.

"It's alright Alice," Joggy said reassuringly. "Ring Danny He has the spare key. He'll collect you. Don't worry about me, I'll be home soon."

Alice stepped aside and the two led him out. As they bar door closed behind them, someone shouted, "Tell the bastards nothing, Joggy."

Joggy sat on the back seat. The Garda climbed behind the wheel. Before he could start the engine, Reilly, sitting on the passenger seat, turned to Joggy. "Did you purchase some nylon rope recently?" he asked in a civil tone.

"Yeah, what of it?"

"Where is it?"

"It's in the boot of my car."

"If I take you to your car, would you show it to us?"

"If it'll get you off my back."

They drove to the car park in front of the Church. Joggy unlocked the car boot, but to his dismay there was no rope.

"When was the last time you saw the rope?" Reilly asked.

Joggy slowly shook his head. "I can't remember."

"Do you always keep it locked?"

"Yeah... most of the time."

"And is there occasion when you don't have it locked?"

"When I'm on a customers property, after all, who'd want to steal used garden tools?"

From an upstairs window, McNeill watched as Joggy was placed back in the police car.

As they travelled to Olbridge Garda station, Joggy, racked his brains, but he could not recall if he had taken the rope out of the boot. He did not think he did. He definitely did not use it. That he was sure of. He remembered buying it in the North Offaly Co-op and afterwards tossing it in the boot. But now as he thought about it, he had not seen it since and he had not missed it. But what was more disturbing to him was what Reilly had on him to make him a suspect. He realised that there was a distinct possibility that the cross words he had with Terry Parker had reached his ears, and now the rope was missing. The implication was not lost on him, nor he reckoned was it lost on Reilly. His stomach began to churn.

The interrogation room was small, sparse and quiet. A pine wooden table with round corners sat in the middle with three sturdy pine chairs; two faced one across the table. The magnolia walls were bare. The only sounds in the room came from the main office -- typewriters, phones ringing, people talking and the odd shout. The room smelt of Jeyes fluid. It was faint, like it had been washed a week ago. *Blood, vomit, was that what they washed away?* He tried not to think about it and instead turned his thoughts to Alice and the children. He had been in the room almost an hour when the door opened and a young Garda with a steel tray came in. On it was cup of tea and a small plate with three bourbon cream biscuits.

"How long more is this going to take?" Joggy asked.

The young Garda shrugged his shoulders. "It takes as long as it takes, I guess," he replied and left.

"Why are we waiting?" Cole asked Reilly

"No harm in letting him stew a little, makes them think... makes them nervous.... wondering what we got on them. Besides, I've got a trick up my sleeve and I need Jackson to fall for it."

Joggy pushed the tray aside, leaned back in the chair and folded his arms. He did not want their food. But somehow he could not take his eyes of the bourbon creams; they and his empty stomach, reminded him that he had not eaten since early morning. He eventually gave in.

Shortly after he had finished, the same young Garda came back for the tray, followed closely by Reilly and Cole. Cole sat opposite while Reilly remained standing. Cole had a large writing pad in front of him. Reilly dropped the thin manila file he was holding onto the table. Joggy said nothing. Instead, like the good card player he was, he waited for them to make the first move.

Reilly took his time. His eyes were locked on Joggy. He took a packet of Benson & Hedges cigarettes and a box of matches from his jacket pocket, lit the cigarette and then placed the spent match back in the box before sitting the match box neatly on top of the cigarette box and placed them on the table. He then removed his wristwatch and began walking slowly around the room.

"Mister Jackson," he said at long last, from directly behind Joggy. "On Sunday the fourteenth of April, did you and Mister Parker have an argument?" He asked in an even tone.

"Yeah, we had words." Joggy made no attempt to look around at Reilly, instead he directed his answers at Cole.

"What was this argument over?"

"He objected to me crossing his daughters land."

"Trespassing were you?"

Joggy did not answer.

When Reilly got no answer, he moved, stood behind Cole and asked another question. "Was this the first time?"

"No," Joggy, still directed his answers to Cole, "we had several rows and they were always over the same thing."

"I see. On Saturday the thirteenth of April did you also have an argument with Missus Harriet Butler."

"Yes."

"What was that over?"

"She put my two calves on the railway line."

"And why did she do that?"

"Pure bloody-mindedness. They had broken out onto her land."

"What did you do about that?"

"You tell me, I'm sure you already know."

Reilly pulled out a sheet of paper from his folder and then slammed it down in front of Joggy. He withdrew the cigarette from his mouth. "This is a copy of a complaint made by Missus Butler," he shouted. Smoke belched from his mouth and nostrils. "It states that you attacked her by driving fast through a large pool of water and saturating her in the process."

Joggy was determined not to allow himself to be dragged into a shouting match. He answered in the same monotone voice he had been using. "That, as I already explained to Sergeant McNeill, was accidental."

"It seems to me Mister Jackson, that you have quite a temper. Did you kill Terry Parker because he kept objecting to your trespass?"

"No I did not."

"Does your son Danny, cross the fields to see Victoria Parker?"

"Not at this time of year, only during the summer."

"So he hasn't crossed the fields recently?"

"No."

"So why was there a trodden grass path, discovered, leading from the back of your house to the back of Parker's sheds on the day of the murder?"

"How the hell would I know?"

A knock came on the door and Cole opened it. A Garda handed him a sheet of paper. He glanced at it and then handed it to Reilly. "What brand of cigarettes do you smoke?" Reilly read the information on the paper and then smiled knowingly at Cole.

"Sweet Afton."

"Did you on Sunday the fourteenth of April stand at the side of Parkers hayshed and lay in wait for Terry Parker?"

"No I did not."

"Then how can you explain this," Reilly shouted again as he slammed the sheet of paper onto the table in front of Joggy. "This sheet of paper says you're a fucking liar. Your fingerprints were found on an empty Sweet Afton cigarette packet there?"

"I can't." Joggy read the one line on the page. *The fingerprints are a match.* "The only way they could have got there is if you planted it."

"We don't manufacture evidence Mister Jackson, we just record what we find."

Suddenly it dawned on Joggy. "Where did you get my fingerprints?"

"You've just had tea, haven't you? You see Jackson, you might think you're smart, but you left a trail wide enough for a blind man to follow. Let me show you how much trouble you're in. You had a motive to kill Terry Parker. A Sweet Afton cigarette box, the type you smoke, with your fingerprints on it was found lying on a trampled patch of nettles by the side of the hayshed. Three Sweet Afton cigarette butts were also found there. Now, since you left your house just before twelve, this by your own admission, and Terry Parker was murdered close to twelve thirty, the cigarette butts suggest that instead of you going to Barterstown House, you crossed the fields and waited by the hayshed. When he came down the yard to feed the chickens you sneaked up on him, snapped his neck and then carried him into the shed. There, you used the blue nylon rope to hang him and hoped that we would think he had committed suicide. We retrieved that half-inch blue nylon rope and it measured thirty six feet exactly. Your rope, a half-inch blue nylon, according to the North Offaly Co-op purchase invoice, was also thirty six feet long."

"You know Reilly," said Joggy, "that is a lovely little fairy tale, and you should tell it to impressionable children, because they are the only ones who would believe it. During the time you say Terry Parker was murdered, I *was* in Barterstown House and as I told you before I have a witness who saw me there; Harry Butler."

"We've interviewed Missus Butler and would you believe it, she doesn't remember seeing you there."

"And you believed her. That only proves Reilly, that you're more gullible than I thought. Of course she's going to say that she didn't see me there; it's herrevenge for me wetting her."

"Missus Butler did say however, that she saw you in Barterstown House the previous Sunday," said Cole. "What were you doing there?"

"Just being curious. The place has been abandoned this good number of years."

"Curious my arse," said Reilly. "Setting up an alibi, that's what you were at. That's when you saw Missus Butler spying on you and being an elderly lady you thought she just might get confused enough not to remember which Sunday she saw you.

Well she didn't and your goose is cooked. So admit it, you did it. You murdered Terry Parker, didn't you?"

"No, I did not."

For the next hour, Reilly circled Joggy shouting at him to admit his guilt. For a while Joggy replied no. Then he stopped talking. He picked a spot on the wall and just focused on it.

Reilly eventually gave up. He put his wristwatch back on and picked up the manila file. Cole rose from his seat and the two headed for the door. "Your guilty, Jackson," said Reilly, and I for one will be glad to see the end of your smart mouth. Escort the prisoner to a cell," he said, to the young guard standing outside the room.

Inspector Murray, through the open door of his office kept a vigilant eye on the interview room. He saw Reilly and Cole leave and shortly after that Joggy Jackson being led to the cells. He then waited a few more minutes before calling Reilly into his office.

"Sir?"

"What have we got?" asked Murray.

"We've got Jackson gift-wrapped for this one, Sir."

"How so?"

"He had motive and opportunity. A trail led from his house to the hayshed. His fingerprints were found at the scene and the exact same length of rope used for the hanging, he purchased sometime earlier. And, his alibi did not stand up to scrutiny."

"Fingerprints! How did you obtain Mister Jackson's fingerprints?"

"From the tea mug, Sir."

"You do know you can't use them in evidence?"

"Yes Sir. They were only used to obtain a confession, Sir."

"And did you get one?"

"No Sir."

"Have that report on my desk, first thing tomorrow morning."

"Are we not jumping the gun here?" Cole asked Reilly when he came back to his desk.

"Of course not," said Reilly. "We've got our man."

"Are you sure? I know he looks good for it, but I would be happier if we did a bit more digging."

"You worry too much, Cole. We're not going to find out anything more than we already know. It's an open and shut case. Now you go home. I'll do the report."

Sergeant Cole lived two miles from Joggy Jackson's home. He had learnt that Mrs Jackson had rung the station on several occasions throughout the afternoon. Rather than phone her back, he decided as a matter of near neighbourly courtesy to call in on the way home and let her know that her husband was still in custody.

Alice answered the door. "Where's my husband?" she demanded, when she saw he was alone.

"I'm afraid Missus Jackson your husband is being detained overnight."

"For what, he's done nothing, he's an innocent man."

"May I come in?"

"Certainly." Alice stood aside and then glanced quickly around to see if any of her neighbours were watching.

Cole told her what they had found and asked if she could shed any light on it.

"Someone is going to great lengths to frame my husband, that's all I can say."

"And what about his alibi; he says Harry Butler saw him in Barterstown House."

"She did. He told me about it when he came home."

"Why would she lie?"

"To get her own back."

"It's a bit excessive for a wetting, don't you think?"

"Have you not met her?" Danny asked.

"I have; scary looking woman."

"And vindictive," said Alice. "She's been like that ever since we moved here twenty two years ago. There's not a neighbour she does not terrorize. But to be fair to her, she has only been nasty to us since the calves broke out onto her land. We had no problems with her before that. Joggy even crossed her land when he went walking and she didn't object. But now we're in her bad books and it's not a nice place to be."

Sergeant Cole stood up. "I wonder Missus Jackson, if yourself or Danny could show me around. It would help me get a fuller picture of your husband's movements."

"Of course, anything that will help."

"I'll show him around," said Danny. There was something about the Sergeant that Danny liked. He appeared fair, open-minded and seemed to want to help. They left the house and then stood on the pathway.

"I want you to play the part of your father Danny, and set out to walk to Barterstown House."

Danny opened a gate into the one acre field and then crossed it, moving left to a gap in the whitethorn hedge. He climbed up the well trodden bank and hopped over the sagging barbwire fence on top.

Cole stood on the grass bank and looked out across the field. He could see Barterstown House in the distance.

"From here, where would he go?" he asked.

"Danny pointed. "Down there, near the far corner there's a gate."

"And is this the route he would take if he was going for a walk to somewhere other than Barterstown House?"

"He would normally cut through Harry Butlers land and onto the railway line. He's only been taking this route lately." Danny then showed him around the rest of the property.

"I can't promise you anything Missus Jackson," said Cole as he was leaving, "but I would be hopeful of getting your husband home by morning."

The cell was a rectangular eight by six, four blank white walls and a grey steel door with a centre hole for food. A toilet, hand basin and a narrow tubular bed, on which he could get no sleep. As it was a Sunday, no solicitors were available. If he needed to engage one, he would have to wait until morning. Later that evening he was allowed make a phone call. He rang Alice and assured her he was alright. The night was long in his brightly lit cell. The hours ticked slowly by and if they had not taken his watch along with his tie, belt and other personal belongings, he would have been able to track them. He craved a smoke and he could have cadged a fag from one of the guards but he wouldn't please them to ask. As he lay on the bed with his fingers interlaced behind his noticeably greying hair, two questions occupied his troubled mind, who was framing him and how far was Harry Butler going to let it go before she told the truth. He hoped that the one night in a police cell would be enough to assuage her wounded ego. As for who was framing him, only one person, for now anyway, fitted into that picture; Reilly. And it was no certainty that it was him. But he was certain of one thing: he was going to pay Harry Butler a visit when he got out.

When Sergeant Cole arrived for work, Reilly, looking pleased, was already in and the report was on the Inspector's desk.

"Have you still got that ordinance survey map," Cole asked Reilly.

"Yeah, why, is there something wrong?"

"I'm not sure, Sir. There's something on it that I want to clarify with Mister Jackson. Could we have him up from the cell?"

Cole unfolded the map onto the interview room table, then spun it around to face Joggy. Reilly watched silently. "This is your property here." Cole, outlined it with the tip of his pen. "And this area next door is Parkers land. Could you show me on the map where you enter onto Parkers land from your property?"

"About there." Joggy, pointed to an area part-way down the left-hand side of his own field.

"And this gap behind the house, why would you not use that?"

"It's too high, too steep; you'd break your neck coming down it."

"Have you ever used it?"

"No."

"Thank you." Cole and Reilly left the room.

Reilly confronted Cole immediately after closing the door. "What are you trying to do? Are you trying to undermine my investigation?"

"No Sir, I'm not. I am trying to do my job."

"Sergeant Cole, can I have a word." The ever-vigilant Inspector Murray called from his office door.

"Close the door Sergeant." Murray said from behind his desk.

50

Since Inspector Murray had not asked him to sit, Cole stood uneasy in front of the desk.

"I've read Detective Sergeant Reilly's report, are you of the same opinion; should we charge Mister Jackson with Parkers murder?"

To Cole, the rhythmic clicking of Murray's pen was not a good sign. He swallowed. "I think it's premature, Sir."

"Go on."

"I called to Jackson's on the way home yesterday evening and examined the area in which Joggy Jackson crosses onto Parkers land and it does not match up to the trodden path we found. The path leads to another gap directly behind the house, a gap he does not use. The gap is on the top of a steep bank. I examined it and found no evidence of it ever being used. Which leads me to believe that it was put there maliciously. And if I take that line, then that leads me to believe that the person who put it there, did not know the area and assumed, being the closest to the house, that Jackson would enter Parkers land through there."

"What's your assessment of Jackson? Do you think he's capable of murder?"

"Everyone is capable of murder, Sir. If Jackson did do it, he must be very stupid."

"I can assure you Sergeant, he's not stupid."

"I know Sir. If he did it I don't believe he would leave that obvious a trail, unless it was on purpose. But the fly in the ointment is Harry Butler. Why would he give her as an alibi, if he knew she would not back him up? Which leads me to believe he may have been set up."

"I see. What about the physical evidence? The cigarette box and the rope."

"They could have been planted, Sir. People discard empty cigarette packets all the time. Anyone could have picked it up, with finger prints and all on it. As for the rope, Mister Jackson did say he didn't always lock his car, especially when he was at a customers house."

"Do you think we should let him go?"

"That's not my decision to make, Sir. But I do believe the evidence we have is not strong enough to hold him at present."

"What other leads have you got?"

"Something happened six months ago to make Parker go all security conscious. He put up a big gate, dead bolted the doors, locked the windows and bought himself a shotgun. I don't believe Jackson was the cause of that, and if he was, I don't believe he would be coming through the front gate."

"Thank you Sergeant," said Murray. "Ask Detective Sergeant Reilly to step in please."

Cole passed on the message. Reilly glared at him. "What did you say to Murray?"

"I only answered what I was asked."

"You better not have left me out to dry," Reilly warned. He walked warily into the Inspector's office.

"Detective Sergeant, go down to the cells and release Mister Jackson. Do not get anyone else to do it and be courteous to the man. Ask Sergeant Cole to drive him home in his car. Then when you come back here, you and I will have a little chat."

"But Sir, he's guilty. I know it. I can feel it in my bones. We have the evidence to prove it, Sir."

"What I just asked you to do Detective Sergeant, was not a request."

"Yes Sir." Reilly sighed and left. A few minutes later he was back. Like Cole before him, since he was not instructed to sit, he remained standing.

Inspector Murray lounged in his chair, his head was down and his fingers were interlaced in front of him, with the thumbs tapping against one another. He took his time before he finally spoke. "Do you know anything about snakes, Detective

Sergeant?" he asked, with his head still down. Slowly he lifted his head for the answer.

"Hmm... no Sir."

"Did you know that the Rattlesnake can hypnotise its prey?"

"Didn't know that, Sir."

"The prey, a mouse or a bird, just stands there staring into the snakes eyes, totally mesmerized. He's so fixated on the snake he doesn't see what going on around him. And because his emotions are all tied up in knots, he allows the snake to devour him."

"Am I supposed to be the rattle snake?" Reilly mentally scratched his brain as he tried to make sense of the Inspector's metaphor.

The Inspector unlaced his fingers and leaned forward. "No, you're the mouse Detective Sergeant. You've allowed your perceived enemy, Mister Jackson, to tie up your emotions to such an extent that you cannot see past him. And I can only blame myself for that. As soon as I became aware of Jackson's involvement in this case, I should have taken you off it. Jackson, did an extraordinary thing in clearing his good friend's name. You became a casualty of his success and unfortunately it left you professionally embarrassed. It was not personal on his behalf, after-all he did nearly pay with his life. Contrary to what you believe, Detective Sergeant, he did not set out to bring you down. But *you* took it personal and in this case you allowed it to consume you."

"But all the evidence is there, Sir. Everything points to Jackson."

"And any half-witted barrister will tear it to shreds in court. Do you want to be professionally embarrassed *again*, Detective Sergeant?"

"No, Sir," he said feebly.

"In my experience, a good Detective not only sees what is there, but he also sees what is not there. You only focused on what was in front of you, Detective. Other clues presented themselves to you in this case but you choose to ignore them. Because of your blind spot, yours was an ill-considered rush to judgement. Fortunately for you, I know you to be a better Detective than that. I want you to take a week off and clear your head. When you come back you'll be reassigned."

"But Sir...."

"I'll have no argument," Murray said sharply. "Take the week, Detective. That's an order."

CHAPTER 5

A small group of reporters were assembled outside the station as Joggy and Sergeant Cole emerged.

"Mister Jackson?" one reporter asked, "What is your involvement in this case?"

Neither Joggy nor Sergeant Cole spoke as they rushed to the metallic blue Ford Escort. With questions flying after them, they drove away. Joggy kept his head down until they were clear of Oldbridge.

"Talk to me." Joggy, straightened up in his seat. "What's going on? Last night Reilly was ready to charge me with murder, this morning you're letting me go."

"Some doubts have arisen over some of the evidence. We're having another look at it."

"The ordinance survey map; was that one of the doubts?"

"Yes, the trail we found leading to Parkers was from directly behind your house. Do you know of anyone who would try and implicate you in this murder? Someone that has connections to both you and Parker."

Joggy thought about it but no one apart from Reilly came immediately to mind. He decided against voicing his opinion. "No, I can't say I can. Does this mean I'm off the hook?"

"Not entirely. You are still very much in the picture and will still be considered a suspect until we can finally rule you out. And that means, you have to stay away from Harry Butler."

Joggy was noncommittal.

Cole had rung Alice before they left. She and Danny were waiting at the gate when they pulled up. Joggy got out. "Remember what I said Mister Jackson." Cole, shouted through the open door. "Stay away from Harry Butler and let us do our job."

"Thank God you're home," said Alice, placing her hands one each side of his unshaven face.

"You look like shit," said Danny, as they walked up the daffodil bordered path.

"You would too if you had the day and night I had. Why aren't you in college?"

"And miss all the fun," he teased. "Did they beat you with rubber hoses or rolled up newspapers?"

"No, they were fine."

"Damn, I thought I'd have a good story to tell my friends."

Over a hot mug of tea and a fry-up breakfast, which he barely touched, Joggy filled them in on everything that was said and done. And then a silence fell. Joggy suddenly rose from the table and grabbed his coat from the back of the kitchen door.

"Where are you going?" Alice asked.

"I'm going to see that Butler bitch and sort this out once and for all."

"You'll do no such thing." Alice whipped the coat from his hands. "You'll do as the Sergeant told you and stay away. The only place you are going to is bed; you've had no sleep."

Sleep came slowly, but when it eventually did, it was deep.

"Excuse me Inspector," said the duty officer as he stood in the doorway. "There is an elderly couple at the front desk, a Mister and Missus Mercer, they say they employ Joggy Jackson and would like a word."

The Inspector followed the Garda to the front desk.

"Mister and Missus Mercer how can I help you?"

"We came to tell you Inspector that you have the wrong man."

"Really, what makes you so sure?"

"Experience, Inspector. You don't get to be our age without developing a sense about people and it's not what they say or do, it's their aura. There is a glow that surrounds good people and Mister Jackson has that glow. Is he still here?" She glanced past the Inspector. "He was to come to us this morning. Maybe we could have a word."

"He's not here, Missus Mercer. He was brought home earlier this morning. I don't imagine he got much sleep last night, so he's probably gone to bed."

"Oh, we'll ring Alice when we go home so," she said to her husband. She looked at Murray again. "Remember Inspector, Joggy Jackson is a good man. He would never do what you accuse him off."

Murray gave a half-smile as they elderly couple turned away. He had barely warmed his seat again when the phone rang. "Yes?"

"Ex-Inspector Matthews is on line two, Sir," said the duty officer.

"Peter," said Murray warmly.

"Martin, on your recommendation I employed Joggy Jackson. Now I hear he's been accused of murder. My family's reputation and safety is on the line here, I can't be seen to employ a killer."

"Peter, calm down. You're jumping the gun a little here. Joggy Jackson has not been charged with murder. He's been simply helping us with our inquires."

"That's not putting my mind at ease, Martin. I need to know if he's going to be charged and if my family are safe around him."

"Look Peter, when your back went out, you came to me looking for someone who could do a couple of hours a week in the garden. I recommended Jackson and I stick by that recommendation. Between you and me and this telephone Peter, I believe there is more to this Parker murder than meets the eye and that Jackson's role in it is that of a pawn rather than a participant."

"So you're saying he's safe?"

There was a short pause before Murray replied. "Yes."

"You don't seem very sure?"

"Look Peter," he said losing his patience, "he's there to do the gardening, not to baby-sit your grandkids. If you don't feel safe, let him go. Now I've work to do, I'll talk to you later. Good day." Murray hung up.

"The Inspector wants to see you," said the Guard at the front desk to Cole when he returned.

Cole tapped on the open door. "Excuse me, Sir. You wanted to see me?"

Murray lifted his head out of what he was reading and in a well grooved action, removed his reading glasses at the same time.

"Yes. Detective Sergeant Reilly has been removed from the Parker case. Detective Sergeant Mark Cosgrove will be taking over and when he does I will need you to bring him up to speed. He is currently finishing up another case, so for the next couple of days, you're in charge."

"Me, Sir," said Cole, clearly shocked.

"I have been impressed by your work to date, Sergeant. You have a smart head on your shoulders; you'll do fine. Just keep me updated. Now close the door on the way out."

Normally Joggy had his tea and sandwiches outside in his make-shift canteen of tea chest, chair and transistor radio, but today Mrs Mercer insisted on inviting him in. Mr Mercer had gone to town on an errand. She was effusively supportive and had said if he should need a character reference they would be only too glad to provide one. She clucked around him like a mother hen and while he was delighted with her support, he found it claustrophobic. He was glad of the break when the phone rang, halting the non-stop chatter. He thought about quietly slipping away but then ruled it out as he did not want to offend her. So instead he allowed his mind to wander.

"Joggy, Joggy," Mrs Mercer's soft kind voice called.

"What! Oh I'm so sorry, Missus Mercer, I was a million miles away."

"I don't blame you, this sordid business would fill your head with all sorts of conflicting thoughts. It must be very disconcerting for you. Would you like more tea?"

"No thank you. You've been very kind. I should really be getting back to work."

So far, to his great relief, his regular customers were very supportive, preferring not to believe what was circulating on the rumour mill. Joggy called in, as per usual, on Wednesday evening to Peter Matthews. The house was a large ivy-covered building, not dissimilar to the Barterstown House he had seen in the black and white photograph. Matthews, unusual even for a retired policeman, was a man of poor posture, sloped shoulders and with an arched back that resembled a weeping willow. Joggy reckoned, lying down, he would be close to six foot four. He was waiting for him when he drove around into the back yard.

"Evening," said Joggy.

"I thought I'd get my Kerrs Pinks in this evening," said Matthews, all business. "A little late I know, but they'll grow anyway." He followed Joggy to the garden and then watched as he prepared the ground. The garden was small and compact. The soil was loose and easy to work and within an hour was dug, manured and ready to be sown. He had enough seed for ten short drills. All the while Matthews sat there silent, watching and evaluating. He sat on one of three white ornate metal chairs that surrounded a matching white metal table on the outer edge of the patio.

Normally, he would light his Briar pipe and then wade into current affairs, whether that be politics, religion or world news and Joggy usually looked forward to these discussions; sometimes wading in with a subject of his own. Matthews was not a man for small talk and the silence, this evening, suited Joggy, fine. It meant he got finished quicker and got home sooner. It was a once-a-week, handy number and Matthews always paid him before he left. This evening however Joggy got the feeling that Matthews wanted to say something. He could almost feel the tension vibrating from him and he also had a good idea what it was about. At last he finished, leaving ten neat drills. Matthews accompanied him back to the car.

"Tell me something," said Matthews as Joggy loaded his shovel and digging fork back into the rear of his car

"How are you involved in this Parker thing."

"I'm not," Joggy replied, closing the boot lid.

"Inspector Murray is a good friend of mine, and he tells me you're helping with their inquires. That, in my time on the force, could mean anything. So in your case what does it mean?"

"It means that someone has been trying to set me up for Parkers death and they've saw through it."

"So they've cleared you?"

"Not exactly. My alibi for that morning, a near neighbour, is at the moment refusing to cooperate."

"Why?"

"I don't know why and I can't find out because I've been told to stay away from her."

"I don't want you to take this personally," he said, as he opened his jaded brown leather wallet and paid over the money, "but I'll have to suspend your services until this Parker thing is cleared up. Being an ex-head of police means I have a reputation to uphold. I don't want to be dragged into the papers. I do hope you understand."

"Well if that is your decision, then I don't have a choice but to accept it," said Joggy.

And the bad news did not end there.

"Katie was sobbing when she came home from school today," said Alice. "It seems some of the children are taunting her and calling names."

"Did she say whose kids they were?"

"Eventually, when she stopped crying. Theresa Conroy's two boys and Maeve Byrne's daughter. You'd think they'd know better than to talk in front of their children. I'll give them a piece of my mind when I see them on Sunday."

"Is Helen all right?"

"A few snide remarks were made in her presence but so-far no-one has said anything to her face. By the way have you seen the Tribune?" Alice took it down from the drying rack above the Stanley range. "Helen got it in Flynn's. They haven't mentioned your name, but it wouldn't take a genius to work out who they are writing about. The story covers most of the front page."

Joggy glanced at it. He then tossed it onto the settee. "Where's Katie?"

"In her bedroom."

"How's my princess?" he asked. Katie was sitting on her bed with her back to the wall reading one of her favourite books; *Marmaduke the Elephant.*

"I wish Marmaduke would jump out of the book and squish them," she said with her bottom lip doing its best to curl up over the top one.

Joggy slid across the bed and sat beside her. "And after Marmaduke has flattened them we'd get a big shovel and scoop them up and then put them in the dustbin."

Katie smiled for the first time that day. "And then we'd get a big rock and put it on top of the lid so they'd never ever get out and be mean to me again."

"That's a great idea." Joggy put his arm around her and pulled her close.

"You feel better now?"

"Now that they're in a dustbin, much better."

"Good. Tell me, how would you like to stay out of school for the rest of the week?"

Katie jumped up and gave him a hug.

Later that night while sitting on the settee in the kitchen, Joggy, after a short period of deep thought, posed a question for Alice. "Do you think evil people cast darker shadows than good people?"

"What a strange question. Where did that come from?"

"Katie. That's what she asked me when I was kissing her good night just now."

"She does come out with the strangest things at times. What answer did you give her?"

"I told her I didn't know any evil people apart from Fred Winter. And at the time I didn't notice whether his shadow was darker than mine."

Father Hayes called on Thursday evening. "God bless all who dwell here," he said as he entered the kitchen. A heavy black Crombie coat and black woollen scarf kept out the cold.

"Evening Father," said Joggy, as he shook hands with him. Father Hayes grip was weak. He had grey watery eyes with dark circles around them. His face was long and thin and there was a slight wheeze in his breathing. They were both the same height.

"You're welcome to the parish," said Alice. "Will you have a cup of tea?"

"Thank you, if it's not too much trouble."

"Oh no trouble at all. Have a seat Father," she said and gestured towards the settee.

Joggy sat by the end of the kitchen table.

Alice removed the hot plate on the stove and placed the kettle over the naked flames. "Will you have something with it? I have some fresh scones, only baked today or I have soda bread, I could butter up a few slices of that for you."

"A scone would be lovely, thank you. You don't get many of them in Africa."

The kettle whistled and Alice removed it and replaced the hot plate.

"Do you smoke Father," enquired Joggy, as he walked across the floor with an open packet of Sweet Afton in his hand. He extended it towards him. One cigarette protruded out further than the rest.

"I do unfortunately, but I'm off them at the moment. So thanks, but no thanks."

"Trying to give them up, are you?"

"Doctors orders. The auld chest was kicking up." Joggy changed his mind about having one as he sat back down. He closed the packet and placed them on the table.

"Don't let me stop you from having one," said Father Hayes.

"It's fine Father. I'll have one when you leave. Your health, is that what brought you back to Ireland?"

"Yes. The arid dusty air out there wasn't helping matters."

"What made you pick Kilpatrick, Father?"

"Oh I'm afraid, Joggy we have little or no say in where we are sent. The Archbishop, with God's help, chooses our lot for us. And I can make no complaint, for he has sent me to a beautiful village with beautiful people."

"Have you settled in, Father," enquired Alice, as she pulled up a chair to use as a table for the tea and scones.

"I have and everyone's been very helpful in that regard."

The children came in from outside. "Ah, Father, these are my two girls," said Joggy.

"Helen here, as she never tires of telling us, is the middle child, while Katie is our youngest."

"You're still brown," said Katie. "You said that you were going to be like us."

"I'm delighted you were listening to me on Sunday, Katie. And I will eventually be like everyone else, but unfortunately it won't happen overnight. It'll take a good few weeks more."

"What are the people in Africa like Father?" enquired Helen. "Are they like us?"

"In some ways. They are a simple, proud and beautiful people with a strong faith. Where I worked was among the country people, farming people. They have little or no education and so they are slow to try anything new. Up to a few years ago the main implement they used for working the land was the *Jembe*. Which in English means a hoe. It took a lot of persuading but we eventually got them to start using oxen to plough the fertile soil. And when I left them they were doing very well."

"Helen, Katie, can ye go to your rooms or outside to play," Alice asked.

"Thank you Father," said Helen, as the girls disappeared outside again.

"You have two beautiful girls," said Father Hayes. "I believe you also have a son?"

"We have, Danny, he's away in college," said Alice.

"What's he studying?"

"Horticulture," said Joggy.

"Taking after you then, Joggy, is he?"

"In a way I suppose he is. The only difference is he'll have all the technical know-how and all the fancy Latin names for everything."

A short silence ensued as Father Hayes bit into the scone and then took a mouthful of tea.

"It's a beautiful spring evening, father, you must be roasting in that coat?" said Alice.

"Not a bit. For the last twenty-five years my body has gotten used to the heat of Africa, so when I come home, I freeze. Like my tan, it'll take my body time to acclimatise."

"And where exactly is home, Father?" Joggy asked.

"West Clare, I still have family there. I couldn't help hearing the gossip, Joggy. You seem to be in a spot of bother with the law?"

"I wouldn't believe everything you hear, father. If my time was to end right now, I would happily stand before God's judgement, knowing that the stain of murder was not on my soul."

"Well I'm delighted to hear that, Joggy. For Our Lord would not look kindly on the individual who committed that heinous act."

"So, do you think you will be left in this parish?" Alice asked, wanting to change the subject.

"I hope so. I find the people here very warm." Father Hayes finished his tea and scone and then chatted for a short while before he eventually stood up.

"Thank you for everything Alice, that was lovely." He shook hands with Joggy and then walked gingerly down the footpath.

"That's not a well man," said Alice as they watched him climb into his car.

Father Hayes turned the car on the road and headed back to Kilpatrick.

CHAPTER 6

His kiss was not reciprocated in the usual passionate way; that was the second clue. The first one was the unenthusiastic way in which she greeted him when he came in the kitchen that Friday evening. For Danny, clapping eyes on Victoria for the first time in five days was normally the happiest part of his week. His heart would jump so hard in his chest, he feared someday it would wrench itself free from its moorings. "What's wrong?" he asked, not waiting for the third clue.

"We need to talk," she said, holding his eyes for only a brief moment before pushing him gently away and dropping her eyes.

"Victoria, has something happened?" He had rung her on Wednesday evening and despite everything, she was in good form.

"Yes," she said abruptly, "My father has been murdered and your father is the chief suspect."

She lifted her eyes to meet his. They were full of tears. "My mother....well....she's not happy with me being with you at the moment."

"But my father had nothing to do with it."

"I don't believe your father had anything to do with it either."

"Do you want me to talk to your mother?"

"No, I want you to leave. I....I...we, we had a chat and think it would be best for everyone if we didn't see one another for awhile."

"What? Are you breaking up with me?"

"Temporarily. It's not for good or anything, it's just until all of this is sorted."

"But this might never be sorted. What if they don't find who did this, what then?"

"I'm sorry Danny, but right now my mother comes first. She doesn't want you here. She's quite upset at the moment and all you do is remind her of what she has lost. I love you Danny, but I can't be with you right now."

Danny could hear it in the tone of her voice that her mind was made up. He turned away and walked out the back door. He did not even glance in the back window as he passed. If he did he would have seen the tears flowing freely down Victoria's face.

Joggy and Alice were very surprised to see Danny walk in. Normally there would be no sign of him until late Saturday morning.

"Any hot water?" Danny asked.

"There's plenty," replied Alice.

Without another word, Danny went straight to the bathroom.

"Must be no hot water in Parkers," said Joggy, carving a piece from his pork chop.

"I think they've had a fight," said Helen.

"What makes you think that?" Alice asked.

She tapped the end of her nose.

Ten minutes later Danny was back out; wet hair, towel around his waist, trailing a cloud of steam. He rushed to his room before anyone could ask him a question. A half hour later he left his bedroom, dressed in black cord jeans, white shirt and blue denim jacket. He made a dash for the front door but Joggy stepped in front of him and blocked his exit.

"What's going on?" he asked.

"Nothing's going on."

"Victoria run out of water?"

"No," he replied brusquely. He brushed past his father and was gone out the door.

For a few seconds there was stunned silence in the kitchen.

"Told you," said Helen. She tapped her nose again. "Sisterly intuition."

Danny walked the half mile to the main road and hitched a lift into Oldbridge. From there he made his way to *The Wayward Mariner*. He sat at the bar and ordered a pint. Nobody knew him so he was left in peace to drink and to brood and as the pub filled up, listen to snatches of conversations in which his father's name was mentioned once or twice. He kept his head down and thought about Victoria and a great sadness came over him. With each subsequent pint the sadness grew deeper and deeper until it turned into anger.

By closing time he had downed eight pints. He staggered out the door and the sharp coldness of the night hit him like a slap in the face. He pulled his denim jacket tightly around him and made his way towards the chipper across the street. He bought a quarter-pounder, curry chips and a can of Fanta, then sat on the windowsill of the chipper and ate them. Groups of people milled around eating and chatting.

Four people stood close to where Danny sat. One of them knew who Danny was and began to speak louder. "You know I was wracking my brain looking for a good name for Jackson. All famous killers have names like, the Yorkshire Ripper or the Acid Bath Killer or Jack the Ripper and then it hit me, the Digger Killer, it has the right ring to it, don't you think; the Digger Killer."

The others laughed. Normally, Danny turned a deaf ear to drunk talk but not tonight. He rose unsteadily and staggered towards his target. The next thing he remembered was being dragged off the man by two Gardai. The man lay on the concrete footpath with blood seeping from his mouth and nose.

"Say Digger Killer now you prick," Danny spat at him.

He was brought to the station and placed in a cell to cool off. Early the next morning he was fetched from his cell. He now stood in Inspector Murray's office.

"Sit down," Murray ordered.

He did as he was told. His head pounded like a pneumatic drill.

"You are lucky that the young man you hit is not pressing charges for assault."

The message sank slowly into Danny's brain.

Murray waited for it to finally register and for the relief to show on his face. "But that does not mean you are off the hook," he said gravely. "We can still press charges for you being drunk and disorderly. Give me one good reason why we shouldn't?"

Danny's eyes watered up. "I'm sorry. I've never been in trouble before. It's just that my girlfriend broke up with me yesterday. She's the daughter of Terry Parker...."

"I see, say no more, I've got the picture." Murray pulled a white handkerchief from his inside pocket and handed it to Danny.

"It's clean. It's never been used. Now mop your eyes and don't worry, I'm not going to charge you this time, but if it happens again I'll have no hesitation in throwing the book at you. Now I've rung your parents. They should be here shortly to pick you up."

"Thank you," said Danny. He returned the handkerchief.

"Keep it as a reminder of, hopefully, your one and only brush with the law.."

Murray walked Danny to the front desk. "You can wait here." He placed a hand on Danny's shoulder. "Stay out of trouble."

Joggy arrived. "Are you all right?"

"I'm fine." And no more was said on the drive home.

"Do you want some breakfast," Alice asked when he came in the kitchen.

"No thanks, I'm going to bed."

Later that Saturday morning Alice did her usual weekly shopping and could not help noticing how people looked differently at her. It seemed to her that every eye in the place was trained on her and everybody was talking about her in hushed tones.

Joggy dropped into the *Cherry Tree pub*, which was attached to the shopping centre. "A pint please," he said.

The young man behind the bar, reddened with embarrassment. "I'm sorry, Mister Jackson" he said, "I've been told by the boss that I was not to serve you. You'll have to leave."

"Why?" asked Joggy, taken aback, "I come in here most Saturday mornings?"

"The boss said that other people would not come in if you were sitting here, I'm sorry."

Joggy left and went and sat in the car and stewed. After loading the messages into the car Alice sat into the passenger seat. Instead of turning left for home he swung right for the centre of town.

"Where are we going?" Alice asked.

"I want to see Reilly and see has he spoken again to Harry Butler. Do you know I was humiliated in the *Cherry Tree* this morning? They wouldn't serve me, asked me to leave. I'm not putting up with this any longer, I want answers."

Joggy marched up to the front desk. "I want to speak to Detective Reilly?" He hated calling him by his formal title but he reckoned if he used his first name he might be branded a trouble maker and not allowed see him at all.

"Can I ask what it's in connection with, Sir?"

"The Parker murder."

"And your name, Sir?"

"Joggy Jackson."

"Detective Reilly doesn't deal with that case any more, the person you want to speak with is Sergeant Cole. Hold on and I'll see if he's available."

Sergeant Cole appeared. "Mister Jackson, what can I do for you?"

"What have you done about Harry Butler? Our lives are a mess. My children are been bullied at school, I've lost a customer and I'm been asked to leave pubs."

"Come through and we'll talk," said Cole.

"How come Reilly was taken off the case?" Joggy asked.

"Another case came up and he was moved onto that."

"More high profile than a murder case, was it?" He tried to keep a smile from breaking out.

"I don't hand out the assignments, Mister Jackson. I just do as I'm told." Cole grabbed a file from his desk and led Joggy into the interview room. "Now, all I can tell you Mister Jackson is that I have re-interviewed Harry...Mrs Butler and nothing has changed."

Joggy was about to say something derogatory, but then thought better of it.

"Do you know the Parker family any way well, Mister Jackson?"

"Only what Danny tells me about them. What do you need to know?"

"It hasn't escaped my attention that the last two owners of the farm have been murdered. Now, our interest in the farm ended with Winters death. Missus Parker told me that they inherited the farm...."

"Terry Parker did not own the farm, his daughter Victoria, does. She was Winter's niece."

"So Winter left it to his niece?"

"Not exactly. Winter died without leaving a will, so the farm then fell to his closest relative."

"But surely Missus Parker was his closest relative?"

"They're not related at all; Victoria was adopted by the Parkers. Her father was John Canavan, the man Winter murdered, and her mother was the fourteen-year-old sister of Winter. She died in childbirth."

Cole's head was suddenly full of possibilities. "Thank you, Mister Jackson, you have been most informative."

"Now that I've helped you, how about you helping me and getting Harry Butler to retract her statement."

"I've tried, twice, but she's not budging. My earlier warning stays in place Mister Jackson, do not approach her."

Joggy left without saying another word.

"She's sticking to her story," he said to Alice as they drove away from the station. "And there's fuck-all that can be done about it."

While Alice put the messages away, Joggy stood at the front door, Sweet Afton in hand, puffing like a man on death-row. It was a beautiful sunny spring day with a hint of summer heat; the type of day he normally loved to spend pottering in the garden. But there was no joy in him today. He did not like the feeling that his life was not in his hands. It was on hold. Other people had control of it and there was nothing he could do about it. Well he could, but he had promised Alice he would stay away from her. She held the key and it only took for her to say she saw him and he would be free again. *But what were the chances of her doing that?* he thought. *What if they never found the real killer? I would be in limbo, permanently connected to Parkers murder and never officially cleared. People would doubt me, they'd never feel totally comfortable around me. The doubt would always be there, did he or did he not?*

"Alice," he called into the kitchen, "I can't do this anymore. I can't stand and wait while other people destroy our lives. I'm going to see Harry Butler."

"No you're not," said Alice, joining him in the doorway. "*We* are going to see Harry Butler."

"What are we going to do if she doesn't change her mind?" Alice asked as they crossed the fields.

"No idea. Let's just hope it doesn't come to that."

Harry Butler was riding her Massey-Brown tractor across the haggard when she spied them climbing through a gap in the whitethorn hedge that bordered their lands. She stopped the tractor outside her front door and disappeared into the house. A few minutes later she emerged into the yard and met them with a loaded single-barrel shotgun raised to her shoulder. They stopped. "Stay back or I'll use this," she shouted.

"Whoah," said Joggy, with his hands up. "We're not here to do you any harm."

"Harriet, we just want to talk to you," said Alice.

"Look," said Joggy, "I'm sorry if you're still mad at me for wetting you, but I was really angry with you at the time for putting my calves on the railway line."

"You think that's what this is all about?" said Harry, with incredulity in her croaked voice.

"But what else can it be?"

"It's not nice being an outsider, is it? People looking at you, pointing fingers, doubting you."

"I don't understand. If it's not about the wetting then why are you telling the guards that you did not see me at Barterstown House? I saw you behind the whitethorn bush and I know you saw me.

"Leverage... without it I have no hope."

"Leverage! Leverage for what?"

"I saw you up at the big house and I could have told the guards that, but that would not get me what I wanted."

"Harriet," said Alice, "could you put the gun down, please, and let's talk about this in a civilised manner."

She glowered at one then the other, then lowered the gun. "One good deed deserves another. I'll tell them the honest truth, but only, if you do something for me."

"Anything," Alice agreed, a little too quickly for Joggy's liking.

"And what would that be?" Joggy enquired.

"I need you to find my daughter."

"Your daughter! You've a daughter?" said Joggy surprised.

"Yes, her name is Cissy."

"And where is she?"

"If I knew that I wouldn't be asking you to find her, now would I?" she retorted sharply.

"I thought that she might have went to Dublin, Cork or Limerick or some place like that and you hadn't heard from her in a while."

"Well she could have ended up in any one of those cities, but all I know is that when she left here, she was going to the shop."

"Oh my God." Alice twigged what Harry Butler wanted. "That was a long time ago; long before we came here."

"It'll be thirty-three-years next August," said Harry.

"Wait now, wait now," Joggy said, catching up, as an old vague memory resurfaced.

"Wasn't she very young; a child I think?"

"She was twelve years old; only a month away from her thirteenth birthday when she cycled out of this yard on my bike to go to Bakers shop and I've not clapped eyes on her since."

"And now, you want me to do what a massive search, with hundreds of men, women and guards couldn't do at the time....find her?"

"That's the deal."

"Oh Harriet, I'm so sorry." Alice moved towards her, her face full of motherly concern. "We were only children ourselves when it happened. I can't imagine what you've been going through all this time."

"Hell. Pure bloody hell, that's what. There's not an hour goes by that I don't expect her to walk in that door."

"I don't know what I would do if anything like that happened to one of my girls," said Alice.

Harriet began to melt. "There's nothing you can do but wait and wait and wait."

Alice placed a caring hand on her arm and Harriet flinched. It was as if she had forgotten what it felt like to be touched by another human being.

"It's all right, Harriet, you're not alone anymore."

The tough external shell slowly vanished and what was left was a broken sad old lady.

Gobsmacked, Joggy looked at Alice as she made further soothing remarks in an effort to comfort Harriet. He could not work it out. Had she not heard or understood the enormity of what Harry Butler wanted?

"Come in, I'll make us some tea," said Harry.

The kitchen smelt of smoke and the furniture was old and the worse for wear, but to both Alice's and Joggy's surprise, the place was clean. The open fire gave a cosy glow and a blackened kettle, suspended on a charred metal arm, boiled steadily above it.

The women chatted amiably as Harry made the tea, while Joggy, in a world of his own, sat at the oil cloth covered table, his mind still boggled by Harry's request.

"Stop, stop" he said loud enough to get their attention. "This, this is crazy. I can't do what you want me to do. I can't magically conjure up your daughter. Sad and all as it is, you have to face up to the fact that after all this time, Cissy is ....."

"Gone.... you needn't be afraid to say it," said Harry as she poured out the tea. "I know she's dead. It's thirty-three-years ago. I'm not a fool. But I still keep a faint spark of hope that one day I will find her. You know," she paused, and holding the tea pot by both hands she looked towards the murky window glass and through it into the front yard. A gentle radiance came upon her face. "Her spirit comes to me. Sometimes when I stand at the front door, I can hear her giggling, the way she used to giggle when she'd chase the ducks around the yard. She had an infectious laugh... it still echoes there. And sometimes I can smell her. She always washed   with Lavender soap."

"You can try, can't you?" Alice looked hopefully at Joggy.

"Don't ye understand? What you're looking for is a thirty-three-year-old needle in a thirty-three-year-old haystack. There was a better chance of her being found back then, than there is now. The trail is ice cold."

"I have the same faith in you that Luke Baker had. You did the impossible for him, why not do the impossible for me?"

"Well I would never give up looking for my child and neither would you," Alice chimed.

"I just want to bring her home," said Harriet, her eyes full of pain.

"Alright, alright, but what happens if I don't find her?"

"Honest effort will be rewarded."

"What does that mean, exactly?"

"I will go to the Garda station in Oldbridge and tell them the truth."

"And what if they don't believe you?"

"They will."

"How can you be so certain?"

"Because, not alone can I clear you but I can point them towards the real killer."

"You saw him?"

"Yes, but I didn't know who he was until recently that is. But then didn't the boy-o turn up again in the most surprising place ever."

"You know his name?"

"Now Joggy, you've been playing cards long enough to know that you never throw down your trump card until the very last." Joggy gave a large sigh. "Ok then. I'll need as much information as you can remember. What happened that day?"

"It was a Thursday, the day before Bonnie Fitzgerald was to be buried. From early that morning the lane had been busy with people calling up to the house. It was late afternoon before it quietened down. I was out of tea. I asked Cissy to go to the shop. She climbed onto my bike, which was too big for her, but she was able to manage it..... I can still see her, pale yellow dress and black boots: A matching yellow ribbon in her hair."

"Is that Cissy?" Joggy spotted the faded photo propped up on the mantelpiece.

Harry took it down and lovingly ran a thumb across the glass. "She was a small little thing, with light red hair. I used to tease her and tell her that it was the same colour as Daisy the cow." Her eyes watered up as she gave the photo to Joggy. "It was taken, out there in the yard."

She was posed, awkwardly straddling her mother's bike, like a tomboy in denim jeans, jumper and a pair of large Wellingtons.

"Jack took that photo," said Harry. "She was his lady. He doted on her. With her blue eyes and cheeky smile, she could ask him for anything and he would get it for her."

"Jack was your husband?" He suspected he was, but since the man was dead before he and Alice came to live here, he just wanted it confirmed

"Her disappearance completely broke him. She was our only child you see. We couldn't have anymore. He died two years later, on the anniversary of the date Cissy left."

"A broken heart?" Alice asked.

"No, I wish it was that." Harry stared down into her tea. It was as if the brown liquid held a vision of her husband there. Finally she looked up again. "Jack shot himself."

An awkward silence fell, broken eventually by Joggy. "Where was the bike found?"

"Miles from here.... a week later, in a sandpit fifteen miles away."

"Was anything else ever found belonging to her?"

"No."

"Did she reach the shop?"

"No."

"Did anyone see her after she left here?"

"No. The only person on the lane at the time was a man white-washing Yarr's cottage. The police spoke to him, but he denied he had ever seen her."

"Had that man got a car?" It occurred to Joggy that her small size probably made it easier for whoever took her.

"No, but his brother had. He picked him up in a van that evening."

"Do you remember their names?"

"Of course I do. You don't think I'd ever forget their names, do you?.... Alo and Bob Coughlin. They lived close to where the bike was found."

"Look Harriet, let's be practical about this. The chances of finding your daughter after all this time, are very, very slim."

"Someone around here knows where she is," she said, bursting into anger. "One of them took her and then hid her from me. They left me behind and moved on with their lives; their children had children." She calmed down again. "I'm sorry about that. I can't help myself. I see what they've got and I feel so angry. Look, I know it's a long shot, but you cleared Luke Baker's name when nobody thought you would. I have every faith in you Joggy."

The feeling was there again. That same sensation he had a few years earlier driving home from Portman Prison: A mixture of excitement and nervousness and an urge to throw up. After the Luke Baker case, he had become a bit of a local celebrity. People bought him pints and stopped him in the street to shake his hand and to say well done. But after a few months it faded away. Looking back now, he had to admit that even though at the time, he was humble and played down his involvement, he liked the way all the attention stroked his ego. Now he was been asked to do the impossible again and it worried him. He likened his situation to that of the recording artist or novelist who has a hit with their first creation but then have to follow up with an equally successful second effort to prove it was not a one-off or a fluke.

"Thanks for the moral support, Alice," said Joggy, as they crossed back the fields. "I thought we were going to confront her, not make friends with her."

"Don't tell me you didn't feel for her. That poor woman is going through hell."

"Of course I have sympathy for her; I'm not a stone. She's stuck in nineteen forty one and hasn't moved since."

"Well at least now we know why she has been such an Anti-Christ to her neighbours all these years."

"Yeah, she doesn't know which of them to blame for Cissy's disappearance.... so she blames them all. But Alice, what she's asking for is the impossible."

"Were you not listening? She's not asking you to do the impossible, she, thanks to me, is only asking you to make an honest effort. And if you had continued to confront her, you would not have got that. Just remember, more can be achieved with honey than with vinegar."

Harriet cleared away and then washed her supper things in warm sudsy water, a tea stained mug, a small egg-smeared plate, a knife and fork and spoon. The heavy metal frying pan was next. Lastly she wiped the soda breadcrumbs off the oil cloth covered tabletop and onto the floor. A couple of waiting brown hens came in from where they had been watching at the open doorway and pecked them from the smooth concrete. When they had completed their task, she ushered them out. Then she paused in the doorway and slowly surveyed the farmyard. The evening was closing in and the shadows were merging into darkness.

It was a ritual now; silently entreating the growing darkness to release her Cissy. She had promised to forfeit her very life if she could just see her daughter one more time. But as always, nothing happened. And as always, she sighed and closed the door. She tossed three sods of hard black turf onto the open fire, then crossed the floor and opened a cupboard door on the bottom of the pine dresser and took out a half- empty bottle of whisky; a cheap brand. She had given up buying the good stuff. Cheap or dear, she found that they both did the same thing in roughly the same time. She closed the cupboard door and grabbed a handless mug from the open shelf, then sat into the armchair in front of the open fire and poured herself a generous portion of the golden liquid.

    She placed the bottle by the side of the chair, took a large sip and settled back into the seat. The first gulp did nearly everything she required it to do; cleanse her palate and scour the grease from her throat, but it could not rid the nagging guilt from her mind. Manipulation did not sit well with her. She was a black and white, yes or no kind of woman. She told herself she had no choice. The opportunity had opened up and she could not resist. He had cleared Luke's name when nobody thought he could. He was her last hope of ever finding out what happened to Cissy. It was a long shot and she knew it. She figured she could have just asked him. But if he had agreed, his efforts, she figured, might have been only half-hearted. She tried to convince herself that this way was better. It would concentrate his mind. She would give him a little time, a few weeks, a month at most, and if he was still floundering, she would set him free. The idea made her feel a little better. But the bubble of guilt did not go away, it just floated to the back of her mind.

CHAPTER 7

Mass on Sunday was no different from the supermarket; all heads turned to gawk when they walked in. After Mass was over Joggy was heartened when people came to him and shook his hand and told him that they did not believe all that they had heard. Heads turned again when they entered McNamara's pub, but this time, from some sections of the patronage at least, he got a cheer. Joggy bowed in mock thanks and then went straight to the bar. Alice, Helen, Katie and Danny found a seat. Alice then looked around the packed smoky room and spotted the people she wanted to speak to, seated together.

"Excuse me," she said, with her hands on the edge of the table, leaning in. "I don't care what your opinion is of my husband, but I would have thought that ye would have had enough common sense not to voice it in front of your children. They are walking tape recorders who take in everything you say and then they think it's great fun to taunt my child with your ugly, ill-informed words. We had to keep her out of the school for the rest of the week, but she's going back tomorrow. And if I hear any of your children say one more ugly word to her, I'm going to sue ye for slander and take everything you own." She then straightened up and walked away leaving a stunned silence at the table.

They finished their drinks, left the pub, and went to Columb's shop, where Joggy picked out his usual Sunday newspaper. He gave it along with the car keys to Alice. "I'll be back in a few minutes," he said. "I'm just going to see McNeill."

The station door was closed. He knocked.

"Joggy." McNeill was surprised to see him.

"Can I have a quick word?"

"Sure, come in." McNeill half smiled. "I take it this is not a social call?"

"God, no."

"Mmm," McNeill grunted his disapproval of the abrupt way in which Joggy had dismissed the notion. Over the last two years relations between them had been cordial... some might even say friendly. He led him into the station office. The sweet aroma of plug tobacco hung in the air. "Have a seat."

"No thanks, this won't take long."

McNeill's pipe sat in a wooden cradle on his desk. A faint wisp of smoke drifted from the mouth. "Ok, so what can I do for you?"

"How hard would it be for you to get your hands on a thirty-three-year-old police file?"

"Intriguing. What case would that be then?"

"Cissy Butler... disappeared nearly three and a half decades ago and has not been seen since."

"Don't tell me, Harry Butler has asked you to look into it for her?" McNeill picked his pipe up and dragged on it twice. "What's she got on ya?" he asked as he emitted a satisfying puff of smoke.

"That's not important. Can you get your hands on it or not?"

"I probably could. At this stage it would be still be open but considered a cold case. What makes you think it's worth looking in to?"

"I don't. I think it's a dead loss, but I've promised her I'd make an honest effort."

McNeill pressed the remaining tobacco further into the mouth of the pipe and then puffed earnestly, never taking his questioning gaze of Joggy.

Joggy squirmed uncomfortably.

"It's the alibi, isn't it? McNeill said eventually. "She has you by the short and curlies." The smile was back on his face. "Isn't retribution a bitch?"

"How'd you hear about that?"

"I've still got friends in high places, you know. There's not much I don't hear."

"So, are you going to help or are you just going to take the piss?"

"What's in it for me?"

"A chance to prove to Inspector Murray, you're not a spent force." Joggy smiled mischievously. "Maybe even get your Detective stripe back."

McNeill's mouth dropped open and the pipe nearly fell. He grasped it quickly and was about to ask how he came upon that information, when he remembered that his former boss, Matthews, was now one of Joggy's customers. "Mmm, yes, well...I'll submit a request tomorrow. I'll ring you when I have it."

"Thanks Ed, I'll owe you a pint or two for that." Joggy left.

Later that Sunday night, Harry Butler lay in her accustomed position, slumped, half-asleep, in her tattered armchair before the dying embers of the fire. The night was moonless and the wind whistled under the eaves. She barely heard the first knock on the porch door. The second knock, louder and more urgent, resonated off the porch walls and shocked her from her whiskey induced stupor. "Who's there?" she shouted, as she reached for her single-barrelled shotgun which lay, butt down, against the kitchen wall close to the fire.

"Open the door," demanded a male voice.

"Go away," shouted Harry. "I've got a gun and I'm not afraid to use it."

"You're bluffing you nosey auld bag. Open this door or I'll fucking kick it in."

"Try it and see what happens," said Harry, raising the gun to her shoulder.

The door received an almighty rap and Harry fired. The recoil knocked her back into the armchair.

"Aghhh," the male voice screamed, before eventually becoming a moan. It lasted for several seconds. She then heard heavy footsteps moving away. They faded into the distance. Harry scrambled to the fireplace and reached for the box of shotgun cartridges on the mantelpiece. With one eye on the door and the other on the box, she made a grab for it and knocked it to the floor, scattering the cartridges. With her heart in her mouth, she knelt down and as quickly as her nervous fingers would allow, reloaded the gun. She stood up and waited, ready to fire again, but nothing happened. After a while she crept closer to the door and warily peered out through the murky side windows of the porch. Seeing nothing she looked through the shotgun hole in the centre of the door. The yard was in pitch darkness and the night breeze ruffled her butchered hair. Then she thought of the yard light and switched it on and had another look through the windows and the hole. The yard was bare; nobody lay on it. She figured he had run away. She then carefully opened the door and stood back, ready to blast anybody that stood in the entrance. But the only thing that came in was the wind. With the yard now lit up and the shotgun in her hands, she felt braver about going out and having a look around. Cautiously, she pushed her head out and looked left; there was nothing. She then swivelled right. The blow glanced off her skull, knocking her and the shotgun to the ground.

He carried her back into the kitchen and placed her in the armchair. Her head lolled to one side. He then went back out and retrieved the gun. As he came back in, Harry revived, the blow having only stunned her. She half lifted her head and looked at him as if he was a fuzzy dream. "You!" she uttered almost incomprehensively.

"I figured you saw me," he retorted angrily. "And now your nosiness is going to cost you your life. I'm going to set fire to your hovel and when they find you, you'll be a charred corpse; the result of a sad but accidental death." He raised his gloved hand and whacked her again across the skull with a short iron bar.

He then struck match after match and offered them up to the old dry thatch roof. The spent matches were then slipped back into the box. Within minutes the roof was ablaze.

The wailing calls of the fire engine's and ambulances lured Joggy and Alice from their sleep. Its call propelled them from their bed to investigate. They followed the sound around the house.

"Oh, my God," said Joggy, as they both stared horrified at the glow that lit up the night sky. They got dressed and with torch in hand made their way back to Butlers. By the time they got there, all that was left of the house were the four walls. The first neighbours they met were John and Kitty Kelly.

"Tell me Harry got out," said Joggy.

"Mercifully, by the skin of her teeth," said John. "She was nearly a gonner. Crawled out seconds before the roof collapsed."

"And where is she now?"

"Ambulance took her off to hospital," said Kitty.

"Will she be all right?" enquired Alice."

"Smoke inhalation and a bad bang to the head, I believe. But she'll be fine. Tough as old boots, that auld one."

"Anyone know how it started?" asked Joggy.

"Accidental by the looks of it," said John. "You know how it is with these old houses, one stray spark and you've got no home anymore."

Shortly after, Joggy and Alice crossed the back yard to the gate that led to the field that separated their properties. With one hand on the gate Joggy stopped and for several seconds stood absolutely still.

"What's wrong?" Alice asked.

"I don't know." He then turned slowly around taking in everything he could see; the sheds, the smouldering house. "I got the strangest feeling just then that I was being watched. It was almost as if someone was breathing on the back of my neck."

"Probably just the night air. Let's get home."

Detective Sergeant Mark 'pit-bull' Cosgrove was occupying Sergeant Cole's chair and office when he turned up for work Monday morning. Cosgrove seldom smiled. He had one expression and wore it twenty-four hours a day. He was forty, blocky and always looked dishevelled. The receding hairline on the cannon-ball head, perched on a thick neck that no shirt collar seemed to fit around, gave the impression of someone you just don't tangle with. But there was nothing thick about his brain, it was sharp and missed very little. "Thanks for keeping it warm."

Cole gave a half-smile, a little disappointed at having to hand the case over so soon.

"Is this everything pertaining to the case?"

"Yes sir."

"Pull up a chair," said Cosgrove, "I could be awhile."

For the next hour Cole was unemployed as he watched Cosgrove read the substantial file from front to back, including the coroner's report. "Do us a favour, will ya?" he said finally. "Get us a cup of boiling water, like a good man."

It narked Cole that Cosgrove was using him as a gofer. But he bit his lip, not wanting to get on the wrong side of his new boss. "No tea or coffee?"

"Na, don't drink it. Get something for yourself as well."

Cosgrove was leaning back in his chair, his hands entwined behind his stubby neck and his glazed eyes fixated on a spot on the ceiling, when Cole came back. He took the cup from Cole. "Was Joggy Jackson ever in the army?" he enquired.

"No, he wasn't," responded Cole, sitting back down with his tea.

"F.C.A?"

"No."

"How thorough and extensive was your search of the hayshed and its surroundings."

"We were very thorough. We went over every inch of the place and didn't miss anything."

"And ye found no matches?"

"Matches, sir?"

"Yes, Cole, matches. Made from wood and sulphur and have the tendency to burst into flame when grated against a rough surface; matches; what you would light a cigarette with."

"No, sir. There were no matches found."

"Well then, whoever lit those three cigarettes found at the back of the hayshed, must have kept them or used a lighter. Now, I see listed among Joggy Jackson's personnel belongings is a box of matches. Find out from...." He looked at the signature on the bottom of the list, "Garda Thompson if he happened to look in the box."

Cole immediately left the office, curses ringing in his head. He couldn't believe he missed that clue. Within a few minutes he was back in Cosgrove's office. "No, sir, he didn't look. But now that I think of it, on the day we turned up in Parker's yard, Jackson was there standing in the back doorway. I saw him light up, but I'm nearly certain he threw the match away."

"Nearly certain doesn't cut it with me, Cole. We are going to have to have a chat with Mister Jackson and inspect his matchbox for ourselves."

Cosgrove picked up a pile of photographs and leafed through them. Again he took his time, before finally making a comment.

"There's no sign of any scuffle marks in these photo's of the yard, particularly around the area where the gun was found."

"We believe he was surprised, sir."

"Not alone was he surprised, but he died instantly. According to the coroner's report his neck was snapped; a clean break. That indicates to me a professional.

Someone with specialist training. Have you ever killed a turkey at Christmas, Cole?"

"No, sir."

"I killed my first one when I was about twelve. It's not easy to snap a neck. The first time I tried I ended up twisting the poor creatures neck like a corkscrew. The head spun right back and the poor bastard ran off. My father just laughed. I thought he might be mad, but he wasn't. It's all know-how, he told me. We caught that poor turkey again and this time I watched more closely. No turkey ever ran away from me after that. So, what I'm saying here, Cole, is that this man has know- how, and I can assure you, unlike me, he did not learn it at his father's knee."

"So you reckon we're looking for a professional, a hit-man maybe?"

"If it is a hit-man, he has a flair for amateur dramatics. The killing was by a pro but setting up Jackson was sloppy. It was as if he wasn't serious."

"Do you think Jackson set himself up and did it in such an amateurish way to take the heat off?" Cole asked.

"Maybe. But if Jackson did set himself up, why did he not leave matches?"

"Maybe he didn't think of them."

"Mmm."

"The case also has a strong Northern Ireland connection, sir. Both Winter's and Parker's families are from there. Parker, before he came down here, was the head of the local Orange Order and they, as you know, have connections with the UVF. I've put in a request to the RUC for whatever information they have on Parker and Winter. So maybe our answers lie in that direction?"

"Maybe, but right now though we have to clear up any lingering doubts on the domestic front," he said rising from the chair. "First up is a visit to the hospital."

"The hospital? Who's in the hospital?" said Cole falling into step.

"Harriet Butler. Someone tried to burn her to death last night."

They found Harry sitting up in bed with a large white bandage wrapped around her head, and she was not in a good mood. "Where's my clothes?" she shouted at a nurse. "I want out of this God-forsaken place."

"You will be discharged as soon as the doctor has seen you," said the nurse.

"I don't want to see any damn doctor, I'm fine."

"I'm sorry, Missus Butler, but you'll have to wait. Those are the rules."

"You know where you can shove your rules, don't you?" She then noticed the two policemen coming towards her. "What the hell do ye two want?"

"Just a few questions about last night," said Cole.

"Who's he?"

"I'm Detective Sergeant Cosgrove, Missus Butler. Believing it might help to lighten her mood, Cosgrove made an effort at a smile. The corner of his mouth lifted. "Do you mind answering a few questions for us?"

"Only if you wipe that damn smirk from your face. I can see it doesn't naturally fit there."

"Did you see who hit you, Missus Butler?" Cosgrove asked.

"No, I didn't."

"Can you recall what happened?"

"Some man came knocking on my door and threatened me. I told him I had a gun. He thought I was bluffing, so I shot at him through the door. I heard him scream, but he must have been play-acting. I thought he was gone. Like an idiot I stuck my head out to check and it was lights out after that."

"What exactly did he say?"

"He said if I didn't open the door he was going to effing kick it in."

"Anything else? Did he give you a reason for being there?"

"He might have, but I can't remember. He did whack me fairly hard, you know."

"Had you heard his voice before?"

"No, it wasn't anyone I knew."

"The doctor says that you were hit twice. He says one of the blows was superficial. Are you sure you didn't wake up?"

"I can assure you it did not feel superficial at the time. He must have hit me a second time when I was out cold."

"Have you received any threats lately?"

"No."

"What about visitors? Did any one of your neighbours call to see you over the last few days?"

Harry paused. Something in the tone of Cosgrove's question made her wary. "You don't know me very well, Detective, or you'd know my neighbours don't come calling."

"So you don't get on with your neighbours?"

"Let's just say they know to keep their distance, and, before you ask, none of them would burn me out."

"What makes you so sure?"

"I know my neighbours."

"Where you live is in a quiet lane, so strangers would stick out. Have you seen any strangers lately?" asked Cole.

"As I told your Sergeant, apart from that man who went up to Barterstown house, no one."

"Missus Butler," said Cosgrove, "someone went to great lengths to silence you last night, and that does not happen for no reason. I believe you know something that you're not telling us. Now I'm going to ask you again, on the day Terry Parker was murdered, did you see someone on the lane?"

"Why are you harassing me, Detective? I've told you all I know."

"Missus Butler, you're playing a dangerous game here; silence will not keep you safe. Whoever did this, will most likely try again."

"I'm well able to look after myself. Now, Detective, I'm tired and I need my rest."

"We're missing something here," Cosgrove said glumly, as they marched smartly down the corridor.

"Do you really think she saw somebody," Cole asked, trying to keep up.

"Yes I do. She practically said so herself. She saw who hit her, I'll swear on it."

"But if she knew, surely she would have told us."

"Not if she has an ulterior motive."

They found Joggy in Cashman's on Cherry Blossom lane. He was mowing the back lawn.

"Mister Jackson," Cole shouted, but Joggy could not hear him above the splutter of the lawnmower. He was going to call again but Cosgrove tapped him on the arm. "He'll see us when he turns back," he said.

Joggy saw them waiting on the wooden step that led to the lawn.

Not having met him before, Cosgrove appraised him. With bibbed dungarees and light blue shirt, sleeves rolled up to the elbow, he looked nothing special and the Detective was disappointed with that.

Joggy pulled up in front of them and cut the engine. It gave a couple of coughs and then shuddered to a stop.

"This is Detective Sergeant Cosgrove," said Cole.

Joggy noted the absence of a first name and thought it was deliberate on Cole's part. But he really did not care. Going by how he dressed, Cosgrove seemed not to have any of Reilly's pomposity.

"Sorry to disturb you, Mister Jackson," said Cosgrove, "but we're making our enquires into the Butler fire last night. Can you tell me where you were between the hours of ten and twelve?"

"I was at home in bed with my wife."

"I see," said Cosgrove. He shoved his hand into his jacket pocket and lifted out a brand new packet of ten Benson & Hedges cigarettes. He unwrapped it, extracted a cigarette and placed it between his lips. He then proffered the pack to Joggy.

Cole lifted an eyebrow in surprise.

"No thanks," not my brand.

Cosgrove then patted his pockets. "I seem to have left my matches back in the station, you wouldn't by any chance have any, Mister Jackson?"

Joggy ambled over to where his coat hung from the stump of an amputated willow branch and pulled a box of Maguire & Patterson matches from an outside pocket and then tossed them to Cosgrove.

Cosgrove caught them. "Thanks," he said.

"And were you out at all yesterday evening?"

"No I was not. I suppose you're going to tell me you found a path from my house to Butlers now?" Joggy said, tetchily.

"Would we find one?" Cosgrove asked, as he opened the half-empty matchbox and inspected the contents. He rooted through the matches before finally selecting one, striking it and lighting the cigarette.

"No, you would not."

Cosgrove took a drag and immediately began to cough. "Then you've nothing to worry about," he spluttered. He handed the matches back. "Good day, Mister Jackson," he said. He coughed again and walked off.

Joggy stood there, with the matchbox firmly in his grasp, looking after them wondering. He knew a non-smoker when he saw one.

Cosgrove and Cole parked on Barterstown lane and walked Butlers short rutted avenue. The smell of smoke and wet charred timber hung heavily in the air. They rounded the gable-end and stood, among the innards of the house in the yard.

"How on earth did she get out of that?" asked Cole. Cosgrove did not answer. Instead he pulled the semi-charred front door closed and examined the gunshot hole.

"She sure as hell wasn't bluffing when she said she fired," said Cole.

Cosgrove again made no comment. He bent down and picked up a broom from the yard. He handed Cole the broom. "That's your single barrel rifle. Go into the porch and close the door behind you."

Cole did as instructed.

"Now open the door and come out cautiously."

Cole stuck his head out and Cosgrove whacked him on the side of the head with his biro.

"Ouch," he whimpered. "What was that for?"

"That was to prove that Harry Butler is holding out on us. The glancing blow she received was on the right side of her head. I'll bet you a penny to a pound she woke up and that's when he hit her for the second time. He would not hit a frail old lady twice, just to be sure. If he simply wanted to kill her, he could have smashed her skull in or shot her with her own gun. Whoever did this wanted us to believe it was an accident. He had hoped that the fire would destroy all evidence of him being here."

"Sergeant McNeill is here, Sir," said the Garda manning the front desk.

"Send him through," said Murray, who after McNeill's earlier call, was expecting him. He replaced the receiver and leaned back in his chair: hands folded across his belly. McNeill appeared in the doorway. "Come in, Sergeant. Have a seat."

McNeill slipped onto the chair.

"You have me curious, Sergeant. You say you want to open a cold case?"

"Yes Sir. The Cissy Butler case."

"The name's familiar. Is she any relation to Missus Harriet Butler?"

"Her daughter; disappeared thirty-three-years ago and hasn't been seen since."

Murray leaned forward, looked out the open door and caught the attention of a Garda. He beckoned him to the office.

"Yes Sir?"

"Go to the archives and dig out a case file from nineteen forty-one, by the name of Cissy Butler. It was a missing persons case." He then turned his attention back to McNeill. "Why the sudden interest in this?"

"It came up in conversation with Missus Butler recently. I thought it would do no harm if a pair of fresh eyes had a look at it."

"I see."

"It's thirty-three-years later, Inspector. People are older, wiser and nearer to death. Guilt comes into play now. Nobody wants to die with that on their conscience. They might be more willing to talk."

"Does Missus Butler know you are looking into this?"

"Not yet. I was going to wait until we had a good look at the file."

"We?"

"We, Sir?"

"You said we. Who are we?"

"Must have been a slip of the tongue, Sir."

"Why is that every time I'm around you McNeill, the hairs in my nose begin to tingle with suspicion?"

"Must be my aftershave, Sir. You might be allergic to it."

"Now you're being facetious and I don't appreciate it."

"Sorry, Sir."

The Garda tapped on the door. "The file you requested, Sir," He placed it on the desk.

"Thank you," said Murray.

It was thick and musty and particles of dust flew from its yellowed pages when Murray opened it. He quietly scanned the first few. "Twelve years of age," he muttered to himself. He now looked directly at McNeill. "Vanished, and without a trace. I've a granddaughter that age. That poor woman must be beside herself!"

"She is, sir."

Murray leaned back in his chair and scrutinized McNeill. His fingers were once again intertwined across his belly and his thumbs tapped in rhythm. "What are you up to, Sergeant? Why are you doing this? I know you well enough to know it's not out of kindness or... empathy for the woman. God knows she doesn't inspire that in people." He raised a hand to stem McNeill's rebuttal. "And... I don't want to know. The same warning as before applies. If anything happens, it will be on your head. Do I make myself clear, Sergeant?"

"Perfectly, Inspector."

Joggy called into McNeill on the way home.

"Well? Any luck getting the file?"

"I have it here." He patted the large brown bulk on the table.

"Have you read it?"

"With fascination. You know, Inspector Murray was right; she did actually vanish into thin air."

"Can I bring it with me?"

"No can do. If anything happens to it I'm responsible."

"I'll take good care of it. I won't let anything happen to it."

"Sorry, can't take that chance."

"Well how am I going to read it?"

"Call back this evening at eight and you can read it here in the office."

At eight, Joggy parked in the vacant car park in front of the Church. So as not to draw attention, he knocked lightly on the station door, but the sound still echoed in the empty street. He glanced down at McNamara's and saw Squeek Malone, his beady eyes peering at him from the doorway. The station door opened and Joggy entered. Squeek turned on his toes, like a ballerina, back into McNamara's.

Almost immediately, Missus McNeill brought Joggy a mug of hot tea and two large slices of currant cake. He thanked her and she then left him in peace. McNeill stayed with Joggy, supervising, making sure he took nothing from the file but the information he was scribbling into a notebook. He took his time, carefully reading every sheet of paper and every scrap of information the file held. Another mug of tea and two hours later, the file was read. Joggy leaned back in the chair and rubbed the corner of his eyes. "Loads of people in that file are now dead. What if one of them took Cissy?"

"Then we're up shit-creek without a paddle."

"Let's hope not. What do you know of the Coughlin Brothers?"

"Heavy drinkers, both of them. Never married. Both would be well into their sixties by now. Alo and Bob have records, but it's mostly for brawling and public order offences."

"Have you met them?"

"Once. We had to wade into a bar brawl and drag them out. They're not particularly partial to the men in blue."

"The file leans heavily on them as the main suspects."

"Yeah, it looks like they put a lot of pressure on them, but couldn't get them to crack. Yarrs, the owners of the house Alo Coughlin was painting that day, were not at home. They did not come back until late that evening. So, if Alo took her he could have kept her in the house until the brother turned up."

"Do you think they'd talk to me?"

McNeill shrugged his shoulders. "Whatever chance you have, I've none."

Joggy left the station as quietly as he could, but Squeek, still saw him go.

CHAPTER 8

"He's gone and you promised me a pint," said Squeek.

"And I'm a man of my word," said Spit Sweeny. "Pat, a pint of your best for my friend." They sat close to the open fire. "That's twice in two days he's been to see McNeill," said Spit, more to himself than to Squeek.

The pint arrived. Squeek admired the large creamy head for a few seconds, before parting his parched lips and pouring a third of the pint down his throat in one go.

"Maybe," he said, licking the creamy froth from his top lip, "he's investigating another case."

"Don't be ridic..." Spit stopped when he realised that Squeek, could actually be right for once.

Reilly lived on the outskirts, a fifteen minute walk from the centre of Oldbridge. He was bored at home so he walked in to meet his son. A bitter wind blew and was more reminiscent of winter than of summer. He waited for several minutes outside the gates of the Christian Brothers as a steady stream of excited teenage boys passed out.

"Hey Joe." Reilly called out to a friend and classmate of his sons. "Is Robert far behind you?"

"He's not here Mister Reilly."

"And where is he?"

"I don't know, Sir," he said sheepishly.

Reilly knew he was lying but decided against embarrassing the young man any further. He stuffed his hands deep into his brown tweed overcoat, turned into the bitter breeze and headed back the way he came. Crossing the entrance to Henry Street he noted the sea of grey milling about at the bus stop. When he reached the footpath he stopped. There among the grey was a red jumper. Curiosity made him walk towards it.

Robert spotted his father in time. "Have to go," he said, abruptly breaking away from Helen.

"Who's the girl?" asked Reilly as his son walked briskly past him.

"A friend, you wouldn't know her."

His father caught up with him. "Do you stick your tongue down the throat of all your friends?"

"No, only the ones I really like."

Reilly looked back towards Helen, who was now heading for her bus. "I've seen that girl somewhere before. Give me a clue, where is she from?"

"Leave it alone, dad. Believe it or not you don't have to know everything about everybody."

Reilly took a mental note of the bus registration number. "I thought we agreed, no distractions until after your exams."

"That was your rule, not mine. And I did not agree to it. You didn't wait for my answer, you just assumed I'd agree."

They turned the corner out of Henry Street and walked for the next couple of minutes in total silence. A school bus passed them. Reilly thought he caught a glimpse of Helen smiling down at Robert. He checked the registration number against the one in his head and it matched. Her face bothered him as they walked quietly along. He knew he had seen her somewhere and only recently. His mind would not let it go, he needed to remember. He thought of the direction the bus was travelling and who it was he knew that lived in those areas, but it was a fruitless exercise as he quickly realised he knew a good few adults but none of their children.

He forced his mind to concentrate on the girl's face, ruddy cheeks and strawberry blonde hair and hoped that his memory would work its magic. She appeared as tiny flashes in his mind's eye but they did not last long enough for him to see where she was. Gradually the flashes grew longer and he could see she was in a crowd and then the picture finally expanded and the girl's face fell into place.

"I don't fucking believe it," he shouted as he came to a sudden halt. His face now red with rage. "You're seeing Joggy Jackson's daughter!"

"So." Robert kept on walking.

That same Tuesday evening, Joggy and Alice called to see Harry Butler. She was still in Oldbridge General Hospital. They were her only visitors.

"We heard you were still here," said Alice as they approached her bed.

"It's not by bloody choice," she said loudly, making sure the nurses could hear her.

"How are you feeling?" Alice sat down on the only chair.

"Not too bad. A bit wheezy. The doctors keep saying that they won't let me out 'till it clears up."

"Treat it as a holiday," said Joggy. "Just lay back and let them pamper you."

"Have you ever been in a hospital bed?" Harry's eyes narrowed.

"No, thankfully," Joggy replied.

"Well if you did, you'd know it's no holiday. They wake you up at six in the bloody morning from a good sleep and a warm bed just to change the bed clothes. Shortly after that they come round with the breakfast. The tea is dishwater, the toast is burnt and the porridge you could hang wallpaper with it. The dinner you wouldn't feed to your pigs, is usually boiled chicken with watery spuds and vegetables. In between meals they talk to you as if you are a child and that's just the nurses. The doctors are worse, they poke and prod you with ice cold instruments and then speak to you as if you're an imbecile. So Joggy, you should book yourself in if this is the kind of holiday you'd like."

"Other than that, I take it, you're having a good time then," he said, his eyes gleaming with mischief. He could not help himself; Harry was growing on him.

"I can see it's pointless talking to you," she said turning her eyes to Alice. "I'll talk to your wife instead. I can see she's the sensible one."

"Where are you going to live when they let you out?" Alice asked.

"For a short while a B & B and then a mobile home."

"A mobile home?"

"One of the nurses here knows someone that has one for sale. It's supposed to be in good nick. I'm going to have a look at it when I get out."

"And what about your home? Will you try and rebuild it?"

"No, for all the years that are left to me, a mobile home will see me out."

"You were a lucky woman to get out in time," said Joggy. "John Kelly reckons you made it by the skin of your teeth."

"Does he now," she said with a touch of sarcasm.

"Did you get a look at who did this to ya?"

"You're the second person that's asked that. I had those two plain clothes boys from the station, Laurel and Hardy, asking me the same question. And the truth is, I did, but I wasn't going to tell them that."

Joggy knew exactly who she was talking about. Her apt description identified the two men that came to see him and poked around in his matchbox. "Why not? Your life could be in danger. He could try again."

"And lose my advantage. They told me they'd never stop looking for Cissy, but they did. If I tell them now, you'll stop looking for Cissy and where would I be then?"

"But I won't stop looking, I promise you."

"I believe you, Joggy and right now you believe that too. But once the incentive is taken away the desire will fade and I can't take that chance."

Joggy considered arguing the point but he could see by the set of her jaw that it would be futile. "Well then, what if he comes after you again. How are you going to stay safe?"

"I'm not afraid to die. But just in case he comes after me again, I'm going to set certain wheels in motion, that hopefully will protect me. I'm going to write a letter and enclose evidence of the man's identity in an envelope and then give them to my solicitors for safe keeping. If I should die they will be handed over to the guards. I'm also going to write a second letter and post it to him and tell him what I've just did. That, with any luck, will keep me alive."

"Smart thinking," said Joggy.

"Do you think you could help me with that?"

"Yeah, but what do you want me to do?"

"To collect me from here and to drive to where I want to go. It shouldn't take more than a couple of hours of your time."

"Yeah, no problem. Just give me a ring when you're ready."

"Now Joggy," said Alice, "that's enough questions for one day. We come in to see how you are and he gives you the third degree."

"No respect for age, that's his problem," said Harry.

CHAPTER 9

Granville's was a coppers pub. And anyone whose business it was to know these things, stayed clear of it. No life preserving terrorist, of either persuasion, would drink there. If one was seen coming out, innocently or otherwise, he was automatically labelled a grass and within a few days his battered body would be found face down in a ditch on the side of a lonely road. The members of the RUC felt safe there.

Chief Inspector Ron Wilkes sat quietly in the corner, reading The Guardian and supping on his Teachers and water. He was a nondescript individual who could blend into any crowd. He had only one distinctive feature; a large brown mole on his jaw-line. He sipped the last of his drink, folded his newspaper, picked up his beige Mac and headed for the toilets. They were around the corner from the bar and close to the side entrance. A few minutes later, a man with a neatly trimmed beard, large clear spectacles and wearing a black Mac, emerged. He slipped, unnoticed, out the side door. In the gathering gloom he made his way down the side street and away from the pub. The square was quiet as he meandered across it, with his hands deep in his pockets and his shoulders hunched against the cold breeze. On the main street he stopped and peered into the windows of the closed shops, while at the same time furtively checking that he was not been followed. Opposite the Presbyterian Church he turned left. A short distance down that street he stopped in front of a narrow alleyway and lit a cigarette, watching all the time. With the coast clear he entered the alleyway. It was pitch black. The only visible light, apart from the cigarette in his hand, came from the entrance to the other end. Half way down, he slipped into a deep doorway and waited.

An hour passed. He was on the verge of giving up when he heard a match being struck. He peered out. At the other end was a man standing in the light, pulling on a cigarette and wearing a Glasgow Rangers scarf. He looked nonchalantly around him before making his way down the alleyway and slipping into the deep doorway. "We've only got a few minutes," he said. "What do you need?"

"The Gardai are looking for what we've got on Terry Parker and Fred Winter. What have you heard?"

"That Parker was a traitor. They haven't stopped gloating since word came through of his death."

"What did he do?"

"He had his so-called good friend, Fred Winter, killed by the IRA."

"Do you know why?"

"It seems Winter murdered *his* best friend, who happened to be a Catholic, years before."

"A slow burner, haw."

"Yeah, the best kind of revenge. He never saw it coming."

"How did they find that out?"

"They captured one of them. He tried to bargain his way out. They agreed a deal and he spilled his guts...after that they put a bullet in him."

"How long have you known this?"

"A good while. I rang Parker anonymously and warned him. But it seems they still got to him. I've tried to find out who they sent to do the job, but so far no luck. These are not the sort of people you ask direct questions of. You have to wait and see what crumbs fall from the table."

"Anything else?"

"Just one other thing. Winter was a member of a secretive group called the Royal Black Preceptory. I've tried to find out who the other members are but again no luck."

"Okay, go safe. I'll contact you if I need you again."

They left the opposite way they came.

Joggy found his friend Tom Baker, in the kitchen in an old tattered armchair in front of the cream Stanley range. He had a heavy overcoat wrapped tightly around him. The fire door of the range was open and his heavy grey stockinged feet, with a big toe sticking out of one of them, sat on the low range shelf.

"Gawnee Joggy, don't come too close," said Tom, through stuffed nasal passages. "I've got the mother and father of all doses on me and I'm getting it hard to shake it off."

"Have you taken anything for it?"

"Naw, it's just a head cold. Don't believe in taking any of that auld rubbish, only makes you weaker. It'll take its own course and I'll be all the stronger for it."

"Have you a drop of whiskey in the place?"

"In the bottom of the dresser. Gawnee, I never thought of that. A hot whiskey would warm me up, right enough."

Joggy dug the bottle of Jameson out of the clutter in the bottom of the dresser and then placed the kettle over the hot plate of the range. He sat down while he waited for it to boil. "So how did you pick the cold up," he asked.

"Got soaked in a shower the other day and like a right eejit didn't change when I came back to the house."

The kettle boiled and Joggy made two hot whiskeys, with sugar but without cloves. He knew there would be no point in asking Tom if he had any.

They clinked glasses. "To better health," toasted Joggy.

"Amen to that," replied Tom.

They chatted for a good while before Joggy got around to the real reason he had called. "Do you remember when Cissy Butler went missing?" he asked eventually.

"Gawnee Joggy, that's not today or yesterday."

"No it's not.... it's all of thirty-three-years ago."

"God, is it that long? I was just ten at the time but I remember, for long years after, it was all people talked about. Every week there was a new theory or a new rumour. Now and then word would come through of a sighting and hopes would rise again.

It was enough to drive any father demented. It's no wonder poor Jack Butler killed himself."

"Yeah, and on the second anniversary too."

"Someone's been doing their homework!"

"Actually, Harry Butler told me."

"Oh! So ye're talking again?"

"We made a sort of bargain. I'd look into her daughter's disappearance and she'll make a statement to the guards clearing me."

"And how does that work? Do you have to find her daughter first?"

"No, I've just to make an honest effort. What do you remember about Cissy? Did ye play together as children?"

"Not that much. She tended to play with the bigger kids. She was two years older than me. That's a big gap when you're a child."

"I suppose it is. Do you remember the Yarrs?"

"Vaguely. They were an elderly couple. They died when I was still a child."

"Alo Coughlin was painting their walls on the day Cissy vanished and his brother picked him up that evening in a van. Now, Cissies bike was found in a quarry not far from their house. There must have been a lot of talk about them?"

"Most people at the time reckoned it was them." Tom sniffled. "People were up in arms over it. I mean, nothing had ever happened to a child around here and then on the one day a stranger turns up... ah ah achoo."

"Gesundheit," said Joggy.

"....a child goes missing," He pulled a large discoloured handkerchief from his coat pocket and wiped his nose; the edges of which were red and sore.

"It's a wonder they didn't try to do something about it!"

"Oh they did. A group of the neighbours, my father included, got together and were fully intent on grabbing the Coughlin's and beating them until they confessed. But, Father Kennedy got wind of it and put a stop to it."

"Your other neighbours, in the cottages at the time, one was Charlie Higgins?"

"Gentleman Charlie, that's what they used to call him; and he dressed like one too. He had two miniature apple trees that stood in the shelter of the back wall and every autumn, he give us an apple; two if we were really lucky. And we'd always be around, because we'd be watching them for weeks beforehand. I can still remember the taste; they were huge, green and absolutely gorgeous. At least in our small hands they looked huge. They were the juiciest apples I've ever ate."

"Would he invite you into his yard and give you the apples or would he bring them out to you?"

"A little of both. What are you thinking?"

Joggy gave a deep sigh. "I don't know what I'm thinking. Right now I'm just fishing. What about next door, the McEvoys, Paddy and Ann?"

"What about them?"

"Anything interesting there?" Joggy took a sip from his glass.

"Well they were brother and sister. Paddy died in a car accident and when Ann passed away she left the house to her sister in America. Other than that I can't think of anything else about them. They were the sort of people who kept themselves to themselves."

Joggy looked towards the window and saw through the grime-stained glass that the evening sun was well down. "Before I head off," he said, "would you like another hot whiskey?"

"Gawnee, if it's not too much trouble."

"No trouble at all."

Joggy was in Mercers when Alice rang to say that Harry Butler was waiting to be collected from Oldbridge General Hospital.

"Where too?" enquired Joggy.

"Home," said Harry.

"Home! But there's nothing there but a burnt out shell."

"There is, if you know what you're looking for."

As they travelled along , Joggy's thoughts returned to Cissy. "Do you mind me asking you," he said after a period of silence, "your farm, was it in your family or was it your husband's?"

"It was mine. I was an only daughter. Why do you ask?"

"Because, you would have known your neighbours, both dead and alive, better than any blow-in."

"I suppose I would."

"Ok, let's travel along Barterstown lane, thirty-three-years ago. We come out of your front yard and turn right. We then cross the railway line. Was it always unmanned?"

"It was, even back then."

"Alright, tell me about the people who lived on the lane then?"

"Kelly's were the first. You know where they live. Sean and Marie were the parents of four children; two boys, John and Vincent and two girls, Beth and Lillian. Sean's father, Albert, was still alive and living with them then. The next house you'd meet was, Harry and Agnes Yarr. They had two boys but they had married and moved away years earlier. You came out of the lane then and turned right for the cottages."

"That's a long lonely stretch," said Joggy. "I should think more-so then than now."

"Yes, well, there wasn't as much traffic on the road then."

"Precisely."

"At the other end of the lane were James and Bonnie Fitzgerald. They had three boys. There was Charles, he was the oldest. Then there was Peter, I think he was a year younger and Leon was the youngest."

"I've heard it wasn't altogether a happy house."

"That would be an understatement. He was a brutal bastard. God forgive me. I can't tell you the amount of times I saw poor Bonnie with black eyes and bruises to her face."

"What was his problem, drink, jealousy?"

"Jealous my foot. He just liked dishing it out and not just to Bonnie but to the lads as well. They were terrified of him. It's no wonder they never came back. Bonnie wasn't even forty when she died. A brain haemorrhage got her. No doubt it was from all those beatings."

"Do you remember what ages the children were then?"

"Of course I do. Charles was nineteen. Peter was eighteen and Leon was fifteen.

The older boys more or less left straight away and Leon took off when he turned eighteen."

"Any ideas where they went?"

"Not a clue. They just vanished and I haven't seen them since."

"But you're leasing their land, so who do you pay that to?"

"Toohey's solicitors in Oldbridge. They collect once a year."

They drove into Barterstown lane, crossed the railway line and then turned left around the gable-end of the house. Harry sat bolt upright and stared out of the front window in abject horror at what lay before her. All her worldly possessions were scattered like confetti across the rough stone yard. Then she caught sight of Cissy's bed and her chest of drawers laying on its side with her clothes, that she had kept all these years, blackened, scorched and scattered around. She slumped back into the seat. Her head dropped and quiet tears ran down her weather-beaten face. She seemed to shrivel in size.

"Are you alright?" Joggy enquired.

"I'll be alright in a minute."

"Look Harriett," he said placing a hand on her arm, "I know it's upsetting, but if you want, I'll come up here this evening and clean up the yard. I'll put everything into one of the sheds and when you're ready you can sort through it."

"Would you do that for me?"

"Of course I would."

"Thank you." She sat there for a few more minutes before she felt composed enough to leave the car. "Now I'd better get what I came for," she said opening the car door.

"Do you need me to give you a hand?"

"No thanks, I'll be fine on my own."

Joggy watched her as she zig-zagged her way across the yard to the turf shed. She didn't hesitate or stop to look at her husbands, Cissy's or her own belongings; it was too painful. She just kept her head down and picked her steps. She stopped at the turf shed, bent down and began to rummage among the sods of turf and then paused as if surprised to find it was still there. When she came back to the car she had Cissy's photo and a medium size brown envelope in her hands.

"How did you get them out?" enquired a surprised Joggy.

"When I came too, I was a bit stupid and I wasn't sure where I was. I saw the ceiling was on fire with the flames rolling along it and for a few seconds I was fascinated by the colours and the movements of the flames, the same way you'd admire them in an open fire. I thought I was in a sort of dream. But then a piece of straw fell down and singed my cheek. That sort off snapped me back to reality fairly quickly. I knew then I had to get out but I wasn't leaving Cissy behind. When I grabbed her off the mantelpiece the frame was hot but I wasn't letting go. I then somehow got to the dresser and found the envelope. It was still behind the plate. The room was nearly full of smoke, but luckily I still had enough of my wits about me to know where the door was. I got as far as the turf shed. I must have blacked out after that, because the next thing I remember was the sirens. That's when I hid these in the turf."

"You must have one thick skull," said Joggy, as he started the car. "You got hit twice and came around twice."

"That was Cissy." She hugged the photograph tightly to her chest. "She woke me up the second time."

"You saw her?"

"No, but I know it was her that saved me."

"Where to now?"

"Burke's newsagents, the post office and then Toohey's solicitors."

At Burke's she bought a manila writing pad and a packet of brown envelopes. She then sat into the back seat of the car and composed the missive. When Harry was not looking, Joggy angled the rear view mirror, but it was to no avail; Harry had the name and address well covered up. When finished, she carefully re-read it and then placed it in the envelope.

As they drove to the post office, they passed Cole sitting in the passenger seat of an unmarked car, parked by the kerb and waiting for Cosgrove, who was in the chemist on an errand for his wife. Joggy did not see him.

"You won't believe who I've just seen together," said Cole to Cosgrove as he slipped behind the steering wheel.

Cosgrove reached across and tossed the paper bag containing a bottle of Calpol and two pink pacifiers in the glove compartment. Cosgrove looked at him with raised eyebrows. "I don't appreciate suspense, are you going to tell me or do I have to beat it out of you."

"Joggy Jackson and Harry Butler."

"That is a surprising combination. Walking or driving?"

"Driving."

"Which way?"

"That way." Cole, pointed towards the High Street.

Costello did a u-turn on the quiet street. "Keep a sharp eye out," he said as he drove slowly along.

Passing the entrance to the main square, Cole called out. "There." They pulled in by the kerb. "I warned him not to go near her and now he's chauffeuring her around town. Should we go and have a word?"

"Not yet. Let's just watch."

"I can see Jackson, he's still in the car, but I can't see her," said Cole. "She could be anywhere." A few minutes later, Harry Butler came out of the post office and walked across the square. She passed where Joggy was parked and into Toohey's solicitors. Cosgrove said nothing. A half-hour later they observed Harry Butler leaving Toohey's. When Joggy left the square and continued on up High Street, they followed at a discreet distance. They passed the railway station and onto the Charleville road. His left indicator flashed on and he drove into the front yard of Boyles B&B. A few minutes later he left, alone.

They followed him until he reached Mercers. Cosgrove accelerated at speed up the avenue after him. He left a cloud of dust and cherry blossoms petals in his wake. Joggy was getting out of his car when they pulled up.

"Mister Jackson," said Cosgrove sternly, "I need a word with you."

Missus Mercer appeared in the yard. "Who are you?" she enquired sharply.

"I'm Detective Cosgrove and this is Sergeant Cole, we just want to have a word with Mister Jackson here."

"And you think that just because you work for the police you can drive into my yard at that speed. What if my grandchildren were here? They sometimes play football on the avenue."

"I'm so sorry," said Cosgrove, who looked suitably chastened.

"Ye might do that sort of thing on TV, but not around here."

"You're right, I just got carried away; again, my apologies."

"Are you alright Joggy? Would you like me to stay?"

"Thank you Missus Mercer," he replied, trying to keep a straight face. "That's very kind of you, but it won't be necessary."

"I'll be in the kitchen, if you need me, just shout. And don't let those two bully you."

"I won't, thank you."

As soon as Mrs Mercer had gone back into the house, Cosgrove turned his attention back to Joggy. "You find this all very amusing do you?" he snapped.

"I think it's hilarious. It's not often I get to see ye boys being berated by an old lady."

"Let's get to the point. What are you doing with Harriett Butler? You were told to stay away from her and here we find you squiring her around town."

"I'm just helping out a neighbour."

"What? This is the woman who will not back up your alibi. What's going on, Mister Jackson?"

"Look, I know this may seem strange but we've talked and come up with a private arrangement. I'm looking into a small matter for her and when I'm finished, she'll make a statement clearing my name."

"This gets better and better." Cosgrove shook his head in disbelief. "This "small matter," what is it?"

"It's private."

"What was she doing in the solicitor's?"

"You'll have to ask Harry Butler that."

"I'm asking you, Jackson, you were there."

Cosgrove's aggressive attitude was raising hackles on the back of Joggy's neck, and under different circumstances he would have bitten back, but Cole was there with him and he felt he owed him. So he kept his replies civil or as civil as he could manage.

"Depositing something."

"Like what?"

"All I know is that it was in a brown envelope. I did not see it. She had it buried in the turf."

"Did she say what it concerned?"

"No." He glanced at Cole. He did not like lying but he felt it was not his business to inform.

"She knows who attacked her, doesn't she?"

Joggy gave a heavy sigh. "Look...."

"Mister Jackson, yes or no. Does she know who attacked her?"

"You'd best ask her that."

"I'm asking you. For the final time, Mister Jackson, before I arrest you for withholding information. Does she know her attacker?"

Joggy called his bluff. "I can't tell you what I don't know."

"You're lying, Jackson. I can see it in your face. This brown envelope she lodged with her solicitor, what do you think was in it? Do you think it had anything to do with her attacker?"

"Look, I'd like to help, but I can't."

"More like you won't." Cosgrove turned to go, but then turned back and came right up to Joggy, pointing an accusing finger at him. "You'd better pray that I don't find out that you've been fucking me around, Jackson," he snarled.

They turned and left. As soon as they drove out of the gates, Joggy went into Mercers and with Mrs Mercer's permission made a phone call.

Boyle's B&B, was a turn of the century, two-storey-grey stone building with a Gothic arched doorway and windows. The gardens were open, bright and festooned with the white, yellow and blue of spring flowers.

"All that's missing are the Gargoyles," remarked Cole, as they made their way along the narrow stone-paved path that divided the lawn in two.

Harry met them at the door. "You've come to see me, have you?"

"Yes Missus Butler," replied Cole. "If it's not too much trouble, we'd like a word?"

"It's a beautiful day," she said, passing them, "let's sit outside." She sat on a bench in front of the kitchen window. Where she could bask in the evening sun and at the same time shelter from a chilling breeze. Cole and Cosgrove remained standing before her.

"Mister Jackson has as good as told us that you know the identity of the person who attacked you," said Cosgrove.

"But he didn't *actually* tell you?"

"He implied it. Who *was* your attacker, Missus Butler?"

"Could you move a little to your left, Detective, you're blocking the sunlight."

Cosgrove moved.

"Thank you," she said as the warm rays of sunlight fell on her again. "And suppose I do know who it is, are you going to keep me safe, Detective?"

"We can place you in protective custody. You would be very safe there."

"Thank you for your offer, Detective, but I have my own way of protecting myself. He knows that if anything happens to me, his identity will end up in the hands of the Gardaí."

"So that's why you were in the solicitors. You've deposited his identity there."

"Did Joggy tell you that?"

"No, we observed you going in there."

"So, you were spying on me?"

"We just happened to observe you and Mister Jackson together."

"If I said my business in Toohey's was not what you think, would you believe me?"

Cosgrove shook his head. "Help us to help you, Missus Butler." Harry hung her head and looked down at her flat brown shoes. The toes were scuffed.

Cosgrove gave Cole a half-wink. "If you don't, within a couple of days I will have a court order and force your solicitor to hand over what you deposited."

"You can do that?"

"Yes we can and we will if we have to."

"And what about a person's right to privacy? Isn't that in the constitution or something?"

"Not if it interferes with an ongoing murder case."

"Oh dear and I thought my business was safe from prying eyes. I suppose I don't have a choice then, Detective?"

"That's very sensible of you, Missus Butler."

"Will tomorrow do, Detective? They're probably closed by now."

Cosgrove looked at his watch; it was past five. "I'll call for you at nine in the morning, will that be all right?"

"Yes, I suppose so," she said, her eyes downcast.

Cosgrove shot Cole a knowing look as they walked back down the path.

Everything was either charred, smoke, or water damaged. Very little of it could be used again. Joggy wheeled a bog barrow with a long handled Slane lying on top of it out of the stone shed that stood next to the turf shed, along with a few other odds and ends to make space for Harry's belongings. There were two beds; he dismantled them both. His plan was to get the biggest items in first. After that the wardrobes. One of them was so badly burned; it was only fit for firewood. Then the two chest of drawers, followed by what was left of the pine dresser. It, along with the kitchen table were in pieces. The chairs were no better. Finally what was left was crockery, most of it cracked or broken, clothes and several books. One of the books took him by surprise, it was Jane Austin's, *Pride and Prejudice.* Somehow he didn't see the Butlers, as classic literature readers. He peeled back the front cover and saw it was a library book, dated from just before Cissy disappeared. He figured it had to have been borrowed by her.

It was late evening when Joggy finished. The golden rays of the sun were already casting long shadows across Barterstown Lane as he took the road home. The shadows dulled the vibrancy of the primroses and the cowslips that grew at the base of the high, thick whitethorn hedge. From beyond came the excited bleating of lambs.

Up ahead, John Kelly leaned on a rusted round-bar field gate gazing at his sheep. He was a tall man with a longish weather-beaten face that tapered to a narrow chin. His silver-grey cloth cap blended well with the greying borders of his brown hair. The cap was angled over his right eye to shade against the dying sun.

"Evening, John," said Joggy, as he joined his neighbour at the gate.

"Lovely time of the year, Joggy," John remarked, still looking out into the field.

"Whitethorn blossoms in the hedges and spring lambs in the field."

Joggy noted the dark circles around his eyes. "Finished lambing have you?"

"Got the last of them last night, thank God. Right now I could happily sleep on this gate."

"Aye, you looked wrecked. There's not much sleep to be had during lambing season."

"Kitty's wiped out. She hit the sack this morning. Probably still there."

"I'm surprised you're not there with her."

"Can't sleep during the day, feels unnatural. But now that the light's fading, I'll head there myself. Just came down to check everything was okay."

"They all look fit and healthy to me," remarked Joggy, as he watched two lambs jostle for their mother's teat.

John half-turned his head towards Joggy. "I've been hearing a little rumour about you."

"I'm sure you have."

"You're at it again then?"

"Afraid so."

"You know most guys our age go fishing or take up golf in their spare time."

"Too boring: I prefer a good mystery."

"Well you won't get a better mystery than the disappearance of Cissy Butler."

"No, I suppose not."

They moved from the gate and began walking slowly towards Kelly's farmhouse -- a large grey square block of a building that stood on a rise a hundred and fifty yards up a gravel side-lane.

"What do you remember of her?" Joggy asked.

"Poor auld Cissy; she was a bit of tomboy. Loved the rough and tumble of the games my brother and I played. She wasn't much for playing with dolls. That's not to say she didn't play with my sisters ... she did. But they were younger than her. She liked bossing them around, being in control, making up games and making sure that they followed her rules. After a while she'd get bored and come back to us."

"Did you see her on the day she went missing?"

"No, but she had begun to change by then." He re-arranged his cloth cap.

Two black-and-white sheep dogs came bounding down the lane to greet them. They circled around excitedly and then fell into step with John, one each side of him. With their mouths open and tongues hanging out they looked up at him as if he was their hero.

"Change, how?"

"When you're young you don't notice these things, but looking back now, I suppose she was becoming a woman. I've seen it in my own daughters. Just when they hit the teenage years, they change. It's like a switch. One minute they're quite happy sitting chatting on your knee and the next you're lucky if you get a goodnight peck on the cheek. You know what I'm talking about, you've got one yourself, Joggy."

"You haven't found one of them with their boyfriend's tongue down her throat have you, by any chance, because I have. It's was hard to know where to look."

"Not yet. But I'm sure it has happened. Not that they would tell you or anything."

"Did you tell your parents when you got your first snog?"

John laughed. "No."

"Well then, I suppose nothing has changed. The day Cissy went missing, there was a man painting Yarr's house. Did you see him?"

"Afraid not, Joggy. Because of Bonnie Fitzgerald's death, our parents wouldn't allow us to leave the farm."

For a few seconds, Joggy fell silent. "Do you remember Charlie Higgins? He used to live in Nellie Roe's cottage."

John smiled broadly. "Of course I do. He had two little apple bushes and they produced the sweetest apples I've ever eaten. It was a huge pity when they died."

"What happened to them?"

"No idea. They just never produced any more fruit after Cissy left us."

"What do you remember of Charlie himself?"

"A handsome, dapper little man. Always clean, always smelt nice, always with a tie and a clean shirt."

"Were any of ye ever in his house?"

"Oh yeah, several times. It was as clean as himself."

"How about Cissy, was she ever there?"

"Yes, she always came with us. Cissy was a bit of a favourite of his. I think it was the tomboy in her that he liked."

"Was Cissy, ever in the house alone with Charlie?"

"No, I don't think so. What are you getting at?" John stopped and stared hard at Joggy. His eyes narrowed. "Are you implying that there was something odd about Charlie?" His voice was harsh.

"I'm not implying anything, John. I'm not trying to sully your memory of the man. I'm just trying to get a handle on him, that's all."

"Good, because he was a lovely man. He never did anything improper to any of us. If we were in his house he'd sit the youngest on his knee and tell us fairy stories. And so all I have of him are good memories."

"Good, that's all I wanted to know. Thanks for talking to me. Good night and have a good sleep."

They parted company and Joggy ambled thoughtfully home. For a short while, John, with a wistful look on his tired face, watched after him. He opened his mouth to shout something but then thought the better of it and turned away.

That night, Joggy slept sporadically. The first time when he woke it was two-minutes-past-one ... then one-forty-one, then twenty-past-two and finally he was mad awake at two-forty-five. And, no matter what he did, he could not get back to sleep. He normally did not rise until seven. Quietly, he slipped out of bed and made his way to the kitchen. He did not bother with the light. The range had been packed down for the night and so the room was warm. He pulled open the curtains and looked towards the western skyline. A blanket of impenetrable darkness lay before him; it masked the horizon and the soft falling rain. He lit a cigarette and stared into the black and tried to make sense of the thoughts that scampered across his brain like a flock of frightened sheep going one way and then the other. *Where are you, Cissy?* The thought was addressed to the dark void in front of him. *Who took you? Was it the Coughlin's or did you somehow reach Charlie Higgins? Or maybe on that lonely sheltered stretch of road between Higgins and Yarr's, someone picked you up. Maybe someone coming from Fitzpatrick's wake? If that's the case I'll never find you.*

He thought about her mother and how for all those years she had kept lit the flickering candle of hope for her daughter. *What must it feel like to lose a daughter?* Having experienced grief, he knew the pain and how it felt when his father had died, but it eventually faded. But to lose a child and not know whether to look among the dead or the living must be much worse: the pain must never go away.

Into his mind came the imagined belief that his own daughter, Katie was taken. He allowed his vivid imagination to take him deep down within himself. And almost immediately felt a terrible loss: the emptiness of the space she used to fill: her vibrant, smiling face: the kisses, the hugs, the feel of her small soft hand in his and then the horror thoughts, of who had her and what they were doing to her and her piteously crying out for him and his sense of devastation and helplessness grew and grew until the pain and anguish was so oppressive; tears began to form.

With a snort he snapped himself out of it, wiped the tears from his eyes and moved away from the window. He turned on the kitchen light and went to the girl's bedroom door. Carefully and quietly he opened it just enough for the shaft of light from the kitchen to stretch and illuminate Katie, safe, warm and snuggled up to her favourite teddy bear, *Pickles.* He closed the door and went and sat on the settee, took a deep drag from his cigarette and prayed a silent prayer that he would never have to endure Harry Butler's pain.

The cigarettes and the matches were still in his hand. He placed the cigarettes on the settee beside him, but kept the matches, turning the box this way and that. *What was so significant about them?* He tried to recall what Reilly had said they had found behind Parkers shed....*three fags and an empty cigarette box.* And then it hit him....*no matches were found. Cosgrove wanted to see how I lit my cigarettes and whether I kept the burnt matches.* He allowed himself a wry smile; for he knew someone who kept burnt matches. He lay down on the settee and before drifting back to sleep, once again thought about Cissy and where she might be.

The receptionist in Toohey's was surprised to see Harriet Butler walk in, escorted by two men in dark suits.

"Is Mister Toohey in?" she asked.

"Yes, but you don't have an appointment, Missus Butler."

Cosgrove flashed his credentials. "We'd like to see him straight away. It's urgent."

The receptionist, a young girl with shoulder length red hair, flustered a little and then got up. "I'll see if he's available."

A few seconds later Mister Toohey appeared before them. "Missus Butler, Detective. How can I help you?"

"These men would like to see what I deposited with you yesterday, Mister Toohey," said Harry.

"This is highly irregular. Are you sure about this, Missus Butler?"

"Yes, it seems I don't have a choice."

"You always have a choice, Missus Butler," said Toohey.

"Let's just get it over with," said Harry.

"Very well, come on through." He went straight for a tall grey filing cabinet and pulled open the drawer with the initials A B. From among the Bs he pulled out a thin buff folder and handed it to Cosgrove.

He opened it. "What is this?" He asked, bewildered, as he quickly leafed through Fitzpatrick's land lease receipts. "Where is the information Missus Butler deposited with you yesterday?" Panic was setting in.

"You're holding it, Detective," replied Toohey, mystified. "Were you expecting something else?"

Cosgrove glared at Harry Butler.

"I tried to tell you, Detective. But you were adamant."

Cosgrove almost ran out of the building. On the footpath, while he waited on Harry Butler to say her thanks to Mr

Toohey, he paced up and down, taking deep breaths to calm himself. "She played us for fools," he said to Cole, his anger palpable.

Cole was faced across the square. He made no reply to Cosgrove's remark. His mind was elsewhere.

Cosgrove stopped walking and glared at Cole. "Did you hear me?" he snapped.

"She posted it." Cole looked back at him calmly.

"What?" he snapped again.

"The identity of her attacker, Sir -- she posted it to someone."

Cosgrove glanced quickly across the square to the post office and knew immediately Cole was right.

Danny pulled into the wide gravel entrance to Charleville Castle and dropped off his sister Helen. He had borrowed his fathers Morris Traveller. It was Sunday afternoon and she was meeting Robert there. He hopped down off the window ledge of the gate lodge and came to meet her.

"I'll be back at five," said Danny. Helen closed the car door and Danny raised a hand in greeting to Robert. Robert returned it.

"Is that your brother?" he enquired, catching her by the hand. He recognised the car from the one that had picked her up from the bus stop.

"Yep, that's Danny."

He pulled her close, leaned down and gave her a short kiss on the lips and then led her into the grounds of the castle. Charleville Castle was popular for walks and there was plenty of people about. A myriad of paths led in all directions. Robert chose a path that swung off to the left and skirted the castle grounds perimeter. The wind rustled the leaves above their heads and the path was mottled in ever-changing patterns of light and shade. "My father knows who you are," he said after a short period.

"And is that a problem?"

"Let's just say he's not pleased."

"Why?"

"It seems your father and mine, don't get on. Does your father know who I am?"

"I don't think so, I haven't told him."

"What's he like, your father?"

"He's fine. He's a dad."

"No, I mean, what's he like, really like?"

"You really want to know?" She looked at him in surprise. His face was dark and thoughtful.

"Yes."

"Okay, well, he's kind and has a wicked sense of humour. He likes long walks and he smokes too much...and he works hard to support us."

"Do you love him?"

"Yeah, of course, what a strange thing to ask."

"I don't. I mean love mine, that is."

"Why's that?"

"He's an asshole. Always telling me what to do -- who I should be hanging out with -- the clubs I should be a member of -- pushing me in the direction he thinks I should go. He wants me to go into the medical or legal profession, says that's where the money and respect is."

"And what do you want to do?"

"I don't know. I think when I finish the leaving, I'm going to take off for a year and see the world."

"That costs a lot of money."

"I have some saved and I can take jobs as I move around."

"Sounds like you have it all planned out."

"Nearly. And do you know what the best part of it is? I'm not even going to tell him. I'm just going to take off and then send him a postcard from my first stop."

As they ambled along hand-in-hand, small birds fluttered nervously overhead and from somewhere in the high branches a wood pigeon cooed.

"What make's you think our fathers don't get on?" asked Helen.

"He told me. *And* he specifically told me never to see you again."

She squeezed his hand. "I'm glad you ignored him."

"I gave up heeding him a long time ago. Now I pretend to listen and just nod. He's delusional if he thinks he's got any power over me."

"And what had he to say about my father?"

"Nothing complimentary. He says he was disrespectful to him, wouldn't address him by his rank, kept calling him by his first name. My father's a stickler for protocol, takes great pride in his rank."

Helen laughed lightly. "Yeah, that sounds like something my dad would do. So, is that it? That's what they fell out over?"

"That, and the little matter of your father proving him wrong. He had put an innocent man behind bars and your father set him free, so to speak."

"Oh yeah." Her eyes lit up as she beamed a smile to Robert. "Luke Baker. I'd nearly forgotten about that."

"Well *he* hasn't."

The path forked to the right and Robert guided Helen that way. A short distance along they turned off the path and made their way towards a fallen tree. Robert gently hoisted Helen onto it. She now sat facing him. Walking side by side he was nearly a foot taller. But now as he stood between her denim clad knees, they were face to face; their heights equalized. They kissed for several minutes, lost, and oblivious to the world around them. They broke and hugged; his head on her shoulder. He held her for a long time. "I think my dad is up to no good." he said eventually. The words partially muffled by her navy sweatshirt.

"What do mean, no good?"

Robert straightened up. "For a while now he's been slipping away on Sunday mornings, saying he's going to the rugby grounds. But when I ask my friends who go to these matches; they say they have not seen him at any of the games."

"Maybe he was there but they just didn't see him in the crowd."

"A small crowd goes to these matches and they're spread out around the pitch. They'd notice him if he was there."

CHAPTER 10

The sweet odour of tobacco smoke wafted out of the stone shed at the end of the walled garden in Heatherville house. Joggy, knew exactly who was waiting for him when he came in for his lunch of cheese sandwiches and tea. "What brings you here?" he enquired.

"Just checking in to see how you're getting on with our little investigation," said McNeill.

"Give us a chance, I've only just started. I'm trying to build up a picture of the people who were here at the time."

"Anything of note so far?"

"No. But if you're looking to be useful, you could track down a few people for me."

"And who might they be?"

"The three Fitzgerald brothers. They once lived in Barterstown House, but have been gone from there since the forties. Charles was nineteen and Peter was eighteen when they left in nineteen-forty one. Leon left in forty-three. None of them have been back since. And the only link I have to them is Toohey's solicitors in Oldbridge. They collect lease money from Harry Butler once a year on their behalf."

"That would make them today ... what?" said McNeill, mostly to himself, as he did the math in his head. "Fifty-two, fifty-one and forty eight."

"Sorry." Joggy poured tea into the white plastic flask cup. "I don't have a second one."

"That's all right. If I find these brothers, do you want me to interview them or do *you* want to do that?"

Joggy washed down the mouthful of food before he replied. "If you don't mind I'd prefer to talk to them myself. Continuity is important here. They may say something trivial that means nothing to you but fits in with something I've already heard."

"Spoken like a true detective. You should have been a cop, Jackson, not a gardener."

"Wash your mouth out with soap when you get home."

"The Coughlin brothers, any plans to go and see them?"

"Been putting it off. After everything I've heard about them, I'm in no rush."

"You're not afraid of them, are you?"

"Wary, might be a better word. "

"Well when you do plan to go, let me know first, will you?"

"Why?"

"So I'll know where to pick up the body of course."

"Ha, ha, ha, very funny."

The report on Parker and Winter, that Cole had earlier requested from the RUC arrived Monday afternoon. It was waiting on Costello's desk when he came back from lunch. He took his time reading it. When he was finished he leaned back in his chair and clapped his hands together. "At last," he said, "meat on the bones.

Cole," he shouted as he marched towards the front door. "My car!"

Cole plucked his jacket from the back of his chair and ran, like an obedient child after a parent, conscious of the sneers of his colleagues as he passed them on the way out. He sat into the passenger seat. Costello dropped the RUC file onto his lap.

"Peruse that while I drive."

Cole quickly browsed the pages. "Shit." he said. "Is any of this verifiable?"

"Of course not, it's all rumour and hearsay and more than likely a hundred-per-cent true. And it's also the real reason why he was killed."

They turned into Parker's avenue. The gates were open.

"Are you going to tell them what's in this report?" asked Cole.

"Are you out of your mind? I want their co-operation. Telling them will only get their backs up and we'll get nothing then."

They pulled up outside the front door.

"You keep your mouth shut," said Costello, as they got out of the car. "I'll do the talking."

Victoria answered the door. "Oh hello," she said, recognising Sergeant Cole.

"This is Detective Sergeant Costello," said Cole. "He's now in charge of your father's case."

"The other man, what happened to him? I thought he was in charge?"

"He's been reassigned," said Costello. "May we come in?"

"Of course, yes... come in." She led them into the sitting-room, where her mother was lounging in an armchair, asleep, close to a dwindling fire.

"Mother." Victoria, gave her a gentle shake.

Her eyes popped open as if she had been in a light sleep. "Who are you?" she asked warily, squinting at the two men. She lifted her spectacles, which were hanging from a gold chain around her neck, and put them on.

"I'm Detective Costello and this is ...."

"Sergeant Cole, yes I know him. Sit down."

"Thank you," said Costello. They both sat on the edge of the settee.

Victoria sat in the other armchair.

Costello took Mrs Parker to be in her fifties. Her oval dark framed glasses parted her shoulder length straight sandy brown hair like a curtain. The centre parting highlighted her greying roots and the corners of her mouth were turned down giving her a sulky expression.

"How can I help you, Detective?" Mrs Parker was now fully alert.

"I believe your husband and Fred Winter were good friends?"

"They were, for nearly twenty years."

"Do you recall how they met?"

"At an Orange Order meeting. Terry joined just after we married."

"I would have thought that he would have been a member long before that. Wasn't his father a prominent member at the time?"

"He was, but they didn't always see eye to eye on things. I have to admit that I was surprised when he told me he was going to join up. I thought it would be the last thing he would ever do."

"Why are you interested in this, Detective?" asked Victoria. "Has it got something to do with my father's death?"

"We don't know that just yet."

Costello turned his attention back to Mrs Parker. "I take it you met Fred Winter?"

"Oh indeed I did. He often stayed in our house."

"Did your husband, by any chance, receive any disturbing phone calls in the last few months?"

Missus Parker looked into the dying fire as she ran her mind back. "Now that you mention it," she said, looking up at Victoria. "You were there at the time." She looked now at Costello. "About six months ago a call did come in. I answered it. He asked for Terry. My husband was down the yard at the time so I asked him for his name, but he would not give it, said it was a private call. Afterwards I asked Terry who it was, but he just fobbed me off, saying it was Orange Order business. Which meant, don't ask. But he did look worried."

"It was shortly after that he bought the shotgun," said Victoria. "Do you think someone threatened him, Detective?"

"It's a definite possibility," said Costello. "Do you think we could have a look at your husband's things, Missus Parker?"

"What sort of things?" she asked warily.

"Paperwork, notebooks, correspondence.... that sort of thing."

"He had a small desk in our bedroom. You can have a look through that if you wish."

They rose.

"And only the desk, Detective," Mrs Parker added firmly. "I don't want you rummaging through my personal belongings."

Victoria brought them upstairs and showed them into her mother's bedroom. The mahogany desk was in one corner. "That's where my father kept anything of importance."

"Thank you," said Costello."

Victoria went back downstairs and left them to it.

"Check the wardrobe," said Costello, when he heard the sitting-room door close.

"Look in the pockets of his jackets and trousers. Open the doors carefully. I don't want them back up here."

A thorough search of the desk and its drawers uncovered nothing of significance.

"Anything?" enquired Costello.

"Not yet. Hold on, I think I have something." He lifted a brown leather briefcase with combination locks from the bottom of the wardrobe. "It was hidden under a pile of blankets."

Costello tried several different combination but without success. "Any ideas of their dates of birth?"

"No, sir."

"Right, nothing for it."

They brought it downstairs.

"Is this your husband's?" Costello asked Mrs Parker

"That was in the wardrobe, Detective," Mrs Parker snapped. "I did not give you permission to search there."

"Do you have the numbers to open this." Costello said, ignoring Mrs Parker's protest.

"We don't," said Victoria. "Dad was the only one that ever opened it."

"Do you mind if we force it?"

"Yes I do," said Mrs Parker, almost panic stricken. She rose to her feet. "Hand that over, Detective."

Victoria rose to her feet also. "Mother, what's going on?"

"Missus Parker, we are trying to catch your husband's killer." Costello, had injected a note of gravity into his voice. "Now, if this briefcase contains information that will further our case, we'll need to see it."

"I can assure you Detective, there is nothing in that briefcase that will help you do that."

"Missus Parker, I appreciate this is a sensitive time in your life, but we are not here to hurt you or your family, we are simply trying to do our job. You can be a hindrance or a help. Which is it to be?"

Victoria could see the fear in her mother's eyes and knew that at any moment now she would start crying. She turned to Costello. "Detective, I think you'd better leave it with me. My mother and I will discuss it and I will contact you later."

Costello was reluctant to do so.

"I promise you, Detective." Victoria took a step forward and placed one hand on the briefcase. "Nothing will be destroyed and I *will* contact you."

Costello had no choice but to relinquish the briefcase. He handed it to Victoria. "I'm holding you to that, Miss Parker," he said, as they left.

As soon as the front door closed, Mrs Parker slumped back into her armchair. Victoria went to the front window and watched them leave. She then turned again to her mother. "What's in this?" She raised the briefcase up from where it had been hanging by her side. "Is it something you didn't want them to see, or was it something you didn't want me to see?"

Her mother looked at her, her eyes brimming with tears. "Sit down," she said gently.

Victoria sat on the edge of the settee and rested the briefcase on her knee.

Mrs Parker sniffed. "I didn't want you to find out this way. In fact, I didn't want you to find out at all. I wanted you to forever remember your father as a good man."

"What are you saying? That dad wasn't a good man?"

"Of course he was a good man." Mrs Parker paused and pulled a handkerchief from her cardigan sleeve and dabbed her eyes. "He loved you and I very dearly. But there was another side to your father; a dark vengeful side." She paused. "Eight, five and twenty four are the numbers."

Victoria lifted the case and rolled the tumblers into position. It popped open. Inside a black diary lay among some loose papers. "How did you know that? I thought dad was the only one who knew the combination."

"Your dad wasn't as smart as he thought he was. He kept forgetting that our bedroom was directly above the sitting room and that sound travels upwards. I heard your father and Fred Winter discussing the contents of that diary. The next day I tried different dates of birth and found mine opened it."

Victoria picked up the diary.

"It belonged to your grandfather. And in it are the graphic descriptions of the deaths of four men he knew. After they were killed, Terry's father believed he was next."

"What's this got to do with daddy's death?"

"Everything. I need to go back to the start." She sighed deeply. "Your father, when he was young had a very good friend by the name of Rory Donovan. Rory was a Catholic. Terry's father had a genuine hatred for everything Catholic. I knew Rory, he was a lovely lad. He was even at our wedding. But, while we were on our honeymoon, Rory was abducted, tied to a tree and severely beaten with iron bars. It was supposed to be a punishment beating; a warning, telling him to stay away from Terry. But something went terribly wrong. Someone came upon the scene and killed him.

When your father found out, he was inconsolable. It was bad enough to lose his best friend in such a brutal way, but what really hurt was finding out that his father was behind the beating. He didn't participate, mind you, but he orchestrated it. His father denied it of course, but he knew he was lying through his teeth. Not long after that, one of the men who had taken part in the beating was found horribly tortured and murdered. The other men then skipped town and travelled to different parts of the world to hide. But it seems they were tracked down, tortured and then killed."

She sat up and looked into the fire as a piece of un-burnt fuel suddenly erupted into flames. The flames seem to draw her away from the present to another time in her life. "I couldn't conceive," she said in a low voice "We tried and tried but I couldn't conceive. We went for tests. I was devastated when they doctors told me that I could not have children. I went into a kind of depression. It took me a good while to come to grips with it. But then one evening Terry came home and all that doom and gloom was lifted."

She look at Victoria and smiled for the first time that evening. "He said that the adoption agency had been in contact and that they had found a little girl and that she was available to be adopted. What I did not know at the time, was that your father had been tracking you and pulling strings so we could adopt you." Her smile disappeared again. "Then your father…"

"Hold on," said Victoria, "back up. Why was dad tracking me? How did he know about me in the first place?"

"Let me continue, Victoria. The answers will become clear in a moment."

Victoria nodded.

"Your father joined the Orange Order; an organisation he detested. It was everything his father stood for and for him to turn around and join them, flabbergasted me. I asked him why and he just said, *it was time for him to take responsibility.* That was the start of the secrets. A few months later Fred Winter spent his first night in our home."

"Had dad got something to do with Fred's death?"

"I believe so. You were born on the same night that Rory Donovan died. Charlie Wright was a friend of Terry's father and also a good family friend to the Winters. I believe that somehow Fred Winter ended up killing Rory Donovan that night. The next morning the brakes on Charlie Wright's car failed and he was killed. It pains me to say it but I believe for seventeen years your father plotted the death of Fred Winter. On the night Fred Winter was murdered, your father went out late and did not come back till near dawn."

"Dad once gave me a key that fitted Fred's bedroom lock," said Victoria. "He asked me to search the room for him."

"Really, did you find anything?"

"I found two things. One was a penknife with some initials scratched into it and the other was a cigarette lighter with an inscription on it."

"You don't remember the inscription, by any chance?"

Victoria went quiet and tried to visualize the inscription. "I think it began with an F. It was a women's name, like a nickname. Flor...florence...Florrie, that was it."

"Oh my God." Victoria's mother went deathly white.

"Mum, are you alright?"

"That was Charlie Wright's wife's name. Fred Winter must have killed Charlie Wright. All these years I've welcomed that man into my home, not knowing he had killed two people. And your father knew and said nothing."

"Who killed the other men?"

"The IRA. They claimed responsibility at the time."

"Yeah, but how did dad know that it was Fred that killed his friend?"

"All of the men were tortured before they died. They must have said."

"Okay, but *they* were the IRA. How did dad find out what *they* found out?"

Victoria's mother did not answer that. She just let it sink in and waited. It took a few seconds before the horrible truth hit Victoria.

"Oh no, he didn't, he wouldn't have. DAD!" she exclaimed, "how could he?" She sank back against the settee. The briefcase slipped from her thighs and fell to the floor. The contents spilled out. Victoria sat there in silence as the ugly truth soaked into her very being.

"I'm sorry, Victoria. I didn't want to tell you, but your father sold his soul to the other side. That is how he found out about your existence and about Fred Winter."

"So I was just a pawn in his game?"

"At the start, that may have been his reason for adopting you. But he quickly fell in love with you. He loved you as if you were his own flesh and blood."

"Yes, but he still used me. He got me to housekeep for Fred, knowing that I would be useful for his plans. Oh my God," Victoria cried out, as she suddenly thought of all the nights she stood at her bedroom window, naked, having her last cigarette before going to sleep and knowing Fred was down in the orchard spying on her. A shiver ran down her spine at the thought of teasing a man who had murdered two men.

"Victoria, what's the matter?"

"I was nearly burnt to death. That's how little dad cared."

"I'm sure he didn't think that way."

"I was just part of the greater scheme. He couldn't wait for me to grow up and play my role. And what about you, mum. How long have you known? What am I asking? You knew from the start, from the time I was adopted."

"I swear Victoria, I did not know who you were until after you were adopted. Terry said it was a coincidence, but that we could never say anything to Fred. Not after the callous way his family discarded you. Joining the Orange Order and then adopting you, did make some alarm bells ring, but I ignored them. Having you was all that mattered."

"So was it the diary that made you face reality?"

"Yes. Everything started to fall into place. But I still didn't know exactly what he was going to do."

Victoria slowly leaned her head back and closed her eyes. Tears slipped from the corners and trickled down her cheeks. There was a long silence before she opened them again. She turned her head towards her mother. "For you, I made the ultimate sacrifice. I couldn't bear to hear you cry yourself to sleep every night. I believed that me being with the son of the man you believed killed dad, was too much for you. So for you, I broke up with Danny. For two years you've known what dad did and you said nothing. And after I broke with Danny, you still said nothing, and I'm certain you could hear me cry myself to sleep. But you let me suffer. What kind of mother does that?"

"I'm sorry Victoria, but he wasn't right for you. He's the son of a labourer. He has nothing. You have a large farm and money. You have responsibilities. You have to think of the future. You have to find someone of your own social stature, and be of the same religion."

Victoria frowned and listened in disbelief. She lowered her head and a few seconds later raised it again. This time she was wearing a smile.

"You're so right mother. I don't know what I was thinking of. I do have responsibilities and I do have to think of the future. And the man I marry should be of the same religion as me."

"Oh that's a great relief. I just knew you'd see sense," she said, beaming from ear to ear.

Joggy set out across the fields for Barterstown lane. It was windy but bright. The uneasy feeling he had in Butler's yard on the night of the fire was still with him. He had reckoned that if the fire was set on purpose, then that person may have hung around to see the results of their handiwork. And if they did, they did not travel to Butlers by the normal route but by the back way. He hoped they had left something of themselves behind. On the lane he turned left. It was narrow, rutted, dark and overgrown with hazel and ash and brambles and briars that reached out from either side to rip at his clothing. The grassy centre-line was the safest path to take. The lane was not dark enough for him not to see his way. Still, he might miss something important, so he had come prepared. He took a small chromium torch from his pocket and then walked slowly and carefully. The ground beneath the grassy centre-line was solid.

The place had an eerie feeling to it, not helped by the rustling of rodents or birds in the undergrowth. It took him an hour to reach the sharp bend that led directly to the road. It was here he stopped when the torchlight shone on tyre impressions. He hunkered down and inspected them. He then withdrew a small notebook and a pencil from his pocket and with the torch clenched between his teeth, began sketching the tyre pattern onto the page. It was a zig zag pattern. When he eventually stood up he was taken aback. Standing in front of him was Sergeant Cole and Detective Sergeant Costello.

"What are doing?" asked Costello, his face more serious than usual.

"Do you know there are tyre tracks here?"

"So I see. You haven't answered my question."

"Just trying to clear my name."

"Sergeant, go back to the car. In the glove-box you'll find a camera and a large torch."

"I reckon these are the tyre tracks of your real murderer," said Joggy.

"Or it could simply be a spot where weekend lovers come to park."

"One way or another, why are ye only looking at it now? Why was this not done at the time of Parkers death?"

Costello's eyes narrowed. "Who said it wasn't? This is just a follow up."

Cole returned with the camera and torch. Costello then held the torch over the tyre impressions while Cole took several photos.

"If it's a follow up, why are ye taking photo's?"

"Did you find anything else?" Costello asked, ignoring Joggy's question.

"No. Whoever did this was careful to walk the centre line. The ground is hard there, so no footprints and as far as I can see, nothing was snagged on the briers. If you wanted to hide your car from sight, would you drive in or would you reverse?"

When neither replied, Joggy answered his own question. "I would reverse. Easier to escape and easier to see if anyone was about. And if that was the case he would have to get out on the right-hand side of the lane which means he would have been brushing against the briars."

Costello, who had been listening but saying nothing, raised his torch and shone it on the area that Joggy alluded to. He worked for awhile examining each outstretched briar and then he stopped. "Sergeant," he snapped as he eyed a small brown fibre caught on a thorn. "Get me an envelope." Cole picked one from his jacket pocket and handed it to Costello. A couple of seconds later he picked off the thread and dropped it in the envelope. He found no more.

"Got any ideas who it might be?" asked Joggy.

"Too early," said Costello.

"It's not too early to suspect someone who has motive to set me up? Someone who wears brown? Someone who keeps burnt matches?"

"Who are you talking about?" said Costello.

"I'm not going to do your job for you. You know who I'm talking about. The question is, do you have the balls to go after him?"

"No one is outside the law, Mister Jackson."

Joggy gave a derisory snort. "That remains to be seen."

The silent atmosphere in the car on the way back to Oldbridge was decidedly tense. Costello's jaw was clenched and his knuckles were white on the steering wheel.

"I think I should just say that I don't believe Detective Reilly has anything to do with Parkers death," said Cole. "But...." He paused, almost afraid to go on.

"Spit it out man," snapped Costello.

"He did say something to me as we left Parker's yard on the day of the murder that I thought was not right." He swallowed before going on. "He said he would give anything to pin this on Jackson."

Costello slammed on the brakes and brought the car to a shuddering stop. "And you didn't think to tell me this before now?"

"I didn't think it was important. He had had a run in with Jackson earlier. He was angry. People shoot from the lip all the time. It doesn't mean anything."

"In a murder investigation, everything means something. Do you know how stupid, inept and unprofessional we looked back there? Jackson's already worked out that we found no matches and now he's doing what we should have done. Why wasn't that lane thoroughly searched on the day of the murder?"

"They found the tracks going to Jackson's and Reilly decided to concentrate on that area. There were no tracks going from Parker's farm directly to the lane."

"That's because he used the track he made to Jackson's and Jackson's own tracks to the lane to hide his own."

"What do we do now?"

"Now we follow the evidence and be damned where it leads us."

CHAPTER 11

Victoria left her mother and drove to Oldbridge Garda station.

"Detective," said the young garda, "there's a young lady at the front desk who wants a word... said her name is Victoria Parker."

Even though he did not show it, Costello was delighted to see she had the briefcase with her. "This way," he said.

Heads turned to ogle the young woman in the tight denim jeans, as he led her to his office. Victoria gave him the combination and then explained in great detail what her mother had told her. A lot of the details Costello already knew. Afterwards he escorted her to her car. Victoria unlocked it and then leaned on the open door. She called after Cosgrove. "By the way, Detective." Cosgrove stopped and turned around. "Do your best and catch my fathers killer."

"We will certainly do that, Miss Parker."

"Because no matter what you may think of my father, in his heart, I believe he was not a traitor."

The whitewashed cottage was set close to a narrow side road. A neatly kept privet hedge marked out the borders of the postage-stamp front lawn and concrete pathway to the front door. Joggy parked opposite the white wooden gate. There was no answer to his front door-knock, so he made his way around to the back. As he turned the corner, a black and white collie, its coat matted into dreadlocks, growled and barked at him. Its bark was hoarse and raspy as it strained hard against a flimsy chain, wrapped around its neck, that looked as if it would snap at any moment. The chain was tied to the corner upright of an L shaped wooden shed, sheeted in slobs, that wrapped itself around to Joggy's left. To his right was the cottage, the backdoor of which was open. He looked warily about him. Through the uneven gaps between the boards of the shed he saw something move. From the inner darkness, a pair of unblinking eyes peered steadily out at him.

"Hello," Joggy called out tentatively.

One of the brothers stepped out of the shed balancing two badly chipped white enamel buckets full of turf. He eyed Joggy with suspicion, as he set the buckets on the ground. "Qui' Bruno," he shouted at the dog, before turning his attention back to Joggy. But the dog ignored him and kept up the racket. "Whoayou?" he asked. His thin lips barely moved as the words came out, melted together. Going on McNeill's description; this was Alo....chubbier of the two, bald and tended to mumble.

"Joggy Jackson. I'm sorry Alo, to disturb you but I was wondering if I could have a chat with you and your brother, Bob."

"From K'patrick?" he asked, recognising the name.

"Yes." Joggy was nervous, though he tried not to show it.

"I herdoyou. Whayu want?" Even though his eyeballs vibrated constantly, their focus never moved off Joggy.

"Well it's a bit of a delicate subject and I'll respect your decision if you don't want to talk to me about it. Is your brother about?" He glanced casually around and wondered where the hell he was. Knowing their reputations, he would be happier if Bob was standing in front of him beside his brother. Alo's eyes darkened and the lines on his forehead deepened. "Go-on."

"It's thirty-three-years since Cissy Butler disappeared and her mother, Harriett Butler, has asked me to try and find her daughter."

"You shouldnbe here...go, now."

There was a hint of warning in his voice, but Joggy chose to ignore it. "Look I'll understand if you don't want to talk about it, but I'd like to have a word with Bob before I do go."

"I said, go, befor..." Alo's eyes looked right and beyond.

Joggy did not turn around in time. "Aaaagh," he shouted as the handle of a shovel crashed against the back of his knees. His legs gave way and he fell forward to the ground. A dirty, clay-covered hobnail boot pushed him over onto his back and the pointed end of the shovel was pressed hard against his sternum. Bob stared down at him, thin, gaunt and with wild eyes that looked monstrous when enlarged by the heavy lenses within dark framed glasses. Alo joined his brother, their expressions, dark and foreboding. Bruno's chain snapped tight as he lunged against it, clambering to join the action.

"All right." Joggy, gripped the edges of the shovel with his hands and grimaced at the burning pain in the back of his knees and the pressure on his chest. "I get the point, you don't need to press it home" he said, urgently. "If you let me up, I'll leave."

The corner of Bob's mouth curled into a smirk as the intended irony of Joggy's remark registered. "So you're looking for Cissy Butler, are ya?"

"Yeah, her mother asked me if I could help."

"And you decided that *now* would be a good time to ask us... what? Thirty-three-years have gone by, we're older now and just maybe, now that we are close to looking at the face of God, we just might want to confess... is that it?" He twisted and pushed down hard on the shovel handle.

"Aaaagh." He tried to twist the shovel from Bob's hands, but to avail. "No, it's not like that. I just wanted to hear your side of what happened."

"What happened and what's going to happen is like Bruno's shite," he spat. "It stinks to high heaven when it's fresh, leave it alone and a crusty skin grows over it and it doesn't stink anymore, but step on it and break the crust and it stinks to high heaven all over again."

He leaned on the shovel again. "For fucks sake Bob," Joggy shouted, "there's no need for this." Despite his grip on the shovels edges, he could feel it cutting deeper into his chest. "If you kill me," he said, finding it hard to say the words. "You'll go to prison for the rest of your lives, you don't want that!"

"We're already in prison; have been for the last thirty-three fucking years. Being in one with bars will be a relief. At least in there they'll look upon us as equals."

Twack.... the short sharp sound rang out and the pressure on Joggy's chest suddenly eased as Bob collapsed to the ground beside him.

"If you don't want a taste of the same," said McNeill, waving the baton in Alo's face, "then back off."

Alo took a couple of quick steps back.

"Where the fuck did you come from?" Joggy enquired, as he massaged his bruised chest.

"I stop you from being killed and that's all you have to say to me?"

"I have other things to say to you, and right enough, thanks would be one of them."

He raised his arm into the air, "Give us a pull up."

McNeill hoisted him off the ground.

"Right now, I'd prefer an answer to my question." He winced as he gingerly flexed his knees, first one then the other. "Where the fuck did you come from?"

"I was watching your back. When you told me you were going out to see these boyos and knowing what they were capable of... I couldn't very well let you go alone, now could I?"

"It would have been nice to know you were there."

"And spoil my fun!"

"You're a sadistic bastard, McNeill."

The dog was nearly rabid; foamed spittle hung from its mouth.

"Shut that fucking mongrel up," McNeil shouted at Alo.

Alo turned, walked quickly to one of the turf buckets, picked up a large black sod and threw it at the dog, hitting him on the head. It yelped and whimpered and backed into the shed.

Bob groaned and sat up, rubbing the back of his head. "Typical dirty fucking cop, hit you when you're not looking."

"That's a tad hypocritical now Bob, wouldn't you say?" said McNeill, "considering what you did to Jackson here."

Bob grunted and continued rubbing his head. "You could have cracked me skull."

"No fucking chance. That head of yours is as thick as a coconut."

"Now what?" Bob tried to raise himself from the ground.

Mc Neill, used his boot to push him back down. "Stay where you are, it's safer for you there. As for what happens next, that's up to Mister Jackson here."

Joggy looked quizzically at McNeill.

McNeill's eyebrows shot up as he nodded at Bob on the ground. "Do you want to press charges for assault and attempted murder?" he enquired.

It took a few seconds for Joggy to work out what McNeill meant. "Not if they answer my questions," he said at last.

Alo gave Bob a look and it was enough for Joggy to know that he had deferred the answering of the questions to his older brother.

Bob gave a deep sigh. "What do you want to know?"

"On the day that Cissy Butler disappeared, did you see her?"

"For the umpteenth time, no."

"She went missing in the afternoon. Where were you during that period?"

"I was white-washing the front walls. Look, all of this shit is on record. Why do I have to answer the same old questions again."

"Because I want to hear your answers," said Joggy. "Now, you would have had your back turned to the road, do you think it was possible she cycled by without you hearing her?"

Bob gave the back of his head another rub as he thought about the answer. "I don't think she could have," he said eventually. "I was told that the bike was old and not in great shape and I know the lane was rough, which means the bike would have rattled or made some kind of noise and I'm pretty sure I would have heard something. Now," he said raising a hand to emphasise his point. "I'm not saying it was impossible for her to sneak past, but I think I would have heard her."

"Did you move away from the house at any time, you know to take a piss or something?"

"Yeah, once. I went around the back, but I was gone for only a couple of minutes."

"Any idea what time that was?"

"No. I had no way of telling the time. It could have been around three, but I'd only be guessing."

Several more questions were asked but nothing differed from the original answers.

"My money's still on those two boys," said McNeill as they walked slowly towards Joggy's car.

"I need a pint," Joggy said, still feeling the effects of his injuries. "There's a grand pub back the road in Foymore. Join me and I'll buy you one."

"Just one?"

"I suppose I could stretch it to two."

The '*Hawthorn*' was quiet. Two men were sat at the bar chatting and another was alone by a window, nursing a whisky and contentedly smoking his briar pipe. The sweet smell of the tobacco lingered in the air.

All heads turned towards Joggy as he made his way to the bar. "Two pints," he said, to the barman, just as McNeill entered, in uniform but without the hat.

"Find a seat and I'll bring them down to you."

They found seats as far from the three men as possible. They sat beside one another on a well worn wooden bench and faced the room. The two men had stopped talking and were now keenly listening. McNeill tapped Joggy's leg with his knee.

"There's two cars outside," he whispered, just loud enough for all to hear, "one's got a tax disc out of date and the other has two bald tyres, when we leave I'm going to do the owners."

The two men at the counter casually finished their drinks, said goodbye to the barman and nonchalantly walked out. The other man stayed put. He was obviously the owner of the bicycle propped against the pub wall.

The barman brought down the two pints. Joggy paid him.

"Was that really necessary?" The barman addressed McNeill. "You just drove away two of my best customers."

"Hey, I'm just doing my job, that's all."

"And then ye wonder," he remarked, as he turned back to the bar, "why the public despise ye."

Joggy smiled at the remark as he grabbed the cold glass with both hands. The chill immediately comforted and cooled the hot angry welts that ran down the centre of his hands. He drank the first quarter of his pint in one swallow. "Ahhhh, I needed that," he said, wiping his lips with the back of his hand.

"How's the knees?"

"Sore. By tomorrow morning I won't be able to bend them." He took another drink. "You could have come in earlier and saved me from being attacked, you know," moaned Joggy, feeling a little sorry for himself.

"There was no reason for me to come in any earlier. But as soon as you were hit, I was on the move. And before you say anything more, there's no point in blaming me for your injuries, if you're going to nose around in other people's affairs, you can expect trouble."

Joggy knew McNeill was right, but he just did not want to admit it to him. "So, you still fancy the two boyos for it, then?"

"Yep."

"Why?"

"Isn't it obvious?"

"Not to me it isn't."

"Look, the people who lived around that way were law-abiding, God-fearing people. Not one of them was ever in trouble with the law. Then a stranger with a criminal record turns up to paint an empty house and a little girl goes missing. Girls of that age have a way of turning some men's heads. Especially one dressed up as pretty as she was. I reckon he saw her and went to talk to her. She wouldn't have anything to do with him, so he got mad and grabbed her. Probably dragged her into the house and after that, well you can guess the rest. Then when the brother turned up they threw her and the bike in the back of the van and brought her with them. They got rid of the bike in the quarry and God only knows what they did with her."

"That's a bit of a stretch, don't you think?"

"No, I don't. Remember, these two guys were no oil paintings and age has done them no favours. They've never had women fawning over them. The respectable ones gave them a wide berth and the whores just used them for what they could get. Cissy was fresh meat and I hate to think what they put that poor child through before they killed her."

"Yes, but Yarr's house was searched from top to bottom and not one single red hair was found, and the same for the van and neither looked like they had been cleaned up. Now I'd imagine, in keeping with that period, that these men where severely dealt with and yet they never confessed. Even Alo, who I believe is the weaker of the two, didn't buckle. Today, thirty-three years later, they still gave the same answers. Either they're fantastic liars with great memories or they're telling the truth."

"If it's not them Sherlock, who then is *your* money on?"

"At this moment my money is staying firmly in my pocket. Having said that, I believe Charlie Higgins, deserves a closer look."

"Why him?"

"He was a bachelor. And by all accounts a good-looking man. And yet he remained single! He liked children; girls in particular. He gave them apples and sometimes had them in his house. This wasn't some dirty, smelly old man. This man dressed well, always wore a tie and a clean shirt. But after Cissy went missing, he never invited another child in again. Why do you think he did that? Did Cissy reach his house? Did he invite her in? And did something go awfully wrong? Could she be buried in his back garden? A strange thing happened after Cissy disappeared. One of his two apple bushes, the ones he picked the fruit from and gave to the children, died."

"That's pure speculation, Joggy."

"Hmm, maybe. I wonder has he any living relatives."

"I could probably find that out." McNeill drained the last of his pint. "Of the two theories," he said, placing the empty glass in front of Joggy, "I'll stick with my own, and for one very good reason; the bike. It was found close to their home in a small private quarry. Not one of Cissy Butlers neighbours knew of the existence of that quarry. The Coughlin brothers were the only ones that knew about it."

"Fine, that is a sticking point, and I concede that the two of them are not exactly the shiniest pennies in the cash-till, but they're not that dull either. If they did do it, and had gotten away without being seen, why on earth would they draw suspicion upon themselves by then dumping the bike that close to their home."

"As you say they're not that shiny."

Joggy shook his head. "Another pint?"

"Aye, why not, you owe me."

Joggy thought about not telling Alice. He did not want to worry her. But then realised he could not hide his injuries from her for long. Especially in the morning as he got out of bed and started to creak and groan like an old shed door. She cried when he showed them to her. "It's all my fault," she said as tears ran down her face. "I should never have got you into this."

"It's not your fault," he said trying to calm her. He came to her, put his arms around her shoulders and pulled her towards him, wincing as he did so. He kissed her on the forehead. "It's my fault. I knew the dangers and I should never have gone there on my own. It was a stupid move."

"No, it's my fault," she insisted, her head resting against his chest. "I'm going to ring Harry and tell her we're finished." He leaned back and looked into her dewy eyes.

"We can't do that." There was determination in his voice. "We've come too far. Besides, as someone said to me not too long ago, would you want me to give up if it was our child that was missing?"

"No, of course not, but it's not our child. It's a child missing over thirty years."

"Yes, and everyone has given up on her, declared her a lost cause and turned their backs on Harry. I'm not about to do the same. If there is a God in Heaven, I will find that little girl."

"How do you know that? You got a crystal ball or something?"

"I can feel it in my waters or at least I could if I wasn't so sore," he said with humour and gave a light laugh. But even that hurt.

Alice knew from the tone of his voice, when there was no changing her husband's mind. "Okay, how can I make it up to you?"

"Later tonight you can rub some salve into my wounds for me, anything that's *stiff* or sore you can massage."

The next morning, with a clear photo of the tyre impressions in his hands, Cosgrove slipped into the station house car park and examined the treads of all the cars present.

"Sir!" Cosgrove, tapped his fingers against Murray's open door. "Can I have a word?"

Murray lowered his copy of the Irish Press and glanced over the top of his glasses. He gave a low irritated sigh. There was an unwritten rule within the station that the Inspector was not to be disturbed until he was finished reading his paper. Cosgrove was well aware of this, but felt this could not wait. Murray folded the paper in half and placed it on the desk. Then removed his glasses and placed them on the paper. "Come in," he said.

Cosgrove closed the door.

"A private word, is it?"

"For the moment."

"Have a seat, so."

"The Parker investigation Sir, has thrown up a surprising element."

"Go on."

"What we have uncovered so far, leads us to believe that Parker was murdered in revenge for what he was up to in the North. His neck was broken and then he was hanged. The person who did this was sending out a clear message."

"Is that your surprising element, Detective?"

"No Sir, we have further evidence, circumstantial at the moment, that points to the possibility of one of our officers being involved."

"Evidence?"

"Motive, an incriminating statement, the retention of spent matches and the tyre treads on his car match the ones found close to the murder scene. The only thing we don't know is if he has any connection with the North."

"You think Detective Sergeant Reilly had something to do with this?"

Cosgrove raised an eyebrow. "I hope not. How should I proceed, sir?"

"With extreme caution, Detective." Murray rose from his chair and ambled over to the window which looked onto a blank wall. He held his hands behind his back and studied his own reflection. He stared into his own unblinking eyes. Investigating one of their own was his and many a commanding officers pet hate. There were no winners. Behind him he could see Cosgrove waiting patiently for an answer. He turned around and sat on the windowsill. "Do you know where Detective Reilly was that Sunday?"

"Sergeant Cole says he collected him at one-fifteen from the bar of Oldbridge rugby club."

"Was he at the match?"

"I don't know, sir."

"I should think you would have found that out before you came to me, Detective."

"I didn't want to stir up suspicion by asking questions."

"You can do it discreetly. Ask Sergeant Cole to have a friendly word with one of his drinking buddies."

"Yes, sir. Thank you, sir." Cosgrove stood up and walked to the door.

"Keep me appraised, Detective."

"Yes, sir."

"Cole," boomed Cosgrove, as he marched towards the front door. "Grab your coat."

Cole moved swiftly after him. He was getting used to these impromptu exits and by now was almost deaf to the snickering.

"Where are we off to, sir?" he asked as he caught up.

"I need a drink."

Dempsey's pub was just open and the morning tea drinkers were dribbling in.

"Do you want anything with your drink, Sir?" Cole enquired as he stood at the counter and admired the selection of confectionery under the small glass case.

"No."

"One tea and one boiled water." He was tempted by what was on display, but decided it was too early for his sweet tooth.

Cosgrove found a seat at the end of the bar counter.

"This is all very cloak-and-dagger, Sir," commented Cole, surprised at Cosgrove's choice of seating. Cosgrove sipped his water and surreptitiously looked about him. Nobody was close and no one seemed interested in them. He leaned into Cole. "On the Sunday you collected Reilly, from the rugby club, who was he drinking with?" His voice was barely above a whisper.

"A couple of lads from the station and the other two I didn't know."

"Are you friendly with any of them?"

"Jack Thomas ... I sometimes go to dinner with him. He's easy going ... affable."

"Good. Make today one of those sometimes. Find out where Reilly was before you picked him up: After eleven and before one-fifteen."

"He was at the rugby match, sir!"

"You know that for a fact, do you?"

"No, his wife told me, when I rang her for his whereabouts."

"So you don't actually know where he was then?"

"Well ... no. You don't actually think he had a hand in this, do you?"

Cosgrove made no comment.

Jack Thomas had the lasagne with chips, while Cole had the cold meat salad. The initial conversation was mostly small talk before Cole swung it around. "Oldbridge are going well in the Provincial Town's Cup."

"They are," agreed Thomas. "Playing Edenderry in the quarters; that's always a tough match."

"They beat ye at the semi-final stage last year, didn't they?"

"Yeah, but not by much and we were short three of our best men that day. It'll be a different story this time."

"I didn't know Reilly was into rugger. I thought tennis was more his poison. On the Sunday of Parkers murder, I was surprised when his wife told me he was at the game."

"Ah, he goes to an odd one, but I wouldn't call him a dyed-in-the-wool fan. In fact when you picked him up, he was only after joining us. He was doing what he normally does; joining in the after-match celebrations."

"So, he wasn't at the match then?"

"No. I don't know where he was; probably playing tennis."

"But his wife said he had gone to the game?"

"That's what he told her then, but *I* can tell *you* he wasn't cheering on the home team."

Before going back to the station, Cole drove out to the tennis club. He was in luck; there was someone in the office: A little old lady with blue rinse hair. "Could I see a list of your membership, please?" He asked, smiling politely, after he had introduced himself.

The old lady smiled back at him. "Call me Elsie," she said.

"Anyone in particular you looking for."

"I'm not quite sure of the name but I'll probably recognise it when I see it." He perused the list and did not make it obvious when he found Reilly's name on it. "I see you have time sheets in front of you, Elsie. What days do they cover?"

"Oh, Sundays only."

"Can a member play a game if he's not on the time sheet?"

"Absolutely not," said Elsie, abhorred at the notion. "It's a hard and fast rule around here; Sundays are sacrosanct; competition only."

"What do you do with the time sheets when ye are finished with them?"

"We store them for one year and then destroy them."

"Good. Could I see the last four Sundays please?"

Not wanting to draw attention to what he was looking for, Cole ran his eyes over the four, but he was really only interested in one of them, and the time slots of eleven to one-fifteen. He thanked Elsie and left.

Cole joined Cosgrove in his office. "No alibi," He kept his voice low. "Wife thought he was at the match, but it turns out he was only just after joining his friends when I collected him. My friend mentioned that he played tennis. I checked it out. Sunday is timesheet only and he wasn't playing."

For the second time that day, Cosgrove closed Inspector Murray's door behind him.

"He did not go to the rugby match, Sir. We do not know where he was between eleven and one-fifteen."

Murray sucked in a lungful of air and then let it out slowly. "You do know how Detective Sergeant Reilly is connected, don't you?"

"Yes, Sir."

"Okay. Do no more about it today. Leave it with me and I'll make a few inquires of my own."

CHAPTER 12

All through dinner, Alice wore an I-know-something-that-you-don't-know expression and it drove Joggy to despair. She answered his questions by humming contentedly to herself. Finally, when they had finished eating, she pulled, with a flourish, a white envelope from her apron pocket. "Ta – da!" she said, and handed him the already opened letter.

"What's this?"

"Read it and find out."

It did not take long. There were only a couple of lines on crisp white stationery with Macken's solicitors printed in the top left-hand corner. He smiled. "Nellie's left me something in her will. I wonder what that could be?"

"It could be money, I'd say she had a bit squirreled away. Or better still, the cottage!"

"Nay, her brother would have got that. It's probably just some memento. It says to call at my earliest convenience."

"It's exciting, isn't it? Alice squealed. "We've never been left anything before."

"What do you think, should I call in tomorrow on the way home?"

"Yeah, do. I'll ring them in the morning and make the appointment."

That evening in the lounge of Hayes Hotel, Inspector Murray and ex-Inspector Peter Matthews sat in two brown leather armchairs. Murray sipped a Scotch while Matthews nursed a Hennessy. They had struck up a friendship shortly after Murray had taken over from Matthews. In the early days, after moving from Limerick, Murray had relied on Matthews to fill him in on the finer points of working crime in a small town. They now met on average once every two weeks and Murray was constantly amazed at the tit-bits of information Matthews would come up with. For a man retired, he still had a finger on the pulse of the underbelly of the town. Like the town gossip, he delighted in filling Murray in on who was on the take, who was cheating on their wives and, among other tit-bits, who was secretly gay and leading double lives. As he spoke, Matthews lit a large cigar. He dragged deeply on it twice and then joyfully exhaled a cloud of sweet smelling off-white smoke. He sipped his brandy. "Owen tells me you took him off the Parker case."

"Unfortunately, I had to. He has a blind spot when it comes to Joggy Jackson. I needed someone that was more open minded."

"So, you put Cosgrove on it... a good man."

"That he is. He and Cole seem to work well together."

"How is the case progressing? Any new leads?"

Murray looked slowly around. Nobody was close to them. "We're forming the opinion that it may have been a Northern hit. It seems that Mister Parker was not as squeaky clean as he led us all to think. He had been involved in some dirty shenanigans up there that may have resulted in his death."

"How intriguing. And I suppose you're not at liberty to say what those shenanigans were?"

"Now Peter, you know better than to ask." Murray's voice was light with humour. He raised his hand and caught the attention of the waiter. "Same again please."

The waiter made his way to the end of the bar and gave in his order.

"Speaking of the North," said Murray, "I've an uncle who lives in Lifford. I've been up to see him on a few occasions, but strangely enough, I've never crossed the border into the six counties. It's a major part of this island and I'm ashamed to say I've never been."

"You'd like it up there .... great cities .... beautiful scenery."

"That's right, I was nearly forgetting; you've family up there."

"Well, yes, they're a bit distant; second cousins, that sort of thing."

"It was your paternal grandfather who came from there, wasn't it?" Murray smirked. "Seen him lately?"

Matthews stiffened and with narrowed eyes studied his friend. Then it hit him. He half smiled in embarrassment. "My wife has too much to say."

"I couldn't believe it when I heard it; a cop who sees ghosts!"

"I've only ever saw one, and it was my grandfather. And I never want to see another. It's not funny," he said testily, noticing the smirk still lingering on Murray's face. "It was very unsettling....gave me the bloody willies. Here's a hard fact to take your mind of torturing me; I'm not the only member of my family to have links with the North: Owen has an aunt in Bangor."

"He never mentioned that to me before."

"Maybe it's because she's a bit of a black sheep. It's alright to convert from Protestant to Catholic but to do it the other way around...." He shook his head, "not good."

"So she was cut off from the family, was she?"

"Yes. But unbeknownst to the rest of the family, Owen goes to see her on a fairly regular basis."

"That's very thoughtful of him. Does your daughter go with him?"

"She did at the beginning, but it seems they had a falling out. She can't bear to be in the same room as her now."

"So Owen goes up by himself then?"

"Regular as clockwork. Once a month, he makes the trip, stays overnight and comes back the next day. This is about the time of the month, so I reckon he'll be heading up some day this week."

"He must be fierce fond of her if he's going up that often."

"I think he feels sorry for her. He used to go up once every six months, but ever since her husband died last year, he's been going more regularly."

"Well it's nice to see there is some altruism left in the world."

"I suppose you could call it that," he replied without any great enthusiasm.

"This doesn't meet with your wholehearted approval, I take it?"

"I have reservations. If he goes to see her out of the kindness of his heart, it would be churlish of me to turn my nose up at it. It's just that I sometimes wonder about his motives. I hope it's kindness and not some plan to wangle his way into her will ... she is a wealthy woman."

"Has she no family of her own?"

"One daughter, estranged."

"I take it he stays overnight with his aunt?"

"He says he does. But I rang looking for him late one night and he wasn't there. I didn't press her on the subject, but she didn't seem not to know where he had gone."

Matthews left Murray home later that evening.

Murray called Cosgrove into his office the following morning. Cosgrove closed the door. "They're getting suspicious outside, sir."

"What they don't know won't hurt them. That's providing no-one's been talking?"

"No sir. The three of us are the only ones that know."

"Good, keep it that way." Murray told him what Matthews had said.

"Should we bring him in, Sir?"

"No. The timings not right."

"But, Sir, we need to know his whereabouts on the night of Butler's fire, and he's the only one that can tell us."

Murray coughed to clear his throat. "Let's just sit on this for a little longer. I have contacted my counterpart in the north and requested all information they and the security forces have on Reilly. I doubt he has gone unnoticed. Travelling that often has bound to have raised suspicions. I have informed them of his imminent arrival and also requested that he be discreetly shadowed. Let's hope he has not been up to anything untoward."

Cosgrove turned to leave.

"I am uncomfortable with a one strand investigation, Detective." Murray leaned back in his chair. "Just because we are waiting on information from the North, doesn't mean we should not be following up other leads. Have you other leads to follow?"

"Information has slowed, sir. But I would not say it has ground to a halt."

"Brainstorming, Detective. It's a ploy, that in my day I found effective. Three or four people, directly involved in the case, would sit around and openly discussed it. The clues were teased out and sometimes we got a result. If we didn't, the case at least got new impetus."

Cosgrove hesitated.

"I know you think you can do it all on your own, Detective. But believe me, two heads are better than one, three better than two and... well, you get the gist."

"I suppose it won't do any harm, Sir," he said but with little conviction.

"Good. Get the file and ask Sergeant Cole to join us."

They two of them sat in front of the desk with Murray presiding like a judge over proceedings. The murder file rested on Cosgrove's knees.

"Okay," said Murray, let's go back to the beginning. Sergeant Cole, you and Detective Sergeant Reilly went to the scene."

Cole cleared his throat. "After I got the call, I rang Detective Sergeant Reilly's house and was informed by his wife that he was in the rugby club and that is where I then found him. We proceeded to Parker's farm. The area had been taped off and secured by Sergeant McNeill and he was waiting for us. Also on the premises was Missus Parker, her daughter Victoria, her boyfriend Danny Jackson and his father Joggy Jackson. Mister Parker was found in a hayshed, hanging by a blue nylon rope from a steel girder. Doctor Kelly arrived and examined the body. He then sedated Missus Parker. Our initial search uncovered an empty packet of Sweet Afton cigarettes and three Sweet Afton cigarette butts. A loaded rifle was also found lying on the gravelled yard alongside an overturned pot of chicken feed. A trail of flattened grass was found leading from Parker's to Jackson's. Fingerprints on the cigarette box were found to belong to Joggy Jackson. A nylon rope of the same length and diameter was previously purchased by Mister Jackson and subsequently was found to be missing from Mister Jackson's car. The autopsy revealed that Parker's neck had been snapped prior to the hanging.

"Detective, what did you make of this information?"

"Our first thoughts were that it was a staged suicide. But after receiving further information on Mister Parkers nefarious activities in Northern Ireland, in which we believe he was involved in the death of several men, including Fred Winter, we now believe his hanging was a warning to all would-be traitors."

"I take it you have discounted Mister Jackson as a culprit?"

"Not completely, Sir. He may have been set up. It was clumsy and amateurish. We know he had words with Parker the week before his death, but by then Parker was paranoid about anyone crossing his land, even people he knew well."

"So why go to the trouble of setting Jackson up in the first place?"

"We don't know, Sir. Everything else was professionally done: the killing, the hanging, and leaving no evidence of himself at the scene. We did however find tyre tread impressions and some brown fibres, at the eastern end of Barterstown Lane.

The fibres we believe belong to a brown tweed jacket."

"Were the tyre threads and the fibre's found on the day of the search?"

"No sir, some time afterwards."

"It's doubtful if that evidence will stand up in court. Sergeant, why wasn't Barterstown Lane searched on the day of the murder?"

"Detective Sergeant Reilly thought he had all that he needed. As far as he was concerned, he had his man."

Murray ruefully shook his head. "Okay, let's go back to Jackson. If the staged hanging was a message to would-be traitors, then what message was he sending by trying to frame Jackson?"

"I believe the killer is local, Sir. The frame-up was not serious. It seems to me to have been done more in an effort to embarrass than to incriminate."

"Why?"

"I don't know, Sir."

"Then it's about time we found out. Ask Jackson in for some friendly questioning, and when I say friendly, I mean it in the good sense. Befriend him. He holds information that he probably does not know he has."

"And what about Harriet Butler, Sir. I believe she knows who the killer is. She must have seen him. Somehow he found out and tried to kill her. Jackson is involved there also. She won't alibi him and yet he's squiring her around town. We spoke to him about it and he told us that they had come to an arrangement. His exact words were; he was looking into a 'small matter' for her."

Murray leaned his head back and laughed uproariously.

Cosgrove shot a bemused glance at Cole.

"I knew it, I knew it, I knew it," said Murray. "The hairs in my nose never lie."

"Sir!" Cosgrove said. "Is there something we're missing?"

"Yes, the reason Butler won't alibi Jackson."

Macken's had their offices on Henry Street. Joggy approached the receptionist. She had the countenance of a spinster. Her greying hair was pulled sharply back and manoeuvred into a tight bun. She wore a charcoal grey woollen suit over a pristine white blouse with a light frill down the middle. It was buttoned to the neck.

"Excuse me, my name is Joggy Jackson, I've an appointment with Mister Macken."

She threw a discerning eye over his work clothes; navy bibbed overalls and black Donkey jacket.

He could see she was not impressed. "I'm on my way home from work," he said.

"Oh, that's quite alright. We get people in here all the time in their work clothes."

She checked her diary. "Ah yes. Take a seat Mister Jackson."

She rose from behind her desk and then tapped lightly on a drab mahogany door that was in need of repainting. She opened and entered. A few seconds later she was back. "Mister Macken will see you now."

The office was small and cluttered with files and law books.

"Have a seat, Mister Jackson." Macken was an elderly white-haired gentleman who had a penchant for dickey bows. The one he was wearing today matched his pin-striped navy blue suit. It had white polka dots. Joggy thought he looked a lot like Noel Purcell.

"Right, let's get down to business, Mister Jackson. As executor of the late Missus Nellie Roe's last will and testament, it is my happy duty to carry out her final instructions."

Alice couldn't settle. At the least sound she was up from her chair and to the door. Finally, Joggy turned up. He looked very despondent as he climbed the path.

"What's wrong?" she asked. "What had he to say? Was it bad news?"

Joggy stopped and looked at her. "You would think that after all the years of bringing up cakes and bread and whatever else she wanted; she would have left us something decent. After all she was my Godmother."

"Oh God, I'm nearly afraid to ask." Her face was now as dark and grave as her husbands. "What has she done?"

He pulled a large brown envelope from his back pocket. "She's only gone and left us everything, the whole kit and caboodle."

"What?" It took a few seconds for it to register. "What? You're fucking Joking," she squealed in excitement. Her hand shot up to cover her mouth. She looked quickly around but none of the children were there. When she looked again at her husband he had a huge smile plastered across his face.

"I'm not joking. May God strike me dead if I am. She's left it all to us. The house, the money, the land, everything."

"How much money?"

"Twelve hundred and forty-five pounds. There was a few bob more, but the solicitor had to take his fees."

"But what about her brother?"

"It seems they haven't spoken in years. She said in her will that she wanted to leave it to the ones she loved most."

"What are we going to do with it?"

"Nothing for the present. Let it settle for now and later we'll make some decisions."

But Joggy had already made one decision, and for the moment he was not even going to tell Alice.

That evening he drove up to Nellie Roe's cottage. He opened the rear door of the Morris Traveller and from among his assortment of gardening tools picked out the long-handled spade. He looked around to make sure nobody was watching, then quickly made his way around to the rear of the cottage and to the back stone wall where Tom Baker had said the two apple bushes once stood. Normally it would irk him to see an unkempt garden or shrubbery, but this evening he was thankful for Nellie's tall, wild overgrown hedges. They gave him the cover to dig for Cissy's remains. Two hours later he came home, flushed and exhausted.

"Where on earth have you been?" Alice enquired.

Joggy flopped onto the settee.

Then she noticed the soil on his boots. "Don't say you've been digging Nellie's garden already. Could you not wait 'till the weekend at least?"

"It's not what you think," he said, still breathing heavily. "Make us a cup of tea will ya and I'll tell you all. You cannot say one word to anybody about this," he warned her after explaining what he was up to. "Certain people around here, John Kelly for one, would be very upset if they knew I was digging for Cissy in Charlie Higgins back yard."

"I take it then you found nothing?"

"No. And I dug several big holes, all about two feet deep. I reckon, he being an old man at the time, that that was as deep as he could dig."

"Is that him crossed off your list?"

"Not yet. It doesn't mean she's not buried somewhere else in the garden!"

"You're not thinking of digging up the whole bloody garden, are you?"

"Not for the moment, anyway." He was quiet for a moment and then concluded. "You know the strange thing about it? I don't know whether to be relieved or disappointed."

A biting wind raked Cosgrove's face as soon as he turned the back corner of Doctor Kelly's.

Bent over, in the lee of a tall laurel hedge, Joggy spotted him as soon as he turned the corner. He continued clipping the hedge into shape

"Excuse me, Mister Jackson, could I have a word, please?" Cosgrove stopped a few yards away.

Joggy straightened up and flexed his back. "Did it feel strange?" He was cold and grumpy and spoiling for an argument.

"Did what feel strange?"

"The word, *please*. It's not one I should imagine you get too much practice in using; that and *sorry*."

Unlike Reilly, Cosgrove did not rise to the bait. "I'm not here to argue with you, Mister Jackson."

"So what are you here for?"

"I came to ask if you could drop into the station, this evening, if that's possible. We have a few things we would like to discuss with you."

"Which is code for what ... interrogation?"

"No, no, nothing like that. We just want to ask you some questions. We'll even provide you with a cup of tea."

Joggy was unconvinced.

Cosgrove could read it. "Look, we believe you may unwittingly have some information in your possession that may help unlock Parker's murder. All we want to do is probe your memory and see what we can come up with."

"Ok. I'll call in before I go home, but you'd better have a packet of ginger nuts with that tea."

As soon as he sat to the table in the interrogation room, a pot of strong tea and a plate with four ginger nuts on it arrived.

"Where's the rest?" Joggy enquired, almost childishly, of the young Garda, as he looked at the four measly biscuits.

"They're in the canteen. Do you want more?"

"Yes I want more, the rest of the packet please, I'm starving. These boys," he grinned and nodded across the table at Cole and Cosgrove, "are not known for short interviews."

The young Garda left and Joggy poured his first cup of tea.

"Let's talk about the nylon rope, Mister Jackson," said Cosgrove, "the one that went missing from the back of your car. When you were initially arrested, you said to officers in the squad car, that you sometimes left your car unlocked. Where exactly would you leave it unlocked?"

"When I was working. There's not a lot to steal. It's mostly run-of-the-mill garden tools."

Cole then pushed a A4 pad and a pen across the table. "Could you write down the names and addresses of your clients please?"

As Joggy scribbled down the names, the young Garda came back with the rest of the biscuits. Finished, Joggy, slipped the pad back to Cole. While the two men looked at the names, he popped a whole ginger nut into his mouth and tried to wash it down with a mouthful of tea.

"Impressive clients," said Cosgrove, raising a solitary eyebrow. "I see you have done some work for Peter Matthews. Why have you written former after his name?"

Joggy's first attempt at an answer was said through a full mouth; it was unintelligible. He held up a finger and took another mouthful of tea.

"We parted ways after Parker's murder," he said at last. "He didn't like the publicity. Said something about minding his reputation."

"Did you leave your car open when you worked there?"

"Yes. It was perfectly safe."

"Could you see your car at all times when you worked?"

"If you mean at Matthews, no." He lifted the tea cup, pressed it against his lips and then stopped. He smiled as the thought hit him. "Strangers stand out, but sons-in-law don't," he said. "It would have been so easy for him to take the rope, an empty fag packet and a few butts from the ashtray."

"We're not in the business of conjecture, Mister Jackson," said Cosgrove.

"Of course you're not," Joggy said dismissively. "When it's one of your own, I wouldn't expect it to be any other way." His voice was flat and cold. Cosgrove took exception to the remark and was about to argue the point when Cole, jumped in. "Why did you buy the rope in the first place?"

"For pulling up old or dead shrubs. I'd spent several hours the previous day digging one out. If I had had a length of rope with me, it would have taken a lot less effort."

"Did you ever see anyone else around Barterstown House?" Cosgrove enquired, his mind now focused back on the case.

"No."

"Well, your friend Harriett said she saw someone up there. Not the Saturday before Parker's death, but the previous Saturday."

For a moment Joggy stopped chewing, then slowly and thoughtfully resumed.

"Neglected to tell you that, did she?" Cosgrove could not resist "By the way, that, 'small matter' you're looking into for her, how's it going ? Any progress?"

"I'm getting there."

"Let's not beat around the bush here, Mister Jackson. We know about your deal with Butler. And it's a dangerous game she's playing. She can identify the killer and he knows that. Has she said anything to you to indicate who it might be?"

"No. And if I knew I would tell you, because like you, I also believe she's playing a dangerous game." He supped the last of his tea. Cosgrove rose up from his chair. "Thank you for coming in, Mister Jackson."

But Joggy did not hear him. He was looking at his feet and his mind was elsewhere.

"Mister Jackson," Cosgrove said a little louder.

Joggy placed the cup back on the table and then looked at Cosgrove.

"She said something peculiar to me once."

Cosgrove sat back down.

"I had asked her about the identity of the man she saw the day Parker was murdered, but she wouldn't tell me. But what she did say was that he had recently turned up in the most surprising place ever."

"Have you any idea what she meant by that?" Cosgrove asked.

"Not the foggiest. But she was a woman who did not leave the farm much, so if she saw him again, he virtually would have had to turn up on her doorstep."

Cosgrove saw Joggy to the door. "A word to the wise, Mister Jackson. Cissy Butler is missing almost thirty five years for a reason; the case is unsolvable. If they didn't find her then, there's no chance of her been found now. I know you got lucky once, but don't expect it to happen again. If I were you, I'd cut my losses."

He turned sharply and came back to his office, Cole was there, his face ashen.

"What's the matter with you?" he asked.

"I think I know who turned up at her doorstep!"

"Spit it out, man."

"During our enquires, we called to Butler's. She wouldn't let us get out of the car. Said we could ask questions from where we sat. I thought she was just being odd, but now I think it was because she was afraid. I think she recognised Detective Sergeant Reilly."

There was only a skeleton staff left on duty when Cosgrove, crossed the virtually empty open-plan room to Inspector Murray's office. He was shrugging himself into a light grey mac when Cosgrove tapped on the door.

"I take it you've gleaned a little extra information from Mister Jackson?"

"Yes Sir, and it seems to tighten the noose further around Detective Reilly's neck."

Murray sighed. He sat back onto the windowsill and listened.

Joggy drove straight out to Boyle's B&B. Harriett came down the stairs and found him pacing up and down the black-and-white tiled hall.

"Why didn't you tell me that you had seen someone else up at Barterstown House?" he asked as soon as her slippered feet set down on the hall floor.

Harriett crossed the floor and sat on the red upholstered stool beside the telephone. She studied him for a second. "Because you never asked," she said finally.

"I shouldn't have to ask. You should have told me. You told the guards."

"How is that going to help you find Cissy?"

"I don't know. What did he look like?"

"I couldn't tell you. He wore a navy anorak with a deep hood."

"What did he do up there? Did he go through the house?"

"I'm not sure where he went. If he was in the house, I didn't see him pass by any of the windows."

"Could he have been one of the Fitzgerald's?"

"How would I know? I didn't see his face. And even if I did, I don't know if I'd recognise any of them again."

"If it was one of them, why was he there do you think?"

"Paying his respects, I suppose!"

"His respects? What are you talking about?"

"To his parents. What do you think I'm talking about?"

"I've no idea. Aren't his parents buried in Kilpatrick graveyard?"

"No, they're not. They're buried in a private grave behind the house."

Joggy picked Danny up from the bus-stop in Oldbridge on Friday evening. On a couple of occasions, he tried to cajole

Danny into explaining what had happened between him and Victoria.

"Change the channel, dad," was all he received in reply. His tone was not curt or sharp; more like tired resignation and his jaw was now set resolutely against all further enquires. And even though it pained Joggy to hear that in his son's voice, he was left with no choice, but to stay out of it.

"I've a match this evening," Danny said, as they parked on the roadside in front of the house. "Any chance of the car?"

"I'll leave you up. I haven't been to a game in a while. Who are ye playing?"

"Mucklagh. It's the second round of the under twenty-ones."

A blustery wind blew diagonally across the field. Joggy stood with his back to it. Shortly after the match started, he was joined by Spit Sweeney. "Not a great evening for a hurling match," said Spit. He hocked up a ball of saliva and sent it sailing down wind onto the pitch.

"True, the wind will play havoc with the ball," replied Joggy. Spit did not attend many matches, which left Joggy suspicious of his presence at this one.

"Chase him down, Wilson," shouted an opposing supporter at one of his players. The man was stout with a ruddy face and a bulbous whiskey nose. He leaned forward as if he was about to chase him down himself. "For God's sake, don't let him get away."

"How's the legs?" Spit enquired, amusement in his voice. Joggy glanced at him sharply. "My, my, Mister Sweeney," he replied as he returned his attention to the match, "what big ears you've got."

"All the better to hear the gossip with, Mister Jackson."

"Who's been talking?"

"That's not important. I just hope Harry appreciates the pains you're going through for her."

"She doesn't know. And I'd prefer it kept that way."

"Won't hear it from me."

Just then, Danny, raced by with the sliother seemingly stuck to his hurley. He left Wilson, in his wake before firing the ball over the bar for a point. Joggy cheered and clapped.

"He didn't take it from the ground," said Spit, admiringly.

"Wilson," shouted the man with the whiskey nose, who was becoming more animated the longer the match went on. "You're not herding cattle now, you actually have to chase after them when they run past you."

"Do you know him?" Joggy nodded in the direction of whiskey-nose.

"I do. That's Wilson's father."

The referee blew his whistle for half-time and whiskey-nose made a bee-line for his son. Joggy felt sorry for the young lad.

"Listen," said Spit. He moved closer. "What Bob Coughlin did to you was a low blow. No pun intended. I have some information for you. Do with it what you will. Bob Coughlin nowadays drinks on Friday nights and Sunday nights in only one pub: Sally Smith's, and he never leaves unless he's had a skin-full. The bicycle is always parked behind the pub against the wall of the car park. And the car park is always in total darkness."

Joggy stared out across the pitch as he absorbed the full meaning of Spit's message. He rubbed the centre of his chest with his fingers. The wound was still tender. It still hurt when he took deep breaths. The ache in his legs had taken several painful days to pass. When he eventually turned to respond, Spit was gone.

Later, on the road, as they drove home from Kilpatrick, they met Victoria in her violet-blue Ford Capri, travelling in the opposite direction. Danny raised his hand and waved. She saw him but did not wave back. He turned in his seat and watched her pass.

"Have you spoken to her recently?" Joggy asked.

"No."

"Do you know where she's going?"

"No."

"That's about the sixth time I've seen her in the last few weeks, heading for Kilpatrick and always about this time."

Danny bit his lip and said nothing.

Danny had got no sleep. *Could she possibly be seeing someone else?* The question burnt a hole in his brain. By late Saturday morning he could take no more of it; he had to know. He rode his bicycle around to the back door of Parkers. He knocked. Mrs Parker opened the door. She was surprised to see him standing there.

"Yes Danny, what do you want?" she asked, recovering her composure.

"I want to see Victoria."

"She's not here."

"Is she on the farm?"

"No, she's gone to Oldbridge."

Danny straddled his bicycle and turned for home. He was about to cycle away when he turned to Mrs Parker. "Is Victoria seeing someone else?"

"Yes. I have not met him yet, but she says he's very nice and is of the same religious persuasion as ourselves. I'm sorry Danny, but it's for the best."

Saturday morning was the first chance Joggy had since he had spoken to Harry, to re-visit Barterstown House. This time he did not go in. Instead he followed a separate grass and weed infested stone path past the gable-end of the house, that nature was successfully reclaiming. He stopped on the brow of a gentle hill. Below him in the corner of what was once a well-kept lawn, was a rectangular railed off area. He approached the wrought iron railings through the high grass. When he looked into the rectangular plot he was surprised to find two faded yellow roses lying on one half of a double grave-- recently trimmed.

CHAPTER 13

It was a Tuesday. McNeill, had slipped unnoticed into the stone shed at the end of the garden at Heatherville House. Joggy, who was half-expecting him to turn up, was not surprised to see him sitting smoking his pipe when he came in for his lunch. He had that smug, cocky, self-assured expression that Joggy detested, and that all cops, or at least the ones *he* knew, seem to wear. But it also meant that McNeill had good news. He poured out the tea -- this time not making any excuses for the one cup – and unwrapped his home cooked ham and spring onion sandwiches.
"So, what have you got for me?"

"Took a bit of digging and some arm twisting..."

"Something that comes natural to you," interjected Joggy.

"But I found two of the three Fitzgerald brothers," he concluded, ignoring the remark.

"Where?"

"Actually not that far from here....just outside Kildare Town."

"Have you spoken to them?"

"No. I thought that was something you'd want to do."

"So, how do you know it's them?"

"Passports. Dates of birth and original home address had to be supplied. Thankfully they both applied for passports or I would have had a tougher time finding them."

"Which two brothers did you find?"

"The two oldest ones, Charlie and Peter."

"And what about the youngest one -- Leon?"

"Nothing. It's as if he fell of the face of the earth."

"Maybe his two older brothers know where he is."

"It's possible. But something's telling me this guy does not want to be found. I did an extensive search. Leon is not a common name. Tried every polling and driving licence register in the country and still found nothing."

"Maybe he just doesn't drive or vote."

McNeill looked doubtfully at him. He reached into his inside jacket pocket and produced a slip of folded paper and handed it across the table. "Those are the phone numbers."

Joggy opened it and quietly scrutinized the numbers and area codes. It was not as if the numbers alone imparted anything of significance to him. They were just numbers on paper. By themselves they were not important. But he knew they held the key to one of two mysteries: if not the disappearance of Cissy Butler then at least he might find out why Barterstown House was abandoned. But then the thought hit him, *what if they won't talk to him?* He decided not to contemplate that now, so he put it out of his mind, re-folded the paper and shoved it into the breast pocket of his bibbed overalls. "Anything on Charlie Higgins relatives?"

"No. That's where our luck runs out. I did however find out that he had one living relative; a niece. But she's in America -- New Jersey to be precise -- and has never set foot on these shores."

He half-looked at McNeill. "Right... well.... thanks for your efforts." He then looked away and took another mouthful of tea. The words were not difficult, he just found them hard to say.

"You will keep me informed, won't you?" McNeill rose from his chair, snuffed out his pipe and stuck in his tunic pocket.

"Yeah, yeah, I'll do that." He hoped McNeill believed him, for he was not sure he believed himself.

The single axle mobile home arrived on Thursday. It was white with light grey stripes; it's alloy sheeting sported a few small dents. With Joggy's help it was placed under an open shed that had four rusted metal stanchions holding up an equally rusted galvanised dome-shaped roof. The caravan was rolled up close to one end of a small rectangle block building with a flat roof. Harriet's husband, when he was alive, had constructed it as a secure place to put farm chemicals. He disliked having them in the house or in anyplace his daughter could accidentally get her hands on them. The electricity supply board were on hand within hours to connect her. Joggy collected Harry from the B&B, and she moved in that same evening.

Reilly was tagged straight after he crossed the border. A nondescript car slipped in behind him, keeping a discreet distance back. He drove straight to his Aunt's house. A few hours later he left and drove another fifteen miles to a large house in the country. The unmarked car drove slowly by just as two men closed the heavy wrought iron gates behind Reilly. They pulled into a lay-by several hundred yards further on and got on the radio to head office. "Sir," one of the men addressed their head officer, "he's just driven up to Jimmy Bolger's house."

"The U D A man?"

"Yes, Sir. Do you want us to stay."

"No, come on in. It'll do us no good if you're made."

Chief Inspector Ron Wilkes was seated halfway down a long table with his wife Sandra and surrounded by a large group of people. They were dining and celebrating the fiftieth birthday of one of their friends. It was Saturday night and the Royal Hotel restaurant was full of smiles and filled with laughter. Ron Wilkes and his wife had driven seventy four miles that day to get there. It was their first weekend away in quite some time. They were booked in for two nights.

The receptionist entered the restaurant and looked around, she then took a circuitous route to come up behind Wilkes. "Excuse me, Sir," she said as she tapped him lightly on the shoulder.

"Yes," said Wilkes, unsurprised.

"There's a gentleman at reception who wishes to have a word. He says you're expecting him."

Wilkes dipped his hand into his jacket pocket and pulled out his room key. "Give that to the gentleman and tell him I'll be with him in a few minutes." The receptionist nodded her head and left.

"Ronnie," his wife said in a low sharp voice, "you promised me there would be no work this weekend." "I'm sorry dear," he said and clasped her hand. He gently rubbed the back of it. "Something important has cropped up. I'll only be gone a little while, half hour at the most and then I'm all yours for the weekend. I promise." He then kissed her on the cheek and left the restaurant.

He looked up and down the hallway before tapping lightly on the room door. It was then opened. "So, what have you got on our friend, Detective Reilly," enquired Wilkes, as he closed the room door behind him.

CHAPTER 14

The Keadeen Hotel was easy to find. He had come through Kildare Town and followed the road past the Curragh racecourse and there it was on the left of the same road on the outskirts of Newbridge Town. It was a large, white, imposing building. Joggy found a parking space. In the rear-view mirror he closed the top button of his white shirt and adjusted his navy tie back into place. It was close to mid-day and a stiff north wind blew. He entered the foyer and looked slowly around as he ran his fingers quickly through his unruly hair in a vain attempt to rearrange what the wind had tossed. The place was all polished brass, shiny leather and dark wood. Large expensive hotels made him uneasy. He felt out of place. A smartly dressed couple passed through the foyer. She glanced at him. A cold eye and an instant appraisal that told her everything; he was not one of them.

Joggy spotted the sign for the lounge and moved smoothly and unhurriedly towards it. He did not look at reception. He did not want them to think he did not know where he was going. Inside the lounge door he stopped again and looked about. It was lightly populated. The smell of strong coffee hung in the air. An elderly couple were at one table; he was reading *the Irish Times* and she, sporting a large black pearl necklace, idly stroked the long stem of her glass of chardonnay with a bejewelled finger. She seemed far away in her thoughts, as she stared out the window. A young family were in one corner, the parents with tea and scones while the two children sat quietly with bottles of orange, sipping through straws.

Two middle-aged men were sitting by the window. They were occupying two of four brown leather tub chairs encircling an oval mahogany table. One stood up, blue chequered shirt and blue denim jeans, smiled, and beckoned him over. As he made his way towards them he wondered how they knew it was him. Then he noticed that their window overlooked the car park and remembered that on the phone he had told them the type of car he would be driving. It was no mistake, they were brothers. They looked alike. The image of their father; tall, with receding hairlines and long faces.

The man standing stuck his hand out. "Hello. You must be Joggy?" His words were slow and drawn out, almost a drawl. A pair of tan cowboy boots with silver buckles on the side, stuck out from beneath his blue jeans. His hand was callused and his face weather-beaten.

Joggy nodded.

"I'm Charlie," he said, "and this is my younger brother Peter."

He shook his hand. It was softer, but like his brother, the grip was firm. The face was tanned but less craggy. Joggy sat in the chair beside Peter. He was a man with a vastly different sense of dress from his brother: light blue open-necked shirt, navy pants, shiny black patent leather shoes and beige jacket.

"Will you have a drink?" Charlie enquired.
They each had a half-empty pint of Guinness in front of them. "Thanks, I'll have a pint so."

Charlie caught the attention of a waiter and ordered. He then turned his attention back to Joggy. His eyes full of curiosity and amusement. "Were you ever up here before?"

"No. Passed on the train once, all right."

"Your drive up was uneventful, I hope?" Peter asked. His words clipped, sharp and clear.

"I had a couple of frights on the road from Portarlington to Monasterevin."

"The two humpback bridges, right?" said Peter.

"You've experienced them as well, have you?"

"The first time I drove that road, I damn near killed myself and my girlfriend. I didn't know the road and I was going a little to fast. I flew into the air going over the first one. We bounced all over the place and into the bargain hit our heads of the roof. And then just as I had regained control of the car and had settled down a little, we flew over the second one only to find that there was a sharp bend on the other side. I slammed on the brakes, but still ended up in the ditch. Thankfully I was able to reverse out without any real damage to us or the car."

"And your girlfriend, did she ever speak to you again?"

"She did worse... she married me."

They all laughed and with it Joggy's initial apprehension fell away. He had expected to find two taciturn and suspicious individuals, but instead they seemed friendly and open.

"You said on the phone that you live close to our home place?" said Charlie.

"Yeah, quite close, just across the fields from ye in fact. We bought Tommy Farrell's place, just over twenty years ago."

"Ahh, right, I have you now so. It's a long time since we spoke to anyone from home. You forget that things change."

Joggy's pint arrived. He looked at it and thought about taking a mouthful, but the churning clouds had not fully settled to black. He decided to let it sit a little longer.

Charlie moved to the edge of his seat and leaned forward. "Your phone call the other evening, Joggy, I don't mind saying, has us intrigued. You said it was a sensitive matter."

"Yeah, it is." He glanced casually at both of them. Peter was now also leaning forward. "Do ye remember Cissy Butler?"

"Cissy! God," said Peter. "I haven't heard anyone speak of her in years. Poor girl just disappeared and has never been seen since. Has she been found?"

"No, unfortunately not."

"Is her mother still alive?" Charlie asked.

"She is, and in good health, considering everything that's happened to her." Joggy then explained.

"She's still in danger then?"

"I'm, afraid so. And she's too stubborn to stay in the B&B, where she'd be safe. She's moved into a mobile home on the farm. She'll be a sitting duck again."

"I don't envy your task. So what made her think that you could find Cissy?"

"I helped clear a friend of mine's name a few years ago. She thinks I can work the same miracle for her. And before ye ask, it's a long story and I'll tell ye about it some other time. Right now I just want to hear your memories of Cissy."

"Poor Cissy," said Peter. "She was a real tomboy you know? Loved horsing about with the lads." He smiled to himself.

"Can't say I ever saw her in anything other than jeans, a baggy jumper, boots or wellies," said Charlie.

"With that short haircut, you would have taken her for a boy," said Peter.

"Did she come up to play with ye often?"

"She used to, but then our father ran her out of the place. His excuse, not that he normally gave excuses for his actions, but on that occasion, he said that she was taking us away from our chores. I don't think he particularly liked her."

"I don't think it was just her," said Charlie. "He just didn't like to see us happy and having fun."

"But it was like water of a duck's back to Cissy," said Peter with a smile. "She'd sneak back and hang around with us, trying to keep out of sight. Eventually he caught her and manhandled her out the front gate. He pushed her and at the same time kicked her up the arse. She went home crying. 'Course she told her parents and they came up to him. But he just told them to fuck off and to keep her at home. He wasn't the sort of man you could reason with." Peter straightened and sat back.

Charlie stayed forward, his head down; he fingered the near-empty pint glass. A silence fell and Joggy's instincts told him not to speak. Slowly Charlie raised his head and for several seconds looked into his brother's pale blue eyes. They had unwittingly raised the lid on their own private Pandora's Box and part of their buried past had slipped out. "What do you think?"

"I'm alright with it, if you are."

"We've already started. Will we tell the rest?"

"That's fine by me."

"He always took his rage out on us...." Charlie was still looking at his brother.

"Beat us with that fucking blackthorn stick of his," said Peter. He now leaned forward again; a pained look in his eyes. It was as if he was reliving every wallop. "It was all knobbly. He didn't care where he hit you – across the head, shoulders, arms, back, legs -- 'till we fell down and curled up into a ball then he would really lay into you."

"Poor Leon – he always got it worse," said Charlie.

"Why was that?" Joggy enquired.

"I think it was because he looked so much like our mother, God rest her soul."

"Like your mother?"

"Yeah," said Peter. "He was the spitting image of mum." He looked at Joggy's puzzled face. "Maybe I should explain. We were young when we left and so delighted to get away from the place, that we never thought about why he was the way he was." He shrugged. "Violence just seemed to come natural to him. He never needed an excuse to lay into us, mother included. It was years later when we heard the reason why. We were at a family wedding in Doolin. A relation of our mothers was getting hitched. There we got talking to my mothers sister. It was she who told us of his past. It seems that he was madly in love with another woman, but they had a row and broke up for several weeks. Then one night he got drunk and met mother, who was also drunk. It seems they had sex that night. About a week later the love of his life came back to him and wanted to try again. He was delighted and they began to make plans for the future. About two months later mum informed him that she was carrying his child. Her father went to him and told him in no uncertain terms he would have to marry her and that he was not going to have the stigma of an unmarried daughter attached to his family. He tried everything to get out of it, even offered to pay for her to go to England and have an abortion. But they weren't having it. When the love of his life eventually found out about it, she promptly dumped him. From the day he married mum 'till the day she died... he battered her. And us when we came along. We all reminded him of everything he had lost. He was a selfish, violent bastard and when we left, we swore we would never have anything to do with him again. We didn't even go to his funeral."

"Actually we didn't even know he was dead 'till we read it in the obits," said Charlie.

"And what about Leon? What happened to him?"

"That's a good question." Charlie gave a rueful sigh. "The truth is, we don't know."

"He was there for just over two years after we left. God only knows what punishment he had to ship -- 'cos we left in the dead of night without saying a word. Leon knew about it and we offered to take him, but he was determined to finish his education."

"Did ye keep in contact?"

"We tried. But *he* kept intercepting our letters. We could not pass on our address to Leon. So we ended up losing contact."

"Did he actually get to leave?" Joggy enquired.

Peter and Charlie looked at one another.

"Well yeah, we presume so," said Peter.

"But ye don't know for sure?"

A heavy silence fell. Then Joggy spoke up. "Are ye collecting the rent for the land around Barterstown House?"

"No. His executor tracked us down, but we told him we wanted nothing to do with the place. Why?"

"Because somebody is."

"Must be Leon," said Charlie a smile lighting up his face. "Thank God. You had us really worried for a minute."

"But what if it's not Leon? What if Leon was never found? Who would the estate go to then?"

"Our father's sister, I presume." Peter's face suddenly grew dark. "What do you mean, if he was never found?"

"I mean if he never left the farm!" The two men looked at one another in dismay.

It was obvious to Joggy, the implication was not one they had ever given any thought to.

"You're not suggesting...." said Charlie, unable to complete the question.

Joggy saw what he wanted to see, so he asked, "Have either of ye been back to the home place recently?"

"No," they said in unison. "Why?"

"Because someone left two yellow roses on your parent's grave."

"Well, that could only have been Leon," said Charlie, suddenly brightening up again. "He would have known they were our mother's favourite flower."

"Why didn't you say this to us earlier, instead of putting us through the wringer?" There was a sharper edge to Peter's voice.

"Sorry....I needed to see your reactions. I needed to be sure about Leon; that ye did not know where he was."

The brothers withdrew back into their seats and observed Joggy with a steady gaze. They thought they had been dealing with a friend, but now they were not so sure. It was as if they were really seeing him for the first time. They regarded him with new interest.

Joggy caught the attention of the waiter and ordered three pints. "Can we talk about Cissy now?" He looked at one and then the other. Their eyes untrusting, their faces impassive. Neither spoke. "Look, I'm sorry men, but look at it from my perspective." He had a smile in his voice. "I don't know you and ye don't know me. I had to find out."

"Okay," said Charlie, eventually. Joggy silently sighed in relief. For a moment he thought he had blown his chance, that he had gone to far and that they were going to clam up. "I suppose you have a point. But it was a dirty thing to do."

Joggy stuck his hands up. "Mea culpa. Won't happen again."

"What do you want to know?" Peter enquired tentatively.

"What age was Cissy when your father kicked her out the gate?"

"About twelve I think. I remember she was starting to sprout boobs. You start noticing these things when you're a horny teenager," he said quickly, suddenly feeling as if he had to explain himself.

"Did ye ever see her wearing a dress?"

"Mass was the only time. Minutes after she was home, you'd see her out in the yard in old clothes."

"How did Leon get on with her?"

"Fine. She spent more time with him than with us. She was nearer to his age."

"I think there was more to it than that," said Peter. "I think she was sweet on him."

Joggy smiled at the idea. "What makes you say that?"

"Ahh, just the way she used to act around him. Whenever he'd pay her any attention, her face would light up and she'd act all giddy and playful."

"How much attention did he pay her?"

"Not much. In fact, he used to get very embarrassed whenever she'd fawn all over him. Actually, I can't be certain..... but I don't believe Leon was into girls."

"That's not fair Peter," said Charlie sharply. "He was only fifteen. You can't be certain of that."

"True. But you have to admit that he had very effeminate ways?"

"That still does not prove anything."

A silence fell.

"Did she ever sneak back after your father threw her out?" enquired Joggy. He did not want the few cross words to deflect them from what he wanted.

"No, can't say she did," said Peter.

"If she did I never saw her," said Charlie.

The three pints arrived and Joggy paid for them. "What about the day of your Mother's wake, was she over then?" He asked when the waiter was out of earshot.

"No. By then my father was not even on speaking terms with the Butlers. They didn't even come up to pay their respects."

"Which was a shame really," said Peter. "Because mum and Missus Butler were very good friends."

"Your mother, it was a brain haemorrhage that killed her, wasn't it?"

"That's what's on the death certificate," said Charlie. "But we know that bastard murdered her. The brain haemorrhage was as a result of all the beatings she took."

"I hope he's being roasted in hell on the end of a pitch fork," said Peter.

"Your father -- did he stay in the house all day, or was he in and out?"

"In and out. He'd always come in when people turned up."

"If Cissy *had* gone up to the house, what sort of reception do you think your father would have given her?"

"Not a good one, that's for sure. He was in a foul mood all day."

"You don't think....,"said Charlie, chewing his bottom lip.

"I'm not thinking one way or the other at the moment. But the fact remains, that Cissy got all dressed up to go to the shop." Joggy shook his head. "No one get s dressed up to go to Bakers shop. But if she was going to call up to see your family and pay her respects...." He left it hanging there and waited.

But the brothers stayed silent, their stomachs churning at the thought.

"The guards interviewed ye, right? What sort of questions did they ask?"

"Basically, had we seen Cissy? Which of course we hadn't. They were very respectful. They watched proceedings, but kept mostly in the background. They did however, discreetly search the house and the farm, even checked our mother's coffin and looked into the grave before she was buried. And for several weeks after, they kept an eye on the grave; inspecting it to make sure it wasn't disturbed."

"And your father, how did he take them being around?"

"He was livid. Not for disturbing the sanctity of the funeral, which he never tired of telling anyone who would listen, but because the spotlight had moved. The talk was no longer about poor him but about the disappearance of Cissy, and everyone felt sorry for her parents."

They ordered another round and chatted for another hour before parting company. Joggy gave them his number and ask them to get in touch if they thought of anything else. Charlie gave his business card. It was for a stud farm called *Linbrook*. It seemed the brothers were the joint owners. Charlie was the hands-on man and Peter was mostly in the office. The men stood up and shook hands. As they walked away, Joggy called after them. "One more thing before ye leave." He approached them. "If he turned up, would ye recognise him?"

"Yeah," said Charlie. "I know it's a long time since we last saw him, but I shouldn't think he has changed that much. A little grey like ourselves, but basically the same."

"You're at it again." Peter's eyes searched Joggy's face. "You know something and you're not telling us. You have an idea where he is, don't you?"

Joggy looked from one to the other. "No, I don't. Not yet." He tried to be sincere, but the twinkle in his eyes betrayed him.

Joggy was hungry. He eyed the bar menu. There was plenty to tempt him, but the prices they were charging were exorbitant.

He left and drove into town to the local Roma Cafe for cod and chips.

CHAPTER 15

Sunday night was so dark, you could barely make out your hand in front of your face. It was ideal cover. He entered a shed in front of the burnt out house and switched on a torch knowing he could not be seen from the caravan. There, he quietly rummaged around the broken and unbroken pieces of furniture Joggy had stored there, until he found what he wanted; a wardrobe door. He switched of the torch and waited. The light was still on in Harriet Butlers caravan.

    Harriet sipped her whiskey. She was not happy. Earlier she had heard what sounded like a footstep outside her door. She had listened—her heart thumping—but heard nothing further. "Curses on ya, Jackson," she had muttered to herself. "for making me hear things." She had argued with him until she was blue in the face; she was safe, she had told him; hadn't she sent him the letter. But Joggy didn't think it was enough. She eventually gave in. But tomorrow, she vowed, things would go back to normal. She placed the cup on the floor and switched off the caravan light.

    He saw it go out, but waited another fifteen minutes before making his move. Harriet by now, he knew, would be stupefied by the whiskey and already comatose. She would hear nothing until it was too late. Earlier he had scouted around the caravan and had found one window slightly ajar. To his relief it was still open. He carefully placed the wardrobe door under the latch of the caravan door and then jammed the other end into the ground. He wanted to make absolutely certain; there would be no escape this time. A settee sat directly under the open window. He struck a match and lit up a cigarette, then took a long satisfying drag as he watched the end glow like a hot coal, before dropping it through the open space onto the wool covering. The wool quickly disintegrated. Then the foam filling caught light and the caravan quickly began to fill with black toxic smoke. He opened the window as far as it would go to let more air in. The fire spread rapidly.

He would have liked to have stayed and watch the end result of his handiwork, but he had to be clear of the area before the Gardai arrived. He got to the lane and took one last look back-- happy--the caravan was now an inferno. No living soul could survive it. He smiled to himself at the thought that crossed his mind; *dead people don't make good witnesses.* Just as he reached his car he heard an explosion.

Joggy sat up in the bed with a start. "Did you hear that," he said to Alice.

"Yeah, what was it?"

"Nothing good," he said as he raced out of the room and opened the front door. He turned the corner of the house and instantly saw the fireball. "Shit," he exclaimed and ran back inside. By the time they got to Butlers, the fire brigade and the Gardai were already there, and Harriet's body was been loaded into the back of the ambulance. It's sirens blared loudly as they drove her away.

Among the smouldering remains was the axle; the only thing left of the caravan. Traces of the noxious fumes still lingered. John Kelly came over. "Joggy, Alice, that poor woman.... what a horrible way to go."

"Well she certainly went out with a bang," said Joggy, absentmindedly. His attention taken. He moved away and circled around to the front of what was left of the caravan. He was unsure of what he was looking at. It was outside the fire-line and badly charred.

Detective Sergeant Cosgrove crossed the yard to him. "Were you here earlier?"

"Yeah, I checked on her around seven. She was her usual pig-headed self."

The area was lit up by the lamps of the fire engine.

"That looks like a wardrobe door," said Joggy, "and I'm pretty sure it wasn't here earlier."

"It probably came from the caravan," said Cosgrove.

"Wrong colour.... that's from the house."

"Are you sure?"

"Certain. Check the shed in front of the house. I put four in there myself."

With Joggy in tow, Cosgrove, took a torch from his car, and then went to the shed. Cosgrove could only find three. "What do you think he used the door for?"

"Probably jammed it under the handle, to make sure she couldn't escape."

CHAPTER 16

Cosgrove was desperate to bring Reilly in for questioning, but Murray made him wait until Tuesday morning. He had been assured by Chief Inspector Wilkes that his report would be on his desk by then. Murray explained to Cosgrove, that he did not want to confront one of their own without the full facts. He wanted an airtight case, with no wriggle room.

The report duly arrived on time and all three men read it, in order of superiority. Murray arose from his chair and stood in front of the window that looked onto a wall, while Cosgrove and then Cole read. Like the view in front of him, he had come to a dead end. The procrastination was over, with a heavy heart, he now knew he had to take action.

"Sir," said Cosgrove, when Cole had finished reading.

Murray took several seconds more before he answered. He sighed heavily. "Bring him in," he said finally. He turned around and faced the two men. "This is no ordinary case. Everything has to be done by the book. Leave no i un-dotted and no t un-crossed. Your every move will be watched. I don't want Joe Public to think that we give one of our own an easy ride. I will have a search warrant within the hour for his home and car. Look in particular for any bank statements. There will be no questioning of Detective Reilly until that has been completed."

"Should we bring him in now, Sir?"

"Yes. But do it as discreetly as possible. The less commotion the rest of the station see the better."

It was 9.22 and Reilly was not due in until 9.30. It was the longest eight minutes of Cosgrove and Cole's lives.

Reilly arrived, as was his habit, exactly on time. Cosgrove hovered around Reilly's desk and waited until he came closer. "Why the long face, Mark. Stuck in the mud with your case, need an expert to help out?" Reilly joked.

"You hit the nail on the head, Owen. That's exactly what we need. Could you come with me to the interview room, so I can pick your brain?"

Reilly raised a neatly trimmed suspicious eyebrow. But the dark thoughts that were on Cosgrove and Coles minds never crossed his. "What about Murray?"

"We've got his blessing. It's fine."

"Oh, well in that case." Reilly said, feeling chuffed. "Lead the way."

Cole followed.

As Reilly dragged out a chair, Cole closed the door behind him and leaned back against it. The noise masked the key being turned. Cole slipped it into his pocket.

"Detective Sergeant Owen Reilly," said Costello in a grave voice, "I am arresting you on suspicion of the murders of Terry Parker and Harriet Butler."

Reilly just smiled with amusement at the two men. Costello then read him his Miranda rights.

"Good one lads, now, joke's over, what can I help you with?"

This is not a joke, Owen," said Costello. "I'm deadly serious. We have certain information in our possession, that leads us to believe that you were involved in both murders."

Knowing that Costello was not a joker, the smile quickly dropped of Reilly's face. "Ye can't be serious. What on God's green earth, could you possibly have that would lead ye to that ridiculous conclusion?"

"We can't discuss that with you at this moment. As we speak your house and car are been searched and based...."

"My house!" He jumped up from his chair. "You can't search my house without my permission."

"We don't need your permission, we have obtained a search warrant. I suggest you sit quietly and wait until...."

"I'll do no such thing...this is a travesty." Reilly strode towards the door, but the two men stepped in front of him.

"Sit down, Owen, you're going nowhere," Costello said firmly. "Calm down and hopefully we'll get to the bottom of this soon."

"This is ridiculous." Spittle flew from Reilly's mouth. "This is the height of bullshit." He stared angrily at Costello for several seconds, then turned away and sat down.

"I hope for your sake, it is," replied Costello.

The two men left the room. As Cole began to close the door he enquired, "Would you like me to bring in some tea and biscuits.

"Fuck off."

Reilly spent the next three hours alternating between pacing and sitting before the door was opened again. This time Costello and Cole were accompanied by Superintendent Murray.

 Reilly jumped up. "Sir, this is a huge mistake, I've nothing to do with the deaths of those two people."

"We'll see. Have a seat, Detective."

"We have concluded our search," said Costello, "and all of this can be cleared up in a few minutes. All we need from you is your whereabouts on the morning of April the twenty-first between the hours of eleven and one fifteen."

"I was at a rugby match."

"No you were not, try again. This time with the truth."

Reilly leaned forward, placed his elbows on the table and lowered his head into his hands. "I can't say."

"You can't say or you won't say?" said Costello.

"Both."

"Where were you between ten and eleven on the night of May the eight, the night Missus Butler's was attacked and her house burnt down?"

"Out walking."

"Did you meet anyone you knew on this walk?"

"No."

"Where were you, again between ten and eleven on the night of May the twenty second, the night of Missus Butlers death?"

"Out walking."

"Did you meet anyone you knew on that particular night?"

"No."

"Where did you go walking?"

"Along the canal."

"You're trying to tell me you walked around for over an hour and you did not meet one living soul who knew you?"

"It happens."

"How often do you go walking?"

"Once, twice a week, it varies."

"And how long would these walks take?"

"An hour, hour and a half, give or take."

"And have you ever met anyone on those walks who knew you?"

"Strangely enough, no."

"So, you have no alibi for Parkers murder, Butler's arson attack and Butlers death?"

"Looks like you'll just have take my word for it."

"You're not helping yourself here, Owen."

"I don't have to tell you anything, I'm innocent."

"Not according to the evidence. You're in it right up to your neck."

"There is no evidence."

Costello opened a thick buff file. "Can you explain how two fibres from a brown tweed jacket of yours, the one you wore the Sunday of Parkers death, came to be found on briers in Barterstown lane?"

"They could be from any jacket. I'm sure I'm not the only person who has one."

"You're the only one that has two pulled threads on the right sleeve."

Reilly went quiet.

"We also found a set of tyre threads in Barterstown lane, that match the tyres on your car."

"Again, I'm sure I'm not the only motorist with those tyre threads."

"No, you're right about that but you are the only one with a distinctive car, and we have three separate witnesses who saw it in the vicinity of Barterstown Lane on dates leading up to and including the day of Parkers murder. One of them remembered the first four digits of the number plate, and guess what? They are the same four digits of your registration."

Reilly did not reply.

"At Parkers, cigarette buts and an empty cigarette box were found, but no spent matches. You're in the habit of saving your spent matches by returning them to the box."

"You're not very observant, *Detective*," he said, emphasising the word. "All the smokers in the station save their spent matches. It's a habit that every other smoker in this station has? It's an old in-house rule," he said contemptuously. "There's not enough there to convict anyone, let alone a Detective Sergeant of good standing, because you do not have one eye witness that places me there."

Costello did not answer. He coldly scrutinized Reilly. He had treated him in the same manner as if he was questioning a hardened criminal, looking for the tell-tale signs of lying. So far he had displayed none of them. But then Reilly was an experienced Detective and knew what to do and what not to do. But Costello had an ace yet to play.

"How do you know Jimmy Bolger?" Cosgrove asked.

"He's one of a small group of people I play poker with. How do you know about that?"

"We had you followed. You recently lost one and a half thousand sterling to him. How did you repay him? And remember, we have your bank statements."

Reilly's cocky façade cracked. The corner of his mouth curled up into a nervous smile and his left leg twitched involuntarily on the chair. "I can't say."

Costello responded with a delight he dared not show. "Did you kill Parker for him? Was that how you repaid your debt?"

"**No.**" Reilly said it with such force that it took everyone aback. "Why would you think such a thing?"

"Because he's a leading member of the U D A. Parker had betrayed him and his buddies. You come along and lose one and a half thousand pounds sterling, then he says kill Parker and it's quits. And what happens? Parker dies and you will not furnish us with an alibi. Is it because you don't have one?"

Reilly was horror struck; all his nonchalance and bravado was gone. "I swear, Sir," he said addressing Inspector Murray, "I did not know he was U.D.A. To me he was just another poker player. We meet up once a month; that's all that's to it."

"So how did you repay him?" Costello asked again

"In cash."

"Where did you get the money?"

"I can't say."

A knock came on the door and Cole opened it. A slip of paper was passed to him. He in turn passed it to Inspector Murray. The Inspector hurriedly left the room and went straight to his office. He then rang reception. "Show them to my office."

"What the hell is going on here, Martin?" demanded Ex-Inspector Peter Mathews, as soon as he entered the office. His daughter was following demurely behind him. She was a short plain woman with wavy shoulder length brown hair and had a motherly figure that was cocooned in a heavy beige wool overcoat.

"Peter, Beatrice, please have a seat and I'll explain what has happened."

"This better be good," said Mathews, flopping down in the chair.

Murray described what had gone on in the interview room and Reilly's reluctance to provide an alibi.

"I see," said Mathews. "I'm sure he has a good reason but right now I can't think what that could be. When you've finished questioning him, I'll bring him home and have a heart to heart..."

"He's not going home tonight ," Murray said abruptly. "He's staying here until I get some damn answers."

Mathews turned to his daughter. "Beatrice, have you any idea what's going on?"

"No, he..I..I've no idea." Clearly she had some idea. Murray had noted how uncomfortable she had been since she entered the office. "Peter, could I have a word with Beatrice?"

"Sure." But Mathews stayed put. He had obviously not twigged what Murray meant.

"Alone, please."

"Oh, yes, of course; those sort of questions."

"Thank you, Peter. Someone will make you tea, if you ask nicely," he said with a smile. Murray came around the desk and sat in the chair just vacated beside Reilly's wife. "Beatrice," he said, his voice full of concern, "Owen is in a lot of trouble and seems very unwilling to get himself out of it. If you know something that may help him, now is the time to speak."

Beatrice was peering down at her hands. One lay on top of the other and she was on the verge of crying, but then sniffed and pulled herself back from the brink. "I don't know where he goes, Inspector. He doesn't talk to me anymore," she said without looking up. "It's been like that for about six months now. When he's leaving the house all he says is --I'm going out. At first he said he was going walking, but then I began to notice things and I pressed him for a proper explanation, but he'd just get angry and storm off to his office."

"You said you noticed things, what things were they?"

She stayed silent for what seemed like ages. Murray was beginning to think she was clamming up. Then she raised her head and looked him square on. "Owen...is a fastidious man, inspector. He takes great pride in his appearance. He has a shower everyday after he comes home from work and if he goes out, he has one when he comes back. The clothes he wears one day he will not wear the next. They are left in the clothes hamper for washing. He tries to be as careful as possible, but I could still smell the faint odour of perfume and it was not one of mine.

"Is that it? You think he's cheating on you?"

"I know he's cheating," she said with cold conviction. "He hasn't come near me in months."

"How can you be so certain? The perfume could have gotten on his clothes from someone brushing against him, in a pub or a crowded space."

Beatrice looked about her, making sure the office door was closed and that her father was not near it. She needed not to have worried, her father was having a deep conversation with two old workmates. She returned her attention to Murray. Her face was a little flushed. "You don't get dried semen stains on your Y-fronts in crowded spaces, Inspector."

"Well there are other ways for that to happen, wet dreams and....well you're a married woman....I'm sure you know what I mean."

"I wish it was that simple, Inspector. But the stains always coincide with his walks."

"Oh dear."

"And Inspector, I'd appreciate it if you did not tell my father this. He's very protective of me and I don't want to hurt him. I'm sure it's just a mid-life crises that Owens going through. He'll come back to me when he gets bored with her."

"That's very forgiving of you, Beatrice. You don't by chance know who this other woman is, do you?"

"I never said I was going to forgive him. I just know he won't break up the home. As for who she is, I haven't a clue. And I don't want to know. Knowing who she is would only drive me crazy. And in my case, Inspector, ignorance is certainly bliss."

"Thank you for your candour, Beatrice. As I said earlier, your husband will be detained overnight. If you call in the morning, we will appraise you of the situation."

"You can hold on to him for as long as you want, Inspector," she said, matter-of-factly. "If he's in here, he's not with her and that can only be a good thing."

Mathews did not seem pleased to be leaving the station without his son-in-law. "I'll be here at nine sharp tomorrow morning, Martin. So you'll have to make up your minds; either charge him or let him go."

Murray called Costello from the interview room. "Any progress?"

"No, Sir. He still won't say."

"I've just had a chat with his wife and she believes he's been having an affair. She found a foreign perfume on his clothes and dried semen stains on his y-fronts, even-though they had not been intimate of late."

"I see. I'll hit him with it and see if he breaks."

Murray went back to his office and stood in front of the window looking out at the wall. He was not a happy man. As far as he was concerned, in his moral code book adultery was one of the worst sins to be committed. To his way of thinking, a man who cheats on his wife, is a man no longer to be trusted.

Costello, once again looked hard at Reilly from across he table. "Are you cheating on your wife?" Costello said it in such a way as to make Reilly believe it was the worst crime he could commit.

"I would never do that to my wife. It's a ridiculous notion, I would never cheat on her."

"It would explain your reluctance to give an alibi."

"I told you, I'm not cheating on my wife."

"Was it she who gave you the money to pay your debt?"

"What part of what I just said, do you not understand, Costello?" he said getting angry.

"All of it. You're lying through your teeth."

"Prove it."

"According to your wife, you're a vain, neat freak, Reilly. A man who showers once, sometimes twice a day and changes his clothes, including his underwear at often as he showers."

"Beatrice was here?"

"And she knows about the other woman; the strange perfume on your clothes and the dried semen stains on your underpants, were dead giveaways."

Reilly's face fell, the bravado finally gone. They continued to question him for another hour but he stayed silent. He had nothing left to say.

"You will spend the night in the holding cells. That should give you enough time to think. Remember what's at stake; your career, your marriage and all that that entails," said Costello on leaving the room. Then with Cole in tow they went straight to Murray's office.

"Has he confessed?" Murray asked.

"Not yet, Sir. But I shook him to his core. He's gone to brood on his situation for the night. It's going to be a long one for him."

"Could his wife have been mistaken?"

"No Sir, he's having an affair all right. I put it to him bluntly and he never said no. And in his denials he never mentioned his wife once by name."

"Do you still consider he has something to do with Parkers death?"

"The evidence is stacked neatly against him."

"What do you think, Sergeant Cole?" Murray asked, more out of courtesy than for any other reason.

"The timing's off, Sir."

"Timing, Sergeant?"

"If Detective Reilly set out to kill Mister Parker that morning, he must have gotten very lucky. According to Victoria Parker, it was she who usually fed the chickens and it was only by a twist of fate that her father decided to feed them that morning instead. And, if as we have surmised Parker had been watched for a number of weeks, then the killer would have known that he did not feed the chickens. I feel that Parkers killer had time on his hands and could wait for his opportunity to arise, not the short window of opportunity that Reilly had."

"People do get lucky, Sergeant," said Murray. "And besides, if he wasn't feeding the chickens, he could have been doing something else. He was always out and about. Gentlemen, I believe we have our man. All the evidence points directly at him.... gift-wrapped like a Christmas present, all we have left to do now is to tie the bow."

Cosgrove flashed Murray a surprised glance.

"I suggest you go home and get some rest," said Murray. "Hopefully, Mister Reilly will be more talkative in the morning."

Cole left immediately.

Cosgrove went to his office. He sat into his chair, leaned back, interlocked his fingers behind his neck and stared at a spot on the ceiling. He hated presents; giving and receiving. Finally, after half hour he snapped out of it, grabbed Reilly's file from the top of the desk and left the building.

Helen stood between Robert's knees as he sat on the shop window ledge and kissed him passionately on the lips. His response was weak as if he had lost interest. "Is there a smell off my breath?" she enquired.

"No, your breath's fine."

"Then what is it?,"

Robert did not answer straight away. He was searching for a good way in which to tell Helen, but none came to him. "My Dad has been arrested for the Parker murder." He blurted. "They've been questioning him all day. Mum called to the school earlier, she wanted me to go home with her. But I didn't want to. What good would it have done, sitting around waiting."

"Oh God, that's terrible. He didn't do it, did he?"

"No, he didn't."

Helen hugged him close.

"I know where he was on the morning of Parkers murder."

"You do... how?"

"A friend of mine saw him that Sunday morning. It was nearly half-twelve. He got out of bed and pulled back the curtain. And there he was, across the road, sneaking out of Ted Corboy's house."

"Who's he?"

"He's the trainer of the Oldbridge rugby team. A big guy; not someone you'd want finding out, that you were shagging his wife."

"Does your mother know this?"

"No, and I'm not going to tell her. My friend only told me after I'd told him what had happened."

"But you'll have to tell the guards."

"No way. He can tell them himself. He deserves all the trouble he's in for the way he treats us, especially for cheating on mum."

Helen tried to talk him into doing the right thing, but he stayed stubbornly steadfast.

The bus came and they parted company.

The cool, unobtrusive atmosphere was what he needed. He was not there to pray. He loved these moments when he could just sit in the silence and allow his mind to drift. Thoughts always seemed clearer in empty church's, as Kilpatrick was this evening. He sat at the back in the shadows for quite some time, watching the multi-coloured rays of sunlight filtering through the stained glass. The light carried to the far wall and illuminated the stations of the cross and in particular the anguished face of Jesus as he heaved his onerous burden to Calvary.

He had a hazy idea of what might have happened to Cissy Butler. The problem he faced was that there were no real clues only tentative indications, and he needed more. By visiting Kilpatrick Church he had hoped for something, divine intervention, anything, but all that came to him was his own clear thoughts echoing back as if from across a snow covered valley. He had talked to everyone that mattered and gathered all the information he could. It was at times like this when he wished Nellie Roe was still alive. Her physic abilities would have come in handy.

"Joggy!"

He jumped and spun in the seat to face the quizzical voice. "Father Nolan, you startled me. I was away with the fairies."

"I'm sorry about that. My steps these days have become shorter and softer. People don't seem to hear me coming any more." He sighed. "I'm not sure whether that's a good thing or a bad thing."

"A bit of both, I'm sure."

"I'm sorry I disturbed you, Joggy. You go back to whatever you were contemplating before I startled you."

"Actually Father, you might be able to help me."

"Of course, if I can." Father Nolan sat into the pew. "What is it?"

"It's Cissy Butler."

"Ah...I'd heard you were involved."

"I think I'm on a fool's errand, Father. Because the answer to her disappearance, I'm beginning to believe, may lie with the dead."

"Yes, well that is a possibility. After-all it has been something over thirty years."

Joggy clasped his hands together as if to pray, leaned forward and rested his elbows on his thighs. He stayed like that for several seconds looking at the floor. Then he raised his head and his eyes were immediately drawn to the last painting on the far wall. "Do you believe that the dead communicate with us, Father?"

"How do you mean? Like a full-on conversation?"

"No. More like planting thoughts and images in our mind."

"Well, religious history is full of spiritual revelations. So, yes, communication....I suppose it's possible."

"The problem I have, Father, is... how do I know which are my thoughts and images and which ones are planted?"

"Has something occurred to you that is outside of what you would consider your normal thoughts?"

"You could say that, Father." He momentarily regarded the last painting again; *The resurrection of Jesus from the tomb.* He looked Father Nolan in the eye. "How do you go about exhuming a body, Father?"

Helen normally had a good appetite, eating most of what was placed before her. But this evening she played and picked at her food. It did not go un-noticed.

"What's wrong, Helen?" Alice enquired. "Not hungry?"

"She's got the love sick blues," Joggy teased.

She smiled grimly at him. "I'm going to my room. Does anybody want this dinner?"

Joggy did not have to be asked twice. He snatched a thick slice of home cooked ham. Nobody wanted any extra potatoes or cabbage.

After everything was cleared away, Alice knocked on Helens room-door and entered. Helen lay on her bed on her back, in the silence. Alice sat on the edge and caressed her hand.

"What's the matter, it not like you to give away a good dinner?"

Helen sat up. "I have a friend," she said tentatively, "His father's in trouble with the law. My friend can get him out of that trouble, but he won't. And I don't feel it's right what he's doing. What should I do?"

"Is it big trouble?"

"Yes."

"Then you should inform the police."

"I can't. I would be betraying him."

"Can you be more explicit with the details, like what sort of crime is he being accused of?"

"Murder."

"Parkers murder?" said Joggy, who had been reading the paper at the end of the kitchen table and had overheard the magic word 'murder' through the half open door. He now stood in the doorway.

"Dad, no one likes a peeping Tom," said Helen.

"I wasn't listening, I swear. But my ears did perk up when you mentioned murder. So does your friend's father have a name?"

"Detective Reilly."

"Really, Reilly!" Joggy's face lit up with a beaming smile. "That is good news. Reilly's in trouble at last."

"Yes, but my friend can clear him. He knows where his father was when the murder was committed."

"And why doesn't your Robert go to the cops with this information?"

"Because he found out that his father was cheating on his mother..... ah very smart Dad. How did you know?"

"Because you would not have turned down your mothers cooking for anyone less. So start at the top and don't leave anything out."

CHAPTER 17

Costello got no sleep. Coffee and adrenaline kept him up. Cole's and Murray's observations had set his mind on fire and had opened up a train of thought that was both disturbing and dangerous. If he got it wrong, he could say goodbye to his career. He woke Cole from a perfectly good sleep and the two then arrived at the Garda station before dawn. He needed two files. The first one was no problem, but the second one was a personal file and he had to do a bit of arm twisting to get it.

An hour later he made three phone calls. One was to Inspector Murray. Who was far from happy when told of the plan. Murray reluctantly decided to go along with it: His decision based on the strength of a phone call he had received the night before. To improve Cosgrove chances of success, he furnished him with an additional piece of information

At eight, Reilly, with dark circles around his eyes, was questioned again. This time he admitted he was having an affair and that on the morning of Parkers death, he was with her. But he refused to name her. He was also with her on the other two occasions, Butlers attack and Butlers death. The money to pay his gambling debt, he said, came from her. The affair, he said, had been over for a few weeks when he accidentally ran into her at the tennis club. He had just acquired the gambling debt and was deeply worried about it. She wheedled the worry out of him and then came up with a plan, she would pay the debt. Highly embarrassed, he admitted that he was to be at her beck and call for sex, wherever and whenever she needed it for one year. He said he had nowhere else to turn, so he accepted the deal.

At nine sharp, Peter Mathews and his daughter Beatrice arrived. From the open doorway of his semi-darkened office, Murray watched Matthews, a big man, lumber up the right hand side of the open-plan room, his back bowed like a coastline blackthorn bush, bent into permanent submission by the will of Atlantic gales. He turned left and headed for Murray. He stopped abruptly. It was as if he had hit an invisible wall. Beatrice had to raise her hand to stop herself bumping into him. He turned sharply back to her, his ruddy cheeks drained of colour. His legs felt as if someone had taken the bones out. "Take a look at Murray's office and tell me what you see," he asked, an air of panic in his voice.

Beatrice took a step to one side and looked, then stepped back into her original position. "I don't see anything other than Inspector Murray in the doorway."

Murray pulled the door closed and moved to meet them. Mathews turned to the sound. "You alright, Peter?" Murray asked, his concern evident.

"Yeah, yeah, I must have gotten a bit of a turn, I'm just not feeling myself." He glanced beyond Murray to the office, but could see nothing.

"Sergeant Cole," said Murray, "can you and Detective Costello take Mister Mathews to the interview room, where he can rest for a little while. " He patted Mathews on one shoulder. "In the meantime I'll see if I can rustle up some tea and biscuits."

"This way. Sir," said Cole and led Mathews away.

Costello glanced at the inspector. Murray nodded.

Mathews was supplied with a large pot of tea and a plate of marigold biscuits.

"Is Owen ready to go home?" Mathews enquired as he sipped the tea, his normal gruff manner slowly returning.

"We have a problem with your son-in-law, Sir, that maybe you could help us with?"

"Problem, what problem?"

"He's being uncooperative. Maybe you could shed some light on what his problem is."

"Well, if you think I can help, of course."

"Owen has admitted to having an affair," said Costello. "He says that he was with her at the time of the murders, but, he won't say who *she* is, and so we have no way of verifying his alibi. Mister Mathews, do you, by any chance, know who *she* is?"

"The bastard, I didn't even know he was having it off with someone else."

"Would you think he's acting out of chivalry or fear?"

"It's certainly not chivalry."

"It's fear then. Who do you think he's more afraid of... you or her husband?"

"Me of course. I don't hold with that nonsense. No one cheats on my daughter and gets away with it."

"Like me, you'd do anything to protect your child."

"Damn sure. Cheating bastards have to pay for their stupidity."

"Would that include framing them for murder?"

Mathews eyes darted from Costello to Cole and back again. "What?"

"A letter, Mister Mathews, from the deceased Missus Harriet Butler, has come into our possession. Her solicitor was instructed, in the case of her untimely death, to hand it over to us." Costello lifted a brown envelope from the file on the table. He opened it and pulled out a white sheet of notepaper. He turned the written page towards Mathews and then back to himself. "I've read it carefully and in it she gives detailed information of seeing you at the time of Mister Parkers death crossing the field from Parkers and entering Barterstown Lane. She also goes on to say how you attacked her in her home; hitting her not once but twice before setting fire to the place."

"Unsubstantiated. Without a live witness, it's not worth the paper it's written on."

Costello had half expected Mathews to make a move for the door or at least remonstrate about his detention, and was a little surprised when he remained calm and seated. It was almost as if he was enjoying it, challenging them to catch him out.

"Framing your son-in-law, was that how you hoped to get back at him for cheating on your daughter?"

"Why would I kill Parker? I didn't even know him."

"That is true. But you didn't need to know him, did you. It was enough that he had Unionist blood on his hands. I've seen your personal file, Mister Mathews. Before you came down here, you were stationed close to the border and was a member of the local Orange Order. According to our sources, the order frowns on murder. So I doubt it if it was one of them that asked you to kill Parker. Fred Winter, however, was a member of a very secretive group called the Royal Prefectory. I suspect you were also a member. Maybe that was part of the oath; to avenge the wrongful death of a fellow member?"

"Pure conjecture."

"You played on your son-in-laws vanity. You knew all about his affair. For him to admit that he was been paid to have sex would be akin to him admitting that his wife was beating him up. It was never going to happen. You went to great rounds to plant evidence....a trail of crumbs for us to find. The problem was; it was too neat. You tried to gift-wrap him for us. Who helped you; Beatrice?"

Mathews jumped up. "Shut your mouth, Detective. My daughter has nothing to do with this nonsense."

"Sit down Mister Mathews, we're not finished," Costello said sternly.

Mathews took a few seconds to compose himself again and then sat down. "As I said before, my daughter has nothing to do with this."

"Ah, but I believe she has. She tipped you off when her husband left the house and you followed him. You then knew how long he spent with her. And so you tailored your cloth to match. An organised man like you could get a lot done in an hour."

A knock came on the door. Cole answered it and a Garda whispered in his ear. Cole in turn whispered in Costello's ear. "You own a premises on Davitt Street, Mister Mathews, is that correct?" Cosgrove enquired.

"Yes, but it's vacant at present."

"In a shed behind it my men have found an Alfa Romeo car similar in make and colour to your son-in-laws and with tyre threads identical to the ones found on Barterstown lane ..... it belongs to you?"

"Yes, so I own a car similar to my son-in-laws. Pride, vanity, call it what you will. I liked his car and I didn't want him to know it. The tyres are like hundreds out there, there's nothing unique or special about them."

"You're right about the tyres and even the car, Sir. But it does have one unique feature and that is its registration; its identical to your son-in-laws. I'd like your explanation for that, Sir?"

"This tea is flowing through me, Detective," he said avoiding the question. "I need to use the toilet." He arose from his chair.

"Let me check to see if the toilet is free, Sir" said Cole. He left the room and within thirty seconds was back.

Mathews lumbered out of the room and turned to his right. The toilet door was thirty feet away at the end of a semi-dark hall. He had only gone a couple of yards when he stopped suddenly. As before, his legs had turned to soft rubber. "Go away," he whispered loudly, and flicked his hand at her, as if swatting a fly with the back of his hand, "you're dead." Realising he may have been overheard he glanced back over his shoulder but nobody came out of the room and no one else was in the hallway. He turned back to face her. He closed his eyes for a few seconds and hoped that when he opened them again, she would be gone. But the apparition remained.... in charred tattered clothing and with hate filled eyes that bored into him from a sunken smoke smeared face. Her right arm slowly rose from her side and a blackened crooked finger pointed at him.

Matthews suddenly felt cold as fear took hold. "Go away, you don't exist," he said un-nerved, his voice almost falsetto.

"Sir," said Costello, from the doorway "are you alright?"

Mathews turned, his eyes wild with fear. "You see her don't you?"

"See who, Sir?"

"Harriet Butler, you must see her. She's standing at the end of the hall."

Costello looked. "I'm sorry, Sir, there's nobody there. Sergeant Cole," Costello called back into the interview room. Cole stood beside Costello. "Do you see anyone at the end of the hallway?"

"No, Sir."

The strength in Matthews legs was almost gone. He leaned a hand against the wall and looked back down the hall again. The pointed finger was now beckoning him to her. He was frozen to the spot. She moved towards him.

"You're dead, go away," he commanded.

"Sir," said Costello, "who are you talking to?"

"Harriet Butler, can't you see her, she's right there." He pointed towards the end of the hall. "But why is she here?" He mumbled aloud, mystified. He pushed himself flat against the wall. "Go away," he shouted, almost hysterical. "You're dead. You burned up, I saw you burn up."

She slapped him hard across the face.

Matthews felt his stinging cheek. "You're not dead...how...?" The slap had shocked him back to reality.

"Thanks to Joggy Jackson, I'm not," said Harriet.

"Peter Matthews," said Costello, "you are under arrest for the murder of Terry Parker and two counts of attempted murder of Harriet Butler." He then handcuffed him and when Matthews turned back to the interview room, Murray was standing in the hallway.

"That was a dirty trick," said Matthews, before disappearing into the room.

Murray put his arm across Harriet's shoulder. "You did great, Harriet. Now let's get you cleaned up."

As this was happening, across the other side of town while erecting chicken wire along a stretch of freshly painted wood fencing in Mrs Mercier's back garden; Joggy had a visitor.

"Rabbit proofing I take it your at?" inquired McNeill as he picked his steps between newly dug drills.

"Little bastards will leave me with nothing if I don't." Joggy had half-expected a visit from McNeill, but just not this early in the day.

The Mercier's were not at home; Wednesday, weather permitting, was a golf day and McNeill knew that. He inhaled deeply. "Ahh, I love the smell of creosote."

"It fairly takes your breath away, all right."

"How did you get on with the Fitzgerald brothers?" McNeill enquired. The small talk was over.

"Fine." He then brought him up to date. Originally he had not intended to tell McNeill as much, but circumstances had changed. He once again needed his help, or more precisely the help of the organisation he symbolized.

"So what's next?" McNeill inquired as he lifted his brier pipe from the side pocket of his tunic. He then took a small leather pouch containing loose tobacco from the other pocket and began to fill the pipe.

The eagerness in McNeill's voice momentarily threw Joggy, knowing as he did that there was not a lot of kudos to be gained in an almost certainly doomed search for Cissy Butler. Unless....and then it hit him. He had obviously heard that Reilly was in trouble and a position was likely to come available. So now there was great kudos to be gained and if by some freak of good fortune Cissy, could be found ....and if in doing so....

McNeill could attach some of the credit to himself, then ....promotion and reinstatement was a distinct possibility.

"I think we need to eliminate the family grave," said Joggy.

McNeill coughed after inhaling the unexpected. "What?"

"The family grave has to be dug up. I've already gotten permission from the Fitzgerald's."

"Did you not read the report? At the time the grave was inspected, before, during and after the burial. It was never disturbed. She's not in the grave."

"She has to be."

"What do you mean, she has to be? If I'm to go along with this hair-brained notion, I'll need more cogent thinking than that."

"Ok, so it's cogent thinking you want? What would you say if I told you I found two yellow roses on Fitzgerald's recently tidied grave."

"Ah... that's better. Why didn't you say that before?" said McNeill, almost laughing. "Two yellow roses on a grave where two people are buried. That's an enormous clue."

"I haven't lost the plot, McNeill," Joggy retorted flatly. "Only one side of the grave was tidied up; her side, and the two yellow roses, which, by the way, were her favourite flower, were lying on her side."

"All that means is that Leon, if it was Leon, had only enough time to clean up one side; nothing else."

"I know it's not strong evidence, but I believe, after hearing the family story, that it's an indication."

"How do you know that the two roses are not for her alone?"

"No one buys two roses. It's either one rose or a bunch of them."

"I can't go to Murray with this. I'd be laughed out of the office."

"Murray doesn't have to know. Keep it low key and local. The family and Father Nolan are going along with it, all I need is for you to give it the official seal of approval. If nothing is found, then, there's no harm done. Missus Fitzgerald will be blessed and reburied and no crime will have been committed."

"Jackson, sometimes you can be very naïve. This has to go before a District Justice and a solicitor has to argue our case...which is a damn flimsy one, let me tell you. I cannot see how I can get this past Murray."

McNeill walked away, puffing on his pipe, the sweet odour of the tobacco mixing with the pungent smell of the creosote. He so badly wanted to impress Murray and finding Cissy, would certainly do that. A few minutes later he returned. "I'll take a chance with Murray. Maybe I can dress it up a little."

"Do you want me to go with you?"

"No. I'll run it by him myself, but as I said before, I think we're pissing against the wind here."

It took the best part of two hours for Matthews to give his statement and for Cosgrove to go over it minutely, tease out the finer details and to make sure nothing was left out. He just could not afford to slip up or make a mistake. It had to be water tight. Matthews signed it without reading it. "Now," he said, "will you tell me, how did Butler survive the fire?" He wanted to know earlier, but Cosgrove would not tell him until the paperwork had been completed.

"She wasn't in the caravan."

"But I saw the lights go out."

"They were turned off from inside the concrete shed beside the caravan. She was bedded down in there. A switch had been rigged up beside the bed."

"And that was Jackson's idea?"

"He was the only one she would listen to. If it had been left up to Missus Butler, you would have gotten your wish." Cosgrove gathered Matthews statement and placed them in the file. He then stood up.

"One last thing Detective, how did she know who I was? I had never met her before."

"The annual Garda dinner dance. Your picture was in the local paper afterwards. Sergeant Cole could you take Mister Matthews to his cell and make sure he gets everything he needs."

Inspector Murray offered to leave Harriet Butler to the B&B, but she refused. She wanted Joggy. A phone call was placed and Joggy called to the station at lunch time. Inspector Murray was waiting at reception with Harriet when he arrived. "Just to let you know, Mister Jackson," said Murray "a statement to the press has been released and any lingering doubts about your involvement in this unfortunate event have now been well and truly dispelled."

"Thank you," said Joggy.

Murray grabbed Joggy's hand and squeezed it tightly. "No, it's we that should be thanking you for keeping this lady safe. Without her help, we might have had a harder time persuading a jury of Matthews guilt." He then let go.

"It can't have been easy for you, Inspector, I know he was a friend."

"Yes, well," Murray said wistfully as he turned away, "such is life."

CHAPTER 18

They drove in silence towards the B&B. Harriet sat brooding on the passenger seat. Small grumbling noises like distant thunder, came from the base of her throat. Joggy had asked how she was as they made their way to the car but she had only grunted an answer at him. He tried to think if he had said anything to upset her but nothing came to mind. He was about to ask if there was a problem, when she spoke. "I suppose that's it for you?" The words seemed to growl from somewhere deep. "Now that they've caught Matthews, and your name has been cleared, Cissy will now be the least of your thoughts."

"I promised you an honest effort, Harriet, and an honest effort is what you will get."

"I've heard that before."

"Not from me you haven't." He explained about the flowers on the Fitzgerald grave.

"I'm gotten together nearly everything I need for an exhumation order. I have a signed affidavit from Charlie and Peter Fitzgerald stating that they had no objection to the grave been opened, Father Nolan said he'd do the blessing and Sergeant McNeill is looking for permission from Inspector Murray to bring it before a District Justice. There's not a lot more I can do, Harriet, until I get the go-ahead."

She made no further comment. The thunder stopped rolling.

After a long lunch, taken on Murray's instructions, Costello and Cole returned to the station. The Inspector called them to his office.

"I've read the statement," said Murray, "comprehensive and detailed. A couple of questions. Are you sure he did this alone?"

"Yes sir," relied Cosgrove.

"Do you think he may have been given encouragement?"

"It's possible. If there is a third party, he's not saying."

"Sergeant Cole, what are your thoughts?"

"He's an Orange Order member, Sir. And from what I have read about that organisation, they're predominantly non-violent. The other organisation that he denies being a member off is called The Preceptory. They're a sort of Knights Templar group; very secretive. Winter was supposed to have been a member also. We don't know anything about them, so they could have asked him. Personally, Sir, I believe he did it on his own and for just the reasons he gave us. Revenge for his fellow Order members and to get back at Reilly for cheating on his only daughter."

"Old allegiances die hard. Perhaps the real reason will come out at trial. Thank you men," said Murray. "And again, good work."

Later that afternoon after earlier receiving a message from Matthews, Murray reluctantly, dropped down to the cells. For several hours he had put it off. He felt betrayed and wanted to distance himself from the man he once regarded as one of his closest friends. However, Matthews still held answers to questions that Murray, for his own peace of mind, needed resolving.

He opened the door and stepped into the cell.

"You took your sweet time," said Mathews.

"Count yourself lucky I'm here at all. Now what do you want?"

"To go home."

"Not in this lifetime."

"You misunderstand. I need some toiletries... a change of underwear... stuff like that."

"I'll have Grace bring them to you."

"I've put my family through enough, I don't want them visiting me as well. Look I'm not asking you to let me out alone, send as many guards as you want with me. At my age, I'm hardly going to make a run for it. Please, for old times sake."

A tense silence ensued as Murray thought about it. "I'll consider it," he said finally, "but only after you have answered truthfully a couple of questions."

"If I can."

"There's no ifs, buts or ands about it, you either will or you won't."

Matthews sighed. "It's not as if it makes any difference at this stage, I suppose. So yes, fire ahead."

"I read the case file of the Canavan murder. It was a short read. Why was that?"

"Because I knew who the murderer was from very early on in the case."

"But Luke Baker wasn't the murderer."

Matthews turned away, his shoulders more hunched over than normal, and stared down at a copy of the King James Bible lying on the bed. For a short while he stayed like that.

Murray heard a slight muttering, and figured he was saying a prayer.

Matthews turned back. "I know.... I knew from almost the very beginning that it was Fred Winter."

"What?" "The answer shocked Murray to his core.

"Then why did you fit up Baker?"

"It's complicated."

"Well un-complicate it."

"It's got to do with allegiances and loyalties."

"Loyalties to whom?...the Orange Order? The Black Preceptory?"

"That's not important. What was important was the request. I took an oath and part of that oath was not to deny a fellow member his request. We are allowed one serious request. Fred Winter asked one of me. He confessed that he had murdered John Canavan. I had no choice. I had to protect him from the murder charge."

"And what of your oath to serve and protect the innocent and punish the guilty. Did that mean nothing to you?"

"Of course it did, but, some oaths supersede others."

Murray gave a snort of derision before asking his final question. "Did someone request *you* to murder Terry Parker?"

"No. No one can request you to commit murder."

"But you had no problem in stitching up an innocent man for murder, had you?"

"I was honour bound...I had no choice."

"Oh you had a choice all right and you picked a murderer over an innocent man."

"I can assure you that his conviction and ultimately his death weights heavily on my conscience."

"And it should...it should weight very heavy."

Murray walked out and closed the cell door without giving an answer. Thirty minutes later three burly guards collected Matthews from the cell, handcuffed him and drove him to his home. Beatrice and Grace, with tears running down their faces, met him at the door and threw their arms around him.

"Could you take the cuffs off so I can hold my family, please?" he asked the lead guard.

"Sorry, Sir. I've orders not to take them off."

"Please," he pleaded.

"Sorry, Sir, I'd be fired if I did."

Mathews turned his attention back to his family. He looked from one to the other. "Beatrice, Grace," he said in a voice that was almost a whisper, "I love ye with all my heart. But I cannot burden ye with a trial and prison and expect ye to spend your days coming to see me. So it ends here. This is our goodbye." He kissed and hugged them both and then made his way upstairs with his three chaperones.

"Do you want me to help?" Grace called after him. "No, this is something I have to do on my own. But thank you anyway."

They entered the main bedroom. Two of the men checked the room while the third stood at the door. Satisfied they were alone, they all stood around the door.

Mathews pulled a small carry-all bag from the bottom of the wardrobe. Inside it was a small black leather toiletry bag. He opened drawers and gathered up bundles of socks, underwear and vests and tossed them into the bag. He then spent a few minutes organising it all. He picked up the toiletry bag and carried it to the bedroom door. "Excuse me gentlemen," he smiled. "The bathroom is across the hall."

One of the men accompanied him in. "Can you excuse me, please, I've some personal business to attend to first."

After checking the room, the guard stepped outside and closed the door.

Downstairs in the hallway, his wife and daughter waited patiently. However, Grace was uneasy. She knew her husband very well. He was a man who said what he meant and meant what he said. And his words troubled her deeply. *What exactly did he mean by them?* Then the realisation hit her. "Stop him," she screamed at the three guards, and began to run up the stairs. But it was too late. The house reverberated to the sound of a gunshot.

McNeill nervously approached Inspector Murray's office door and knocked.

Murray peered over his glasses and beckoned McNeill to enter. "What can I do for you Sergeant?"

"You know I've been looking into the Cissy Baker case, Sir?"

"You mean we, Sergeant. You do have a partner, Mister Jackson!"

"Yes, Sir."

"Nothing has happened to him, I hope?"

"Oh no, Sir."

"Good. So what is the problem?"

"Well, Jackson has this theory, Sir, and has insisted I put it to you for consideration."

"Go on."

McNeill laid out Joggy's theory, and then waited for Murray to throw him out of the office. But to McNeill's surprise it did not happen. Murray, instead leaned back in his chair and gave it serious consideration. Finally, after several long silent minutes Murray roused himself. "Okay, this is what we're going to do. Missus Butler has been through a tremendous ordeal of late. I know she is not everyone's cup of tea, but she is a mother who has lost her only daughter. She has been a terrific help to us and I believe the onus is now on us to help her. If there is even a slender chance that her daughter is in that grave, then we owe it to her to put it in front of a District Justice."

McNeill left the station stunned at the turn of events. He later rang Joggy with the news. In turn, Joggy rang Father Nolan, who had asked to be kept in the loop. The matter would come before the Court in two weeks time.

Two weeks later, on a murky Wednesday evening, on his way home from work,

Joggy called into Kilpatrick Garda station. He closed the door behind him.

McNeill opened the hatch. He did not have to speak; Joggy could read the bad news in his face.

"What happened?" Joggy asked.

"Leon Fitzgerald had his solicitor there."

Stunned silence.

"I know. We were as stunned as you are now. If there hadn't been a dissenting voice, I'm pretty sure we would have had a good shot at getting that exhumation order."

"Was Leon there?"

"No. His solicitor was acting on his behalf. He basically laughed at the evidence we had and the Judge agreed. So what now?"

"It's over, isn't it? There's nowhere else to go."

CHAPTER 19

Gutted, Joggy sat on the top step and stared out at the countryside and into the distance, his mind absent of all thought. Alice ran a soothing hand across his shoulders as she made her way to the kitchen to serve up the dinner.

Joggy could not eat his dinner; his stomach was in a knot at the thought of breaking the news to Harriet Butler. An hour later, he drove back into Oldbridge and out to the B&B to where she was staying. She met him in the front hall.

"You've a face on you like a constipated hound dog," said Harriet. "If it's more bad news, spit it out."

"I'm afraid it is Harriet. The Justice turned down the exhumation order. Leon Fitzgerald has resurfaced and put a stop to it."

"Why would he do that?"

"I suppose he wasn't happy with us disturbing his mother's remains."

"Are you sure it's her remains he's afraid we'd disturb?"

"It's possible he has other reasons, but we'd only be speculating."

"So what are you going to do now?"

"There's not a lot I can do." He shrugged his shoulders. "The grave was my only clue and without the exhumation order...."

"So that's it, you're going to give up?"

"Well...I wouldn't say I'm giving up...but...there's nowhere else I can think of to look."

She stared hard at him in disbelief. Her last cherished hope of being reunited with Cissy, had just evaporated and the pain of bitter disappointment seared her heart like a white hot poker..

Anger took over and she directed it at the man in front of her. "Joggy Jackson," she said,. "I really thought you were different; made of sterner stuff, not the kind to give in at the first setback. But it seems I was wrong. I placated you, gave you what you wanted... and now you've thrown it all back in my face." She rubbed her left arm and grimaced. "Get out," she barked, "you're as worthless as the rest of them."

He knew there was nothing to say. He had run out of ideas. There were no words left that would appease her.

She banged the door behind him.

When he got home, Alice was waiting with her coat on and her handbag by her side.

"The hospital just rang, Harriet's been taken ill," she said.

"Did they say what was wrong with her?"

"A heart attack."

"Oh God! How come they ring us?"

"It seems she had the number written into a notebook in case anything happened to her."

Joggy explained to Alice, as they drove to the hospital, what had earlier transpired.

"The disappointment must have brought on the heart attack," he said, as guilt tied his intestines into animal balloons.

"Poor old dear. She had such faith in you finding her Cissy. Was there nothing you could have done?"

"Like what?" The words came out sharper that he would have liked.

"I'm not accusing you of anything. I know you made an honest effort."

Honest effort. Had he made an honest effort? Had he done everything in his power to find Cissy, or had he just taken the easy way out? Clearing his name had been the initial driving force. He posed another question for himself. *"What if my name was still not cleared, would I have given up so easily?"*

They parked the car and then made their way to reception and from there to the ward. "How is Missus Harriet Butler?" Alice enquired of the matron on the ward.

"Are you family?" she enquired.

"She has no family. We're her closest friends."

"She's had a coronary seizure. She's asleep at the moment. Unfortunately, her vital signs are weak. Prepare yourselves for the worst. People in that age group, if they have nothing left to live for, just give up."

"Can we see her?" Joggy asked.

"Certainly. But please, do not try and wake her. She needs her rest."

She was surrounded by tubes and wires and the high red colour she had, was gone from her face. Her breathing was slow and shallow. She looked fragile...far from the battleaxe they once knew.

Alice held her hand; it felt rough and calloused. She gently stroked the back of it.

Joggy stood for several minutes looking down on this small and shrivelled woman and the knot of guilt tightened. He then moved forward, bent over and whispered in her ear. "You listen to me Harry Butler. I know you for the stubborn mule you are. I know you're only pretending to be asleep. You were right, I did give up too quickly and I'm sorry about that. But if you give me another chance I promise you, I will do everything in my power to find Cissy. And this time, I won't let you down."

"Can you find Cissy? Alice asked in surprise as they walked to the car. "I thought you said that you didn't know where to look."

"I don't. I had to say something. I had to give her hope. It's all she's got left."

"But all you've given her is false hope."

"It's better than no hope at all. Besides, it buys me time."

"That's if she heard you."

"Oh she heard me all-right. I wouldn't put it past that old biddy to pretend to be asleep."

"So what's next?"

"I'm going to go back to Barterstown House and let it talk to me."

The following evening, Joggy made his way across the fields to Barterstown House. As he walked up the rutted driveway he extracted the faded photo from an inside Pocket. He looked at the yellowed image of Fitzgerald, standing beside his car in front of the house. It was from another era. The house in all its splendour with its wide gravel yard and ivy covered front walls with the sun glistening off its waxy leaves, looked back at him.

He imagined how it must have been with the constant trickle of cars and people making their way up the drive and into the front yard to pay their respects to his wife. The men shaking hands and the ladies imparting hugs and kisses. He moved around to the back, ducked under the scraggly privy arch and then stood and faced away from the house. He could see nothing. The hedges were now too high and overgrown. Nothing else had changed, not even the raucous cries of the rooks overhead. A bizarre thought occurred to him as he craned his neck and gawped up at them perched in the high branches. *Their ancestors probably saw what happened to Cissy!*

Beyond the hedges the sheds still stood in formation, in front and in an unbroken line to his right. Beyond them, about two hundred yards away was Harriet Butlers farm. Charlie Fitzgerald had said he remembered Leon, sometime in the late afternoon, leaving the house by the back door and going for a walk down the backyard. Why he remembered that detail was because afterwards his father had gone to look for him and on failing to find him, came back in calling him all sorts of names. Later, when Leon returned with mud on his shoes, he explained that he had gone for a walk on Barterstown lane and had not heard his father calling for him. His father told him he would deal with him later. He dealt with him on the night after his mothers burial: it turned out to be a vicious beating.

Joggy set off down the back yard. The line of sheds eventually gave way to an open field, that had a tractor path scoured into it and led onto Barterstown lane. It was deeply rutted and from the many hardened ridges, Joggy, surmised that it would have been quite muddy when in use and that was how Leon probably got the mud on his shoes.

Through the sparse whitethorn hedge that bordered the land, he had a very good view of what was left of Butlers house and their entrance onto the lane. He stood there for quite some time with the sounds of rooks cawing and the lonely low of a cow in the near distance as his only company.

In his minds eye he could see Cissy, cycling out her gateway in her black boots and pale yellow dress. He silenced his mind from all distractions. And as it was that evening in Kilpatrick Church, thoughts came, disturbing thoughts.... and again he was not at all sure if they were his.... or someone else's.

That evening he made some phone calls and followed that up by a visit to the council offices the following afternoon.

It took nearly two weeks to put everything into place. Saturday morning came dry and bright. Joggy crossed the fields to Barterstown House and waited at the entrance gate. After a short time he began to pace back and forth like a soldier on guard duty. He would stop and anxiously glance at his watch, ten, fifteen, twenty minutes passed and still no sign, then he'd pace some more. Then he heard a far-off sound. He stopped and listened intently... then smiled. He unbolted the rusty flat iron gate and with a mixture of lifting and pushing, eventually got it opened wide enough for the J C B to pass through. A car followed. It stopped and Joggy slipped onto the passenger seat.

"Nice to see you again, Peter," said Joggy as he shook hands with the driver. They followed Charlie in the bouncing JC B up the driveway, around the back of the house and down to the grave.

"There was a picket fence around it," said Joggy, as the three men stood in front of the grave, "I took it down and threw it away. It's rotten....not worth putting back up."

"Last chance to back out," said Charlie, not looking at either of the two men beside him. When nobody voiced a doubt, he climbed back into the J C B and started it up again. This was the moment. There was no going back now and Joggy felt the bile in his stomach climb up his neck like some hidden serpent. He felt like throwing up but instead swallowed it back down. The acid burnt his throat. Charlie raised the bucket and the hydraulic arm reached across the grave, dipped, then bit into the soil at the head of the grave. He dragged about four inches of grass and soil of the top, gathered it up and dropped it to one side. Peter and Joggy kept a tight eye on what was been deposited for telltale signs of bones or clothes.

A few minutes later a car pulled up behind them. It was John Kelly. Joggy went and spoke to him. Kelly then got back into his car and drove off. When John Kelly got home he rang Sergeant McNeill.

The men kept a sharp eye on the depth of their dig. Charlie had dug the hole wider than the original grave. This was to allow, when the time came, for both Joggy and Peter to climb down beside the coffin and slide a rope under it.

They were getting close. The J C B was halted and Joggy climbed into the grave. Using a spade, he dug the last few inches until he heard the sound of metal on wood. He removed the remaining earth from the lid. The narrow bucket of the J C B then cleared the space both sides of the coffin. The two men climbed back down again and with the use of a spade and a shovel, levered the head of the coffin off its resting place, just high enough to slip a slim lath underneath. They then did the same with the other end. Two loops of rope was slid underneath and then secured to the teeth of the J C B bucket suspended above.

Joggy hoped the coffin would not break in half. He tapped on the wood and the sound reassured him that the timber was still surprisingly solid. Charlie pulled gently on the lever and the coffin began to rise slowly. Peter climbed out but Joggy stayed and waited until the coffin had cleared the lip of the grave.

Above him another car came to a halt and Sergeant McNeill jumped out. "Stop, stop," he shouted, as he came running towards the J C B. He crisscrossed his arms several times indicating for Charlie to cut the engine. With the coffin left suspended in mid-air, Charlie complied.

"Where's Jackson?" McNeill barked at Peter.

"I'm here," said Joggy as he climbed out of the grave.

"You're in one large steaming pile of trouble now, Jackson. Exhuming a grave without an exhumation order is a serious matter." He extracted a notebook and a stubby pencil from his tunic pocket. He licked the nib. "Now I want your full names." He pointed at Charlie, who was sitting in the cab of the J C B with the door open, his trouser leg riding high exposing the tan leather of his cowboy boot. "We'll start with you."

"This," said Joggy, "is Charlie Fitzgerald and the other gentleman is Peter, his brother."

McNeill tilted his cap back slightly and scratched his scalp. "I see," he said, with a bemused look. "Never-the-less, you still need an exhumation order."

"Fuck the exhumation order," said Charlie, becoming agitated. "She's our mother. We didn't need an order when we were putting her in the ground and we sure as hell don't need an exhumation order to take her out of it.."

"I can't ignore the law," said McNeill.

"You do when it suits you," said Joggy.

"You keep your mouth shut Jackson, you're in enough trouble as it is." However, McNeill, figured he needed guidance. He looked towards the squad car, raised a hand and beckoned. Father Hayes was sitting in the passenger seat. "Maybe he'll shed some light on what to do next."

Fr Hayes alighted the car and came forward. "This is reprehensible behaviour," he said angrily. "From beneath his thick white beard he scowled at everybody. "I demand you put the coffin back immediately."

"No," said Joggy. "We want to know the truth, Father? We want to know if Cissy Butler is in that coffin?"

"Don't you think you've done enough harm for one day? Desecrating this lady's grave is a sin against God and man. Now replace the coffin."

"You heard Father Hayes," said McNeill, finding his voice again. "Now lower it back into place. These shenanigans have gone on for far too long."

"She was our mother," said Peter. "We have a right to know if anybody else is buried in there with her."

"One way or the other we're opening the coffin," said Charlie. "It's up to you Father, which is it to be; with or without your blessing?"

There was a short silence before Fr Hayes spoke. "Well it's highly undesirable, but it seems to be the only way to put a stop to all this nonsense."

"Lower the coffin onto the grass," said McNeill,

While waiting for the coffin to be slowly lowered to the ground, Joggy, turned around and looked down on the final resting place of Bonnie Fitzgerald. It was now mid-day and the sun shone directly down, lighting up the six-foot-deep crater. The bottom, where the coffin had lain, was smooth.

"What makes you so sure that Cissy Butler is in this coffin?" Fr Hayes enquired of Joggy.

Joggy turned back just as John Kelly appeared on the crest of the hill. He was the only one facing that direction and saw him. He then ran his fingers back through his mop of unruly hair. Seconds later Kelly was gone again.

"Because two yellow roses were left on the grave."

"But surely they were for both parents."

"Only one side of the grave was tidied up and both of them lay on that side."

"Maybe whoever left them didn't get time to clean it all."

"I told you Jackson, that was the reason. But, oh no, you wouldn't listen," said McNeill.

"Shut up McNeill," Joggy barked and turned his attention back to Fr Hayes. "Only one half was cleaned up because that was the half he wanted to clean; the people he loved were buried there."

"He? You mean Leon Fitzgerald? You think he meant the roses for Cissy Butler and Missus Fitzgerald?"

"Well the second rose certainly was not for *his* father; he hated the very ground that man stood on."

"Attitudes do soften with distance and time, you know."

"I've heard enough," said McNeill. "Let's open the coffin and clear this up once and for all. He looked to Charlie who nodded his consent. Peter did likewise. He then looked to Fr Hayes for final approval. Fr Hayes shrugged his shoulders. "It looks like I don't have a choice."

They gathered around the coffin. Charlie had a hammer in one hand and a nail bar in the other. Then McNeill noticed that one man was missing. "Jackson?" He called out. Joggy was again looking into the grave "We're about to break open the lid."

"Don't bother," said Joggy. "I was wrong, she's not there." He turned back to face McNeill, ashen faced. "Cissy, was never in the coffin."

"What? And what the fuck was all this about then?" McNeill shouted. "Mark my words, I'll do you for this, Jackson."

Joggy pointed a finger at the hole in the ground. "She was under it."

They all stood at the edge of the grave and peered in.

"On the day she disappeared," said Joggy, "Cissy, was wearing a pale yellow dress."

A patch of pale yellow material was protruding up through the smooth earth.

"But," said McNeill, mystified, "a tight eye was kept on this grave. How on earth did she get in there?"

"Footprints...undisturbed footprints," said Joggy. "That's what the guards were keeping an eye on. When she was buried here on the night before Missus Fitzgerald's funeral, the footprints covering the floor of the grave, were all they had to replace."

"Everyone get back." McNeill ordered, suddenly taking charge. "This has just become a crime scene." He then marched to the squad car to radio for assistance.

Charlie, clearly stunned, looked to Peter. "Dad? Do you think it was him?"

"It's possible," said Joggy, recovering his composure. "But to be sure, we need to go to where I believe it happened."

"And where's that?" enquired Fr Hayes.

"To the sheds at the back of the house."

"How do you know this?" Charlie asked.

"I don't know for sure, but I have a plausible explanation."

"Ok," said Peter, "lead on."

They moved towards the back of the house and had only gone about twenty yards when they noticed that Fr Hayes was not with them.

"Father, are you coming?" Charlie asked.

Father Hayes had a rosary beads in his hands, his head was bowed in prayer. He looked up. "I've just started a decade!" he said.

"Father, we need your help," said Joggy. "Cissy will still be here when we get back. She's going nowhere."

Fr Hayes seemed doubtful for a moment, but then he blessed himself and placed the rosary beads back in his pocket. As they moved off again, McNeill, returning from his car, shouted after them. "Where do ye lot think you're going?"

"To the scene of the crime," said Peter.

McNeill moved towards them.

"Don't you have a body to guard?" said Joggy. He did not want McNeill to be party to what he hoped was about to happen.. "It wouldn't do your career any good if you were responsible for losing Cissy, a second time."

McNeill stopped and scowled. He suspected Jackson was up to no-good and he desperately wanted to be there, but he also realised Joggy was right, He couldn't leave.

Joggy brought the three men pass the sheds to the open spot on which he had stood only two weeks previous. He turned to face the three men. "What do ye see?"

"Butlers," said Peter.

"Precisely. But more importantly, you have a clear view of the entrance to Butlers."

Joggy turned his gaze on Charlie. "You told me about an incident that happened on the evening before your mothers funeral. You told me that Leon had gone out the back for fresh air and that your father had told ye not to leave the farm, so when your father noticed he was missing, he went looking for him, and when he did not find him, came back in a foul mood."

"Yeah, what of it?"

"How long was your father gone for?"

"Not long....maybe ten minutes or less."

"It was late afternoon, right? Approximately the same time Cissy left her house?"

"Yeah?"

"What if Cissy did not turn for the shop but in this direction and he had then encountered her in the yard looking for Leon?"

"You think our father killed her?"

"It's a possibility. He was a violent man with a short fuse. He had warned her off before. He could have lost it and hit her with something; realised he had killed her and then put her body in a shed. It would certainly explain the foul mood he was in when he came back."

"Your speaking ill of the dead, Joggy," said Fr Hayes. "No matter what he did in life he does not deserve to be accused of this."

"Don't worry, Father," said Peter, "he deserves to be spoken ill off."

"Still, I would prefer to hear facts, not theory."

"I hate to put a dent in your fender, Joggy," said Charlie, "but her bike was found fifteen miles away in a quarry. How did it get there?"

"He rode it, and probably jogged home."

"Your saying a man in his early fifties, who by the way was passed out in an armchair by nine from drink, woke up in the middle of the night, buried Cissy, rode fifteen miles to a quarry and then jogged all the way back before first light?"

"No, I'm not. I'm saying Leon did."

"Leon?" said Charlie. "But you just said our father did it."

"No, I said it was a possibility. My real belief is that Leon was responsible."

"You think Leon, murdered her?" Charlie was clearly outraged by the suggestion.

"Murder," Joggy shook his head, "I don't think so. I think it was an accident."

"An accident?" said Peter.

"Leon had told ye he had gone for a walk down the lane and ye saw no reason not to believe him, after-all, when he came back, he had mud on his shoes."

"Leaving the farm and knowing the consequences.... ask yourselves, why would Leon do that? Why would he encourage his fathers wrath? It was probably the worst thing he could have done."

Everyone was silent. Joggy left the question hanging and waited for a reaction, but no one was forthcoming... not even Fr Hayes.

McNeill paced up and down in front of the grave, his mind on Joggy Jackson. He was up to something; he could feel it in his waters. But he was tied to this damn grave and he could not move. Then he heard a car and his hopes lifted, but it was only John Kelly. He had passengers.

Alice stepped out of the front passenger side and opened the rear passenger door. She then helped Harriet Butler get out. They made their way to the grave.

McNeill had the area taped off. "I'm sorry Missus Butler I can't let you come any further."

"Is it true?" said Alice. "Have ye found Cissy?"

"It would seem so. But we won't know for certain until her remains have been exhumed."

"I have to see her," said Harriet, on the verge of tears. "I will know if it's my little girl."

"I'm sorry," said McNeill.

"Please," said Alice, "she's waited a long, long time. Let her go to the edge of the grave and look in."

McNeill sighed heavily. "Okay, but it'll have to be quick."

Alice and Harriet warily approached the edge and peered in. When Harriet saw the patch of pale yellow material sticking out of the brown and tan soil, she screamed. "My Cissy, my Cissy, and made a move to climb down into the grave.

Alice wrapped her arms around her and stopped her. "It's all right, Harriet, it's all right," she murmured, "We have her. Cissy's come home." She turned her around and held her close. After a short while she led her away. But Instead of bringing her back to the car, Alice veered left and steered her towards the back of the Fitzgerald house.

"Where are you taking me?" Harriet asked.

"Joggy said to me earlier that if his hunch paid off and he found Cissy that I was to bring you to meet the Fitzgerald brothers. You do want to meet them, don't you?"

"Not right now. I want to be alone."

"I know you think you're not up to it, but it's important. Joggy wouldn't ask otherwise."

Harriet stood still and gazed at Alice's concerned face. The last thing she wanted was to have to make polite conversation with people from her past. But Joggy had found her Cissy, like he promised he would and now he needed her for some reason she could not fathom. "I'll not stay long," she said finally. "I'll see what he wants and then we'll go."

"Fair enough," said a relieved Alice.

They moved off again.

"Personally, I believe Leon never left the farm," said Joggy breaking the silence.

"And he didn't answer his father because at the time he was between a rock and a hard place. Let me put to you what I think really happened. Leon was fifteen and bored. He was too young for people to sit and chat to. They preferred the older members. So, thinking he would not be missed, he went for a walk. He came as far as here and that's when fate conspired against him. Because, at that very same moment, Cissy Butler was leaving her yard. She probably glanced in this direction and saw Leon. Remember, she was sweet on him. She came to him, leaving her bike at the gate. To be out of sight... remember she was banned from the farm... Leon probably brought her into one of the sheds, maybe the one on the end, where some farm machinery was kept. And that's where he was when his father came looking for him...with Cissy. And that, I believe, is also where she died.

The mud got on his shoes when he retrieved her bike from the gate. What do you think, Father, is it possible?" Joggy asked.

"I really wouldn't know. But it does seem a bit much for a fifteen year old."

"Sorry to burst your balloon there, Joggy," said Charlie, "but it seems this time you're full of hot air."

Led by Fr Hayes, Charlie and Peter turned to go back, but came to an abrupt stop when they came face to face with Harriet and Alice.

"Missus Butler," Fr Hayes, blurted.

Harriet gazed at him in silence, her mouth ajar, then asked, "How do you know me? "

"I'm the new local curate."

"I guessed at that...but that still does not answer my question."

"Someone must have pointed you out at mass to me...I can't quite remember."

"I don't go to mass." Her suspicion heightened. There was something familiar about him. Harriet scrutinised his face... the light blue eyes... the nose not quite straight... even with the beard...there was a distant familiarity of those features. Where had she seen them before? Then her eyes shone in remembrance. "You haven't changed one bit," she said. "You were the only one that resembled poor Bonnie!"

"Leon?" said Charlie.

"I'm sorry," said Fr Hayes, "you're mistaking me for someone else."

"I'm not mistaken," said Harriet. "I knew you as well as I knew your poor mother. You were her baby. You were always with her. Why are you now hiding and using your mothers maiden name; Leon Patrick Joseph Hayes Fitzgerald?"

"Leon?" said Peter as he and Charlie came and stood beside Harriet. "My God. I didn't recognise you with the beard, but now that they say it... it is you."

"What the fucks going on, Leon?" Charlie asked.

Fr Hayes raised his voice. "I'm telling you, you're mistaken."

"And I'm telling you we're not," said Joggy. "If you have any shred of respect left, Leon...now's the time to talk."

"I'm not...." He said plaintively.

Joggy cut him short and yelled at him. "You are or you were until you became Fr Hayes. I know you want to do the right thing because a few moments ago you defended your father from my cock and bull story. You could easily have let him take the blame... after-all, he made your life a living hell... but you didn't... because you knew the truth."

Fr Hayes was stunned into   silence.

"Last chance," said Joggy, "Talk to us ...or talk to McNeill."

Thirty three years of hiding had come to this. Something inside him slithered off the shelf it had been clinging so precariously to all these years and fell into the abyss. Tears filled his eyes. He took a step forward and clasped Harriet hands in his. "I'm so sorry, I'm so sorry," he sobbed, his composure completely shattered. "I killed Cissy." He fell to his knees. "I'm so sorry, I'm so sorry."

"What!" said Harriet, taking her hands back and starting to cry. "You...wha...how?"

"I smothered her....I was so terrified of my father that I smothered her."

"You'd better explain," said Joggy. "Take your time."

Leon wiped the sleeve of his coat across his eyes. "It was like you said, Joggy," he sniffed, "bad timing. Cissy saw me and came to me and wrapped her arms around my waist. Which terrified me because I thought, at any moment, Dad would come out and see us. So I moved us into the machinery shed. I sat on a seed barrow and Cissy stood in front of me and we just talked. Then suddenly out-of-the-blue she kisses me, full on the lips. A quick kiss and then she sat beside me and was quiet.

After a few minutes she started to giggle. Probably at the thought of what she had just done. But then I heard my father calling for me. I told Cissy to be quite, but she seemed not to be able to stop. My father was getting closer and I was petrified of him finding us. Again I told Cissy to stop and she did for a few seconds but then she started up again. I grabbed her and put my two hands over her mouth My father was now outside of the shed where we were. Cissy struggled but I held her firm. I was so sure he'd hear us. But then he went back to the house. When I was sure he was gone, I let Cissy go. She just collapsed to the floor. I thought she was play-acting.

But when she didn't move I checked her pulse and was horrified to find none. I'd killed her. In my panic, I did not realise that my hands had also covered her nose. I didn't know what to do or who to turn to. A long time later, I left the shed and collected her bike. Father became drunk and fell asleep around nine. Peter and Charlie were tired and went to bed early also. I then did exactly as Joggy said. I was a very fit young man back then. "I'm so sorry Missus Butler The only way I could atone for what I did to your daughter was to give myself to God."

With all the strength she could muster, Harriet slapped him hard across the face. "You should have told me," she shouted. "If not then, in the years after, but you didn't, why?"

"When it happened, I was too afraid. I was only fifteen. But then the years just slipped by and it just got harder. I've prayed for you, your poor husband and Cissy ever since. Ye have never been out of my thoughts."

"It was obviously an accident," said Joggy, "an unfortunate accident. Harriet, what do you want to do about it?"

"What do you mean, what do I want to do about it?" She asked, as if it was the most stupid question she had ever heard.

"Well now that we know the truth, do you really think that justice will be served by sending Leon to prison?"

"That's where he belongs for what he did to Cissy."

"I'm already there," said Leon. "That's what the last thirty-three years has been like in my head. I can't get her out of my mind. And she will remain there until the day I die."

"And where do you think I have been?" said Harriet. "My poor husband killed himself because of what you did."

"I know. I'm so sorry....if I could bring him back, I would."

Alice placed her arm across Harriet's shoulder. "Let me have a quiet word with you," she said softly and gently turned her away.

"You'll not change my mind," Harriet said sharply.

They walked far enough away to be out of earshot.

"Joggy's right," said Alice. Justice will not be served by sending Leon to prison. Like you, he's been in hell all these years. Look at him Harriet, worry has made him an old man. It was no wonder his brothers didn't recognise him."

Harriet turned her head around and had a good look at the forty-eight-year-old Leon. She had to admit, he looked at least sixty. She then turned back to Alice.

"You have every right to be angry," said Alice. "He took Cissy away from you and that is unforgivable. But he was a very frightened fifteen-year-old kid when it happened. Harriet, if you're looking to blame anyone, then blame the man who made him that way."

Harriet took another hard look at Leon.

"All I'm saying, Harriet, is to think of what Bonnie and Cissy would have wanted you to do."

She turned again to Alice. "Let's go back to the car, it's getting cold."

Alice looked at Joggy.

He mouthed, "What's she doing?"

Alice could only shrug her shoulders as she joined Harriet.

"What now?" asked Peter.

"I guess we wait," said Joggy.

"There's sure to be an investigation," said Charlie.

"I don't care," said Leon. "I deserve everything I get."

"You have a lot of good to do yet," said Joggy. "This is not the time to throw your life away. No good will be served with you going to prison."

"It's out now, Missus Butler will see to that," said Peter.

"Maybe, maybe not. Have some faith men," said Joggy. "They'll have to find Leon first."

"What do you mean, they'd have to find Leon first, shure he's here?" said Charlie.

"No, Father Hayes is here. As far as McNeill is concerned Leon Fitzgerald is in the wind. But right now all of that is immaterial. If Harriet Butler stills wants her pound of flesh, then there's nothing we can do."

"You knew who I was, didn't you?" Leon enquired.

"I only knew for certain when you turned up with McNeill."

"How?"

"Father Nolan was the only one I told about the exhumation order. So when Leon objected to it, I guessed it had to be you. But even that wasn't enough, I had to be certain. That was part of the reason I got Alice to bring Harriet down here. If anyone was going to identify you then it had to be her. One thing puzzled me though, how did you know about the quarry?"

"Friends of mine from secondary school told me about it. They use to boast about all the shenanigans they use to get up to in it." A short silence fell. Then Leon asked, "What do you think she'll do?"

"Probably turn you into McNeill. She's a stubborn auld Biddy and right now madder than a hive of angry bees. If your boss has any sway over the living, then now is as good a time as any to send him a quiet prayer."

McNeill cut them off before they could reach the car. He had been pacing up and down and hated not being privy to what was going on. And he knew something was going on. "What have ye been doing? This is now a police investigation and I need to know exactly what has been said."

Alice waited. She wanted Harriet to answer.

Harriet looked back and saw the four men in the distance, emerging from the back yard. Leon did not look up, his head and shoulders slumped in dejection. She returned her gaze to McNeill. "We've been raking over the coals of the past," she said, "and they burned for a short while, but they've gone cold again." She then brushed past him and opened the rear passenger door of John Kelly's car and climbed in.

"Wha..?" said McNeill.

"She means it's over," said Alice, as she slipped in beside Harriet.

John Kelly drove the car in a semi-circle that took him past the four men. Alice winked at Joggy.

"The jobs oxo boys," said Joggy. "Leave McNeill to me." He looked at Leon.

"Head up, Father. Remember, you have to travel back with the Sergeant and he's going to grill you. He doesn't suspect you of anything, so put on the act of your life and just be Father Hayes again; a man who knows nothing."

"Missus Butler says ye have been raking over old coals?" McNeill directed his question at Joggy, "what did she mean by that?"

"I thought if I brought Peter and Charlie back to their childhood, they might remember something of what happened to Cissy, and I thought Father Hayes, being impartial, might be able to throw a cold eye on things, but we were not able to come up with anything."

Police cars could now be heard coming in the near distance.

Joggy placed his hand on McNeill's arm and led him a short distance away from the others. "Listen, I know you're a bit mad with me right now for going behind your back and opening up the grave without your consent, so, if you want it, you can have the credit for finding Cissy. You can put any spin you like on it, we'll back you up."

"Why are you doing this?"

"Isn't it obvious? We want to stay out of jail."

McNeill gave a quick half smile. The carrot was too tempting for him not to go for. It would do his promotion prospects the world of good. But still he could not help thinking that Jackson was up to no good. But what? "Ok," he said finally and they rejoined the others. McNeill then spun the storyline that everyone was to follow.

EPILOGUE

Cissy's autopsy showed no signs of physical damage and to the people who now actually knew the story...it was a relief: it proved that Leon was telling the truth. The police once again questioned everyone involved. But the investigation eventually settled on finding the missing link: Leon Fitzgerald. And after months of exhaustive searching the investigation stalled... they failed to locate him and the case once again went into cold storage.

After a short period of deep contemplation, Fr Hayes, decided against turning himself into the police. He agreed with Joggy's analysis...no good would be served with him going to prison. Six months later he returned to the missions.

Harriet Butler interred her beloved Cissy in Kilpatrick Cemetery. Father Nolan performed the service. She would not hear of Fr Hayes doing it. The community and especially her neighbours got together and raised enough money to knock down the old house, clear the site and erect a comfortable port-a-cabin home for her. She was moved to tears at the unveiling, but despite this, managed to warn them that "*their cattle were still not welcome on her land.*" They hoped she was teasing.

McNeill was invited to call on Murray in Oldbridge Garda Station. He was cautiously excited. Reilly had been demoted to Sergeant and posted to the Beara Peninsula. He knocked on Murray's door.

"Enter," Murray requested.

McNeill closed the door behind him.

"Have a seat," said Murray. He had a buff manila file opened in front of him.

McNeill figured it was his personal file. Murray made several facial expressions before he spoke again. It was as if he was trying to suck something out from between his teeth. "I have been interviewing all relevant candidates for the vacant Detective Sergeant position and I thought it only fair to talk to you too."

"Thank you, Sir," said McNeill.

"But I have a problem with you, McNeill."

"What would that be, Sir?"

"I don't trust you."

"Sir, I have done everything by the book for the last two years and I don't believe, in that period of time, I have given you anything to worry about."

"Really?"

"Yes, Sir, really."

"Then explain to me how everyone had the same story concerning the discovery of Cissy Butlers body?"

"Because they were all there and saw what happened, Sir."

"Verbatim...word for identical word...it never happens."

"I can't explain that, Sir."

"I can...Jackson had something to do with it, hadn't he?"

"No, Sir."

"That's not what I'm hearing on the grapevine."

"With all due respect, Sir, the grapevine is not evidence."

"It's as reliable as yours, and that's not saying a lot. So, I'm back to my original problem...I can't trust you. Ironically, if you had allowed the course of events I heard on the grapevine happen...you would have had a decent shot at promotion."

"Bye the way," said Murray, when McNeill reached the door, "On your way out, don't forget to congratulate Sergeant Cole on his promotion."

McNeill sat into his car and then slammed himself hard back against the driver seat. He closed his eyes and screamed, "Jackson, you fucking bastard."

Joggy was charged with the felonious crime of, 'Desecration of a grave' and a file was sent to the DPP. After several stressful months, word finally came back that no legal action would be taken.

Danny sat in the pew beside his family at eleven o clock mass on Sunday. He was restless and worried and was wishing for the mass to be over. During the previous week, he had received a short curt letter from Victoria. She wrote, *Don't believe everything my Mother told you. I will explain more when we meet after eleven mass on Sunday.*
Love, Victoria.
Danny did not go for communion. Instead, he sat, deep in thought and stared at the floor. Helen jabbed an elbow into his side. He looked sharply at her.

"You're missing all the action," she whispered.

"What?" said Danny, not in tune with her.

"Look who's going up for communion," she said.

Danny eyed the long queue. Then his eyes lit up when he spotted the tall blonde, slim figure of Victoria. Father Nolan slipped the tiny disc into her open mouth and Victoria, with everyone aghast, walked proudly back down the aisle. She glanced at Danny and smiled.

After communion was over, Father Nolan stepped up to the microphone and began reading out the local upcoming events. He surprised everyone with his first piece of news. "Today, as you may have noticed, we have a new recruit. Miss Victoria Parker, for several weeks now has being taking religious instruction from me, and last Wednesday evening was baptised into the Catholic faith. I would like you all to make her feel welcome. A round of applause broke out.

"So it was Father Nolan you were seeing all these weeks?" said Danny, as he leaned back against Victoria's car. "Yeah, sorry if I worried you, but I had to tell my mother a lie to keep her from finding out."

"What's your mother going to say when she finds out?"

"She can't say anything. It was her idea. She told me not to marry anyone of a different faith."

FOOTNOTE

It was dark in the car-park. A distant street light silhouetted Bob Coughlin as he made his drunken way towards his bicycle.

"Evening, Bob," the voice said.

"Who's that?" said Bob. "If it's money your after, it's all drank."

The voice came forward to the outer reach of the distant light.

Bob squinted. He could barely make out the features. Then his face lit up. "Ah, it's yourself. I've been meaning to thank you."

"I didn't do it for you." The voice took another step forward and drove his fist into Bob's solar plexus. He immediately collapsed to the ground and vomited. As he lay in his own puke trying to catch his breath, he watched in agony, as the voice walked away.

THE END.

Made in the USA
Charleston, SC
14 October 2014